Call of the Wolf

The Viking Chronicles

D1764919

A Novel By:
Dr. Paul Perkins

ISBN-13:978-1505632323
ISBN-10:1505632323

Cover design by Paul Perkins
Cover Photo of Stein Zupancic by DiamonEyes

Printed in the United States of America

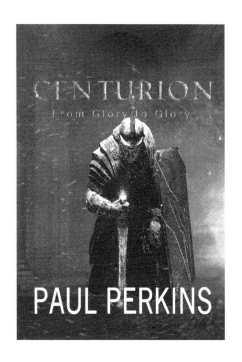

First 3 Chapters FREE

www.craivingsomethingmore.com/centurion

Special Thanks
To my editing team:
Janet Murphy
Rachel Perkins
Beta Readers

Other Novels by the Author

Centurion: From Glory To Glory
Viking Chronicles Book 1: Call of the Wolf
Viking Chronicles Book 2: The Wild Hunt
Viking Chronicles Book 3: The Priest's Son

For other books go to:
Amazon.com
www.cravingsomethingmore.com

Dedication

I little reck... to reach her risked I have my life oft...
Though I be slain within the arms of my beloved,
Sleeping in the Sif-of-silken-gowns' embraces:
For the fair-haired woman feel I love unending
-The Skalds-

To Rebecca, the fair-haired woman whose
unending love motivates me to be the best I can be.

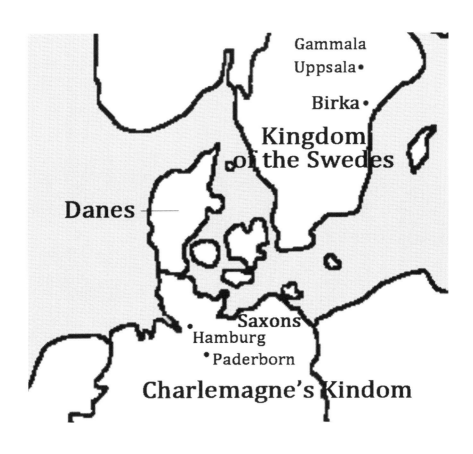

Gammala
Uppsala•

Birka•

**Kingdom
of the Swedes**

Danes

Saxons
• Hamburg
• Paderborn

Charlemagne's Kindom

Cry of the wolf
Book 1

Wake early
If you want
Another man's life or land.
No lamb
For the lazy wolf.
No battle's won in bed
Go you must
No guest shall stay
In one place forever.
Love will be lost if you sit too long
At a friend's fire.
—The Hávamál

Prologue

In the beginning darkness lay over the abyss, its length and breadth too large to fathom. It lay at the center of created space. On one side of the abyss was the land of Niflheim, filled with cold, mist and darkness. From its depth sprang twelve large rivers overflowing half of the abyss with blocks of ice. On the other side lay the land of Muspelheim, filled with fire, warmth and brightness. A flame whose sword sent great showers of sparks into the abyss guarded it.

In the course of time Niflheim and Muspelheim mixed and a mist rose and froze to create Ymir and his cow that nourished him. Soon more giants appeared, two from Ymir's sweat and two from his feet and they struggled with one another until they gave birth to Odin, Vili, and Ven. Together the brothers fought with Ymir and vanquished him. From his corpse the universe was created.

In the beginning Odin fashioned Midgard from the flesh of Ymir, and the mountains from his broken bones. From his skull he created the expanse of sky, supported at its four corners by the four dwarves Nordi, Surdi, Austria, and Wstri, from whose names come the four points of the compass. From Ymir's brains the clouds were formed and from the sparks of Muspell they created the sun, moon, and stars to give the world light. Golden chariots carried the sun and the moon. Two riders, Day and Night, were charged with guiding their course across the sky. The Wolf who intended to devour them pursued them. On occasion the Wolf was successful and caught them in his mouth, but it heard the terrified cries of the people of Midgard and released them, only to continue his pursuit.

In the beginning Odin took the branch of an ash tree and created a man named Askr and from the branch of an elm tree he created a woman named Embla. They were placed in Midgard and from them sprang the human race. Through the centuries humanity flourished under the protective watch of the gods, and in the course of time a child named Magnus was born.

In the beginning God created the heavens and the earth. The earth was without form and void, and darkness was over the face of the deep. And the Spirit of God was hovering over the face of the waters. And God said, "Let there be light." And God saw that the light was good. And God separated the light from the darkness. He called the light day and the darkness night.

In the beginning God said, "Let there be an expanse in the midst of the waters, and let it separate the waters from the waters." The expanse above the waters God called heaven. He then separated the water under the heavens into one place and the dry land he called earth and the waters he called sea. And God said, "Let there be lights in the expanse to give light to the earth, two great lights, one to rule the day and the other to rule the night." God said, "Let the earth sprout vegetation yielding and bearing fruit after its kind." God said, "Let the waters swarm with living things, the sea with living things, and the land with all forms of creatures. Let them be fruitful and multiply after their kind." And God then said, "It is good."

In the beginning God said, "Let us create man and woman in our image, after our likeness." Out of the dust he fashioned the man and called him Adam. Out of the man's rib he fashioned a woman and the man called her Eve, for she would be the mother all living things.

In the Beginning they lived in a garden that was watered by the three rivers of Pishon, Gihon, and the Tigris. God said, "Let the man and woman have dominion over the fish, birds, and livestock over the whole earth." He blessed them and commanded them to be fruitful and multiply and fill the earth and subdue it. Throughout the centuries humanity flourished under the protective care of God, and in the course of time a child named Charlemagne was born.

War raged in the heavenly realm and the forces of the King of Kings fought against the gods of man. The serpent, the mischievous Loki, beguiled the ignorant and blinded the eyes of the wise, and led them down a path they were not meant to walk. And the war of angels and demons spilt into Midgard, the realm of man. Nation rose against nation, clan against clan, brother against brother, until the earth was soaked with their blood.

Each generation of innocents tried to break free of the chains binding it to the gates of the damned, but fate refused to loosen its hold and the struggle continued. Heroes were born and died, forgotten but in the memories of long lost hope.

The Coiled Rope
739 A.D.

Vidar knew that not all stories of adventure involved dragons and heroes. Too many that began with possibility ended in tragedy. For every successful hero countless others died in obscurity, and he, Vidar, son of Strom, would not be one of them. He was tall with long blond hair. His father had tried convincing him to cut it, to give him a more fearsome look, but he would not listen. He enjoyed the mane as it was. He had practiced until he could swing his ax with precision, and spent countless hours throwing it at trees, stumps, and small animals. His reputation was spreading as one of the best warriors the village had to offer.

Using his newfound renown for his own pleasure, Vidar had seduced a number of the young lasses, and his reputation was a cause of concern for every mother. But of all the girls that had caught his eye only one had caught his heart, the lady Svenheld. As she had grown, her father had given her the name Svenheld, but she would never reveal her true name. She had a slender waist, but an even slenderer neck that drew attention to her face and eyes. Her look could melt the hardest heart or bore through the thickest stone. She was gentle to the needy and harsh to the unjust; she was the desire of most men, but none could tame her. It seemed that she and Vidar were destined—or so he thought.

His arrogance turned her gaze away, but his handsome face drew it again. She disliked his treatment of others' misfortunes, as if they were cursed by the gods and unworthy of mercy. He exuded an air of superiority as of royal blood, and his attitude of entitlement soured her desire—or so she thought.

"Why do you ignore me so?" Vidar inquired of the maid.

"And why is my attention any concern of yours?" she said playfully. Her teasing enticed him all the more.

"You know there is no one else for you but me, and your sad attempts to avoid the truth only prove you a more generous reward." Vidar swooped in to block her way, but Svenheld was quick and graceful as she ducked his advance.

"You think your prowess with an ax and your good looks can win my heart?" she asked.

"So you think I am handsome?"

"I think *you* think you are, which only confirms your delusion." Stopping and looking him squarely in the eyes, she said, "I am not a prize to be won or a foe to conquer. I will choose a husband who is strong in battle, but gentle in bed. From what I hear you have not proven yourself in the former, and your prowess in the latter is said to be lacking." She pushed past him, while he feigned a sense of hurt.

Although Vidar was sure of himself in both categories, she was correct in regard to battle. He had done nothing, gone nowhere, to prove himself worthy of honor. His father had introduced him into the community and now he waited for an opportunity. Ships came and went all the time, but captains were particular with whom they took, oftentimes bringing along the young only when accompanied by a guardian. Since his father seldom sailed, he was left to convince another to take him along.

Caldar was the only sailor in Birka who would give him a chance. Everyone else thought him too much trouble, but Caldar was a hard man, born of the sea. He was the total opposite of Vidar, short, with a balding head, and his face worn and scared by battle and disease. He was married, but only because the girl was an orphan and no one else would have her. He supposed it was his fate to look after the down and out, yet he was not known for his compassion. He consented to look after Vidar because it suited him to order someone around. He knew that the sea would make Vidar into a man, or kill him. Either way the village won.

"Boy," he yelled at Vidar. "If you're going to sail alongside of me you need to have some skill."

"I can wield an ax like no other—"

"The sea will kill you before an enemy. Coil the rope and then I will show you how to tie off the ship."

"How much skill does it take to tie a knot, let alone coil a rope?" Vidar felt the task was beneath him, but he knew the only way onto the ship was through Caldar. The rope proved to be more difficult than he expected. He would wrap it one way and it would go another.

Caldar laughed, "Maybe you should throw your ax at it."

"Or at you," Vidar said under his breath. "So what am I doing wrong?"

"Ah, the pompous ass asks for help," Caldar mocked.

It was all Vidar could do to restrain himself. No one near his age ever treated him like this, and if they did he put them in their place.

"You have to let the rope coil in its own direction; to fight it only brings frustration." Caldar showed him how to let it drop in a circle. When it started to resist, moving in the wrong direction, he

13

slightly twisted the rope in his fingers and it coiled, as it should. "Like that," Caldar said. "Life's a lot easier if you don't resist."

Resistance was all Vidar knew. He was argumentative with his parents and always skirting the community laws; on a number of occasions he would have been severely punished if not for his father's intervention. Some said the lashing would have done him good.

"Caldar, when do we get to sail?" Vidar was impatient.

An answer didn't come directly. Caldar wanted his protégé to learn patience, and he also liked to taunt the boy. "In good time. The summer is almost gone and the ships will be returning. We will not sail until the next thaw." He could see the frustrated disappointment on Vidar's face. "Maybe you should take the next months to temper your attitude and find a woman to settle down with. Once we set sail the girls left behind will soon be forgotten."

Vidar could never forget Svenheld, but maybe she would forget him. He decided to approach his father, asking him to make arrangements with Svenheld's family. Which wouldn't be all that easy. Her family was as proud as she was beautiful, and the thought of giving Svenheld permission to marry a young man like Vidar was out of the question.

"He is reckless," her father said. "As honorable as it is to die at sea and in battle, I must think of what you will be left with if he does not return. The sea is dangerous enough for seasoned sailors but for an insolent whelp such as Vidar? He is as likely to die on his first voyage from falling overboard as from dying in battle"

"Now, now," her mother said. "I agree with your father." That was unexpected. Svenheld thought surely her mother would encourage her to wed.

"I am not sure I want to marry Vidar anyway. He is so, so, so infuriating." But her mother could see that Svenheld's heart spoke differently.

After many more words Svenheld finally went to bed and her parents were left alone. Sitting in the evening glow of the fire they spoke of their family and clan. They whispered of Vidar and his weaknesses. They decided that in the end they would leave it up to their daughter.

"Vidar isn't the first arrogant Norseman I've known," her mother said. She nudged her husband and he gave her a knowing look.

Pulling her close he silently invited her to his bed. "If I could change so can he."

She smiled, "Who says you've changed?" The night passed with passion and dreams.

In another home not too far away, Vidar's father tried to prepare his son for the worst. "They come from an honorable family, and are honored in the community. Other young men have no doubt sought her hand."

"So you do not think we are worthy? Are we not as honorable as any? Father you may not be rich but you are honest and hardworking. If anyone deserves the hand of Svenheld it is someone in this family. That leaves me."

Vidar's parents were proud of him despite his reputation, and he honored them as nobly as other children in the community honored their parents. In the months to come, it would prove to be this characteristic that made Svenheld fall in love; on the day of their marriage she was the happiest of all women.

But as it is for most Vikings, the winter months passed in preparation for the coming spring. Spring signaled the thaw of the passages and opportunity to sail. Vidar's thoughts were consumed by it, and a tinge of resentment made his new bride sullen.

"I know you must go, but why must you be so eager?" Svenheld asked. "We have been married less then a year and you think of nothing more than the sea." She was hesitant to tell him but she thought he should know. "I am with child."

"That is wonderful!" he said. Holding Svenheld close he kissed her passionately. "To think there will be another me running around. Thoughts of you and the baby will keep me, even in the darkest nights, until I return home. You will be my saving grace."

When the time came to say goodbye Svenheld stood with the rest of the wives as their men set sail. Family surrounded her; in the event her husband did not return, she and his child would be looked after.

Pain
741 AD

By his second year aboard ship, Vidar had earned the respect of his crew, at least for his ability to wield an ax. His strength increased with each stroke of the oar, and his long hair became a mangled mane that struck fear into the villages they visited. His responsibility was not to negotiate trade, but to guard their goods. One look at him gave everyone pause. They couldn't tell if he was ferocious or mad. He let them believe both.

He loved this life, and though he cherished Svenheld and his son, he couldn't wait to be at sea. Svenheld named their son Kory, he was strong and had Vidar's eyes. He would teach his son everything his father had neglected, and at the first chance take him to sea; fifteen years seemed far away. During the long nights when the water was calm his thoughts would drift to his family, but he had little time to daydream. He need to focus his energy and not wasted it on sentimentality.

At home, Svenheld tended to her duties. She wasn't the only single mother, so plenty of others commiserated with her. The difference was that they tended to complain about their husbands, while she appreciated hers.

"He's too fat," one would say.

"Mine's too ornery," bemoaned another.

"You're lucky," said one. "My husband drinks too much and beats me." There was silence.

"I hate it when they drink too much." They all laughed. Though violence in the home was uncommon, recourse could be sought under the law.

Svenheld often listened without saying too much. Vidar was loud and proud, his arrogance getting him into trouble on occasion, but at home he proved to be gentle, and a good husband and father. She was glad to have chosen him over all the other men in the community. The hardest moments were at night when the baby was asleep and she crawled into bed alone. It made it hard to sleep and her dreams were restless. Yet, in all her life was good.

"The wind is picking up!" yelled the captain. "Steersmen, keep the bow of the boat into the wind. Don't let the waves pound against the side or we will be swept over." Most of the sailors were hugging the side of the ship, balancing their weight to buoy the boat. The rain was starting to beat down harder and the captain's voice was disappearing in the wind.

Vidar was the least experienced of the crew, but others still got sick when the waves grew too large. They groaned under the physical and mental strain of the storm. The water was cold and the salt stung their eyes. Because of the salt it was useless to drink but as the wind blew it against their faces they could not help but swallow. Its distaste made the sick feel even more nauseated.

The captain was standing at the bow shouting something, but no one could hear. He cupped his hands and thrust his arm out pointing toward the mast. The sail had not been secured and began to unfurl. The wind whipped its ends and frayed the rope that struggled to keep it in place. Vidar stood to make his way to the mast when a wave washed across the bow and down the deck. The water was strong enough to knock him off his feet and sweep him against the railing. He hit his head, and a momentary darkness clouded his eyes.

"Are you all right?" A crewmate was kneeling over him.

Rubbing the top of his head he replied, "I think so. It's only my head." His ventured humor was lost in the gale. His crewmate slumped back, groaning.

The captain, seeing no one was able to help made his way toward the mast, and Vidar, regaining his feet, strove to meet him halfway. By the time they reached the mast the sail had whipped itself free and was blowing in the wind. If the crew wasn't sick, incapacitated on the deck, they may have been swept overboard as the sail flung back and forth.

"Get the other end!" the captain shouted. "We have to secure it before it's torn beyond use." It would be a long way to row home, and the crew already looked too weak to man the oars.

Grabbing the end of the sail, Vidar struggled to wrap it in any manageable way. He had to dodge the rope tied to it, and twice already it had struck him in the face. The salt water burned his eyes and made it difficult to see. Squinting, he doubled his resolve and tucked more and more of the sail under his arm.

"It's too big to carry under your arm," the captain yelled. "Throw it on the deck and roll one of those useless bodies on top of it."

Rolling heavy bodies on the sails wasn't easy but at least he wouldn't be carried away if the wind caught the sail. It took close to thirty minutes to stow the sail, and by the time they were finished not even the gods could wake them from sleep. Vidar slipped back to his position, proud of what he had done. None of the others would remember this night, but he would. It was the night he saved the crew.

Smoke rose from the chimney as Svenheld stoked the fire. Vidar had left her a fair amount of wood for the summer and she was careful not to use too much, but it was coming to its end. If he didn't return soon she would have to chop more herself. Not that she couldn't do it, but she had plenty of other chores to occupy her time.

The harvest promised to be fruitful this year. The plot of land they owned wasn't very big, but Svenheld was able to grow a variety of vegetables, cabbage and leeks being her favorites. Vidar liked the carrots and turnips best, but the barley took up most of her time. Before he had left, Vidar tilled the ground and planted the grain, but Svenheld had to weed and water the seedlings. Birka had rich soil and ships came from miles around to trade in their markets. She hoped this year would bring enough to purchase another cow. Theirs was growing old and not producing as much as she liked.

She had reserved this morning for harvesting the patch of raspberries that grew in the forest not too far from home. Holding Kory's hand, because he insisted on walking, Svenheld hiked the quarter mile to her destination. It took her longer than it should—the toddler was distracted easily, and every bug, rodent, and bird caught his attention so Svenheld would stop and name the creature before moving on. He was the light of her life and she would not hurry him for the sake of chores. Of course, trying to pick berries with him was a chore in itself. He delighted in their taste but became infuriated with the thorns. Yet, he was persistent. Every time a thorn pricked him he would scrunch his face and reach back in a bit more carefully. When he cried Svenheld would stop what she was doing and pick him up.

"Pain," she said, "makes a Viking strong. That is why the gods give us so much." She would look at his furrowed brow and say, "Don't let the thorns win, and you will grow up and be as strong and brave as your father." Placing him back on the ground, she showed Kory how to slip his hands past the thorns until the reward of the sweet berries brought a squeal of delight to her ears.

The sun was descending behind the trees and Svenheld knew it would be dark soon. Picking up her harvest and her son, she was able to make the trek home at a quicker pace. The fire had died down long ago, but enough coals were left for her to bake a small pastry. It was a favorite dessert that her mother had taught her to make. She took the berries and smashed them together until the juice ran out and the seeds floated to the top. After kneading the dough she folded it over pushing down the edges until only one end was left open. Taking the berries she carefully poured them into the opening and then pressed the remaining dough until the fruit was fully enclosed. Placing large leaves around the berry-filled bread she placed it beneath the coals and left it there to bake. That evening she made five of the berry breads, and tomorrow she would take them to market.

Black Raiders
741 AD

Heroics notwithstanding, Vidar was ready to set foot on dry land. Three weeks of sailing and rowing was taking its toll. This year they had gone east, making their way around the Horn of Jutland, when the captain decided to return to port for trading.

"The land of the Franks is rich with goods. Our furs will fetch a grand price and our stores will be filled with trinkets for our wives," Caldar assured them.

It was a dangerous venture. Trading with the Franks had not always been profitable. Their war with the Saxons had made everyone suspect, and the ragged Vikings often engendered fear and distrust, a valuable commodity in battle but not in trading. The Frank's wares, however, were of the highest quality and the captain felt that it was worth the risk. He even passed up the Danes to procure his treasure. What the captain didn't expect was the heavy winds and rough seas.

It wasn't clear how far they were driven off course; all they cared about was the land they saw ahead of them, which meant they weren't going to be driven over the earth's edge. The gods had spared them this time, and when they approached the coast their exuberance could be heard on the shore. The small village overlooked the sea and the quaint hovels that lined its lane reminded them of home and the families they had left behind.

"This is strange." Vidar had become friends with the captain and always made his way to his side when they landed. "There is no one here."

"Anyone here?" yelled the captain. "We are interested in trade." But all that echoed back was the empty wind.

There were inhabitants in the town, but when they saw the Vikings' vessel they weren't sure what to make of it. They had seen similar ships but none ever ventured onto their shore. Three men were dispatched to get a closer look and when their eyes fell on the visage of these terrible men their hearts fainted and they ran back to the village in a panic.

"They are monsters from the sea!" they exclaimed, breathing heavily. "Their ship is adorned with the devil's mast and the creatures it vomited look as if they have seen the devil and turned mad themselves. They carried axes, swords and shields as easily as we carry bread. We must hide ourselves lest they carry us away."

And they did just that. Every woman and child hurried off to the next village and every able-bodied man hid behind closed doors, weapon in hand. They were unnecessarily frightened, but prudent nonetheless. These were uncertain times and caution was always the better part of wisdom.

The closer the Vikings came to the village, the more nervous the inhabitants became. When Vidar and the captain were at its very edge, a man stepped into the street. He was the largest man in town and so it was laid upon him to engage the strangers. The villagers hoped to convince their visitors that he represented the average man and scare the creatures back into the sea. It did not have its desired effect, because the Vikings were glad to see someone.

"I am Eric, captain of this crew. We have been sailing long and ask for your hospitality. Is there a place we can find some food?"

To his chagrin, but not surprise, the large man stood as if dumb. This was not unusual in their ventures to new lands. The language barrier was inconvenient but not insurmountable. He had initially chosen the Franks because he understood their language. Based on the look on the villager's face he would have to try the few words he knew in a couple of different languages. But it was to no avail. Though the man's face lightened up when Eric said hello in the Frankish language silence fell between them because it was all the Saxon knew.

"This is ridiculous," said Vidar. "Let's leave or take what we want. Otherwise we will be here all night."

"It is easier to take what we want, but it will only be good this one time. If we can establish trade then we can come back year after year."

Vidar would not be put off and with dramatic gestures said, "They don't have anything of value except for small animals. Let's take them and be gone." Eric saw that young Vidar's words were being well received by his men. They had been at sea for a long time and they were hungry and tired, both catalysts for mutiny.

Vidar's tone and movements hadn't gone unnoticed by the villagers and their fear was being exacerbated tenfold. Vidar brandished his ax, a motion which seemed threatening to people hidden in their homes. One man, who happened to own a bow and two arrows, had been positioned toward the front. Villagers believed that in the event of an attack, he could at least hit one man and the rest would run away. They didn't know much about Vikings, so in panic he let lose his arrow, but the Vikings' reaction was a total surprise.

"Ahhhhhh!" Vidar yelled as the arrow borrowed into his thigh. The archer had been aiming much higher.

"Shield wall!" the captain shouted, and they pulled Vidar under its protection. The large man hurled something that sounded like an oath and disappeared behind a door.

"Are we still going to stand around and argue?" Vidar said with his teeth clenched.

Eric motioned to one of the men to stay behind with Vidar and said, "We cannot let this go unchallenged. Steadily move the wall forward. When we reach the edge of the first building separate into two groups and kill anyone you find."

"I am going," Vidar said. He snapped the shaft of the arrow, but when he stood he fell back in pain. The arrow's head had struck bone and settled next to it. No one disputed Vidar's bravery, but he was of no use to them now.

"Go," he said and slumped back, grimacing, and grabbing his leg. "And if you find the man who shot me, let me kill him."

There was little resistance from the villagers. When the Vikings broke into the homes any man who had not run away quickly died. To Vidar's later disappointment, even the large brute was seen scurrying like a dog up the hill. They searched the houses but didn't find anything of value. There were some utensils, goats, and chickens. One of the men found a house full of bread. They were so ravenous that they immediately tore into their booty.

It is sad it happened this way, Eric thought, *but they brought it on themselves*. His sympathy dissipated quickly as he returned to his injured crewman. He bent over Vidar and looked at the wound. "This doesn't look good. We have to get the arrowhead out of your leg. We can't do it here; we're too exposed." Eric motioned for two men to carry Vidar to the ship.

Vidar was angry about everything: getting injured, missing the fight, and now the indignity of being carried to the ship. "Let me try and walk." Wrapping an arm on one of the men's shoulders he tried to stand. He put too much weight on his bad leg and clenched his teeth as the pain worsened. His head started spinning. At the combination of pain and blood loss, he finally lost consciousness.

Pain shot through his leg waking him instantly. Vidar was lying on the deck toward the stern of the ship with two men bent over him. Caldar was holding him while Eric held a bloody knife.

"What are you doing?" Vidar yelled through his teeth.

"Hold still, I told you we had to remove the arrowhead." Eric was making another attempt. "Hold him still or knock him out."

Vidar was given a piece of leather to bite down on. He held the side of the ship as the crewman restrained him. The pain was excruciating, not because Vidar's flesh was being sliced, but because Eric was a poor surgeon. He couldn't find the arrowhead and kept digging until the tip of his knife hit bone. Vidar passed out, which made the operation easier. "There," Eric said, and he held up the prize. "Now that it's out his life is in the hands of the gods."

Pouring seawater over the wound, they prepared Vidar for the final procedure. The only way to stop his continued bleeding was cauterizing the wound. It was dangerous, but they built a small fire in the center of the ship and heated the blade of the knife. When it was hot enough Eric pressed the knife over the gaping wound to seal it. Vidar groaned but didn't wake. The stench of burning flesh drifted from stem to stern and the other Vikings thanked the gods it wasn't them.

If he survives, Eric thought, *his leg will be lame and his days at sea over*. Pity was not the Viking way, but better Vidar die in battle than languish on land, an all-but-forgotten remnant of a warrior. Eric shouted, "Head for home!" This trip had proved worthless and was becoming tiresome.

Colors swirled and shifted, disappearing into a puff of smoke. Through the haze, fiery eyes bored through Vidar's soul. In the distance were the halls of Valhalla, and he longed to enter those doors. He listened intently for the beating wings of the Valkyrie, but the sound never came. The laughter in the distance mocked him as a failed warrior, neither victorious in life nor glorious in death.

He woke to searing pain in his leg and sweat beading on his forehead. He was alive, but he had mixed emotions. The long voyage home allowed him to come to terms with his lot. If not for his wife and son he would have thrown himself overboard. Instead he longed for Svenheld's arms and Kory's giggling. He drew his covering across his body and fell asleep, hoping his dreams would be more glorious.

A cold wind blew from the north, an unusual change in direction and temperature. It did not bode well for the community of Birka, and most women worried about their husbands, though most wouldn't admit it. The market was busy, but the mood subdued. Svenheld was trying to corral her son as she carried a basket of vegetables.

"Can I help you with that?" came a woman's voice. It was Ingrid. The two had been friends since childhood and it was always good to be together. Ingrid was shorter than Svenheld and much wider. Her husband sailed on a different ship, but both he and Vidar were still at sea. Ingrid picked Kory up and made funny faces at him.

He laughed and squirmed to free himself. When she placed him on the ground he ran off behind a stall and peeked out to see if she was following.

The childless are so much lonelier than others, thought Svenheld. Ingrid had not produced any offspring and Svenheld heard the whispering. The women of the community would not pity her in public, but in secret spoke of her misfortune.

"If she does not bear a child her husband might leave her," one had said.

"He won't leave her; no one else would want him, or her," another responded.

"They are cursed by the gods," an older woman proffered. "I have seen this before, and the gods will end their line for sure."

The others nodded in agreement.

Svenheld remained silent. It didn't do any good to confront them but she felt a little guilty for not speaking up for her friend. When they were together she tended to overcompensate and spoke glowingly of Ingrid's future prospects; Ingrid was never encouraged. At the moment Svenheld and Ingrid enjoyed their time and each were comforted in their friendship.

"I am worried, Svenheld." Ingrid said. "Something is in the wind. I was about my chores this morning when my left eye began twitching. It wasn't noticeable at first, but it progressively got worse."

"What do you think it means?" Svenheld asked.

"My mother always said that when the right eye twitched a baby would be born, but the left signaled someone's death." She reached into her pocket. "I picked these up this morning for good luck." Ingrid held out a couple of acorns. "Take one for protection."

Svenheld did, not because she believed it would actually protect, but because her friend did.

"I am sure our husbands will be fine. They are strong and capable warriors and sailors. Besides, Vidar would never allow himself to be harmed. Kory is his delight and he is determined to see him grow up to be a man." As the words left her mouth she realized the pain they would bring to her friend. She could do nothing to assuage the pain so she didn't even try.

They were silent for a moment when a sudden commotion drew their attention. People were gathering on the beach and around the dock. Even the Earl made his way toward the crowd. Svenheld could see him speaking to two of his warriors. They had stayed in Birka to provide protection for the women and children. It was a necessary precaution but a dull assignment. Apart from breaking up fights between the older boys trying to establish an adolescent pecking order, there was little excitement. Something, however, had caught their interest.

"Make way for the Earl!" one of the men yelled. "Make room so he can see."

The Earl stepped onto the dock and walked its length to the end. He couldn't quite tell whose ship was approaching. No one was expected for at least another two weeks, but sometimes expeditions were cut short. The water swelled and fell to the rhythm of his heartbeat, and when its markings were close enough to see his breast beat harder. He turned to the two men with him.

"Take the women and children out of the city to the south caves." He spoke quickly and his companions understood. What he tried to avoid, however, happened. As soon as his men tried to calmly gather the people someone shouted.

"It's the black ship!"

"It can't be!"

"It is, I can see its sail." The woman pointed across the water and when everyone comprehended the situation they began to shout and push as they ran toward the village.

No one knew where to run, but they believed that if they kept moving they would be safe. In the bedlam that ensued people pushed and shoved, knocking old women and young children to the ground. It wasn't like anything Svenheld had ever seen. With all the commotion she had forgotten about Kory.

"Kory!" she called. "Kory, where are you?" There was no answer—she couldn't hear above the screaming and running. She hoped someone had picked him up, but she wouldn't leave without knowing for sure. "Kory! Ingrid, have you seen Kory?"

Ingrid shook her head, and joined the search. They were able to garner the help of two other women, but no one could find him.

At that point she realized that she had put these women in danger. Looking toward the beach she saw the ship, with its pure black sail, land on the shore. At least twenty men stood in a staggered formation. Each wore a heavy leather jacket and long leather trousers. Holding weapons in both hands, they stood challenging the men of the village. If Vidar were here he and the other warriors would drive these men back into the sea, but they weren't here, and the *Black Raiders of the North* sought one thing: slaves.

Svenheld had never seen them before, but her father used to threaten his children into obedience with the myth, or what she had assumed to be a myth. The black raiders were a clan far to the north, forged in the frozen tundra and hardened in the icy sea. Their resources were said to be so scarce that their only recourse was to steal and plunder other villages. For all their toughness though, they were cowardly; they waited for the men to leave and would lay siege to a city in their absence to capture the women and children, killing the few men who remained.

The southern caves provided protection in times like this and were used to hide the families while the warriors did battle. But there were no warriors in Birka, at least not enough to fend off the black ship. The earl thought it best to retreat to the cave and use their defensive position to its greatest strength. But some of the villagers, greedy and foolish, returned home to gather as many of their possessions as possible. Svenheld wouldn't leave until she found her son, and by that time the black warriors were upon them.

They showed no mercy. They were ravagers and only interested in taking easy prey. Of those who failed to escape were eleven women, five boys, nine girls, and a smattering of the old. The latter were killed immediately. The others were dragged off and loaded onto the ship. Svenheld had hidden Kory and herself behind some crates in the community hall. It was everything she could do not to scream at the men and attack them for hurting her friends and family. What kept her still was the little boy in her arms. For him to survive she would have to stifle her grief.

"Search all the buildings and set fire to them. If any of the hiding rats attempt to escape, kill them," the captain commanded.

Cowering behind the crates, under some old grain sacks, Svenheld and Kory waited for them to leave. The spreading fire quickly sucked all air from the room. If they didn't move, their hideaway would soon become their tomb.

Smoke and Fire
741 AD

Young Magnus was standing near the Earl when the leader of Birka first spoke to his guards. Amid his fascination with their conversation, the imminent danger didn't register on his little mind. Not until the call to head for the caves did he quicken his steps. In the panic he could think only of his mother. She would be at the farm, and his father had left the night before to hunt. He had run these woods many times and knew all the short cuts between town and home. Ducking branches and leaping over fallen logs, Magnus hurried to his mother.

Bursting into the barn where his mother was feeding the cow he yelled, "The Earl told us to go to the caves."

"Slow down, Magnus, and take a deep breath. What are you saying about the Earl?"

"A ship with black sails was coming, and the Earl said we had to go to the caves."

The look of horror on his mother's face sent a shiver through him.

"Where is father? We have to tell him."

"He will be fine. Find your sister and follow me." His mother collected some food in a bag and scooted her children out the door and into the woods.

Only a few paths led to the caves, so the family met up with others as they fled the marauders. No one spoke except to ask if they had seen a relative or friend. It wasn't easy trying to evacuate 400 women and children, but the Earl's word was final and no one hesitated to follow his command. If he had raised an alarm the situation must be serious, and without the warriors the village was vulnerable.

Vargr was tracking a small she-wolf when a flurry of birds rushed overhead. Something had spooked them and ruined any chance to stalk his prey. The she-wolf would be on alert now and he might as well let her win for the day.

What caused the flurry? He thought.

Hiking up the small hill, he climbed the tallest tree that would support his weight. When he looked down over the landscape he could see the top of the community hall and smoke billowing from its roof. Quickly he descended the tree, missing branches and scraping skin. The minor pains went unnoticed as he found the ax he had laid against the trunk and sprinted toward the town.

The caves were not far from his position and he learned of the black ship as he passed the families running for safety. He asked about his family, but nobody knew where they were. They must have been behind them. He couldn't think of them now. The city was in peril, and the Earl would be making a stand; he needed to help. When he arrived at the beach the ship was gone, the community hall was in flames, and the bodies of several dead men lay on the ground.

Svenheld gasped for air and Kory lay limp on the floor. She had to find a way of escape. Coughing from the smoke she stooped to pick up her son. Pieces of the burning thatch were falling all around. She covered her mouth as best she could with a scarf, but when a beam fell next to her, the flying sparks set it on fire and she instinctively dropped it. Like the building around her, her hopes were going up in flames. She couldn't stop coughing and fell to the ground. Lying still for a moment she noticed the air was easier to breathe. It was still smoky, but it gave her a little more energy. In the distance the smoke cleared slightly and she could see the door. Dragging her son, she pulled them both away from the inferno.

Coughing, Svenheld fell to the ground, praying that the gods would spare her son, but when she caught her breath and the smoke cleared from her eyes, her heart sank. Standing in front of her was an imposing figure, covered from head to toe with animal skins dyed black. On his head was a leather helmet studded with bone, and the mask covering his face gave the appearance of a demon from Heldigard. He didn't say anything as he held a large ax in one hand and a shield in the other. It was too much to hope that he had not noticed her and Kory.

Lifting his ax he waved to another of his crew who quickly grabbed Svenheld and dragged her toward the ship.

"My son, do not hurt my son," sobbed Svenheld.

There was a pop in Svenheld's arm as the warrior yanked her away. She couldn't see Kory through the soot and mud, and withheld her prayer since it hadn't worked before. Svenheld didn't go willingly; if Kory was to die she would rather be killed fighting, but she didn't know where her son had been taken. She kicked her assailant one more time, but then the hilt of his sword struck the side of her head, and whatever hope she had faded into unconsciousness.

When Caldar called for the oars to be stowed he stepped to the bow of the ship and looked for the clamoring crowd of women and children who would celebrate the return of their men. He looked forward to seeing his wife and son, and on the beach he could barely make out their form. He waved and was unsettled when they didn't wave back. He saw a crowd but no sign of celebration.

The deck hand caught the rope and tied the ship to the dock. As captain, Caldar shouted orders and commanded his men until all was stowed in place. Vidar was the first to leave, assisted by his comrades; he made the long walk down the plank amid the pitying eyes of both warriors and women. Those eyes, empty of concern or sympathy, said that something was wrong. All waited for the Earl to speak.

The Earl was young, but still a commanding figure. He waited at the end of the pier for the captain and all of his men. The crew was so preoccupied with both mooring the ship and awaiting word from the Earl that they did not notice the gaping hole in the center of the village, framed by the burnt structure of the community hall.

The captain pushed through his men until he was face to face with the Earl. "What is it that places a dark cloud over our arrival?" He could see his wife in the back of the crowd.

"Birka has been attacked." The Earl let his statement sink in. "All of our ships were away, and those warriors who were left were no match for the Black Marauders."

Vidar had heard the stories of the black ship and her crew. They were ruthless warriors who preyed on weak and unsuspecting villages. Shunned by the Viking community, they became renegades and brigands, respecting not even their own people. They instilled fear in women and old men, but were loathed by true warriors. They never approached strong villages or towns but waited until they could ransack without resistance, as had been the case with Birka.

The Earl related the tale and when he was finished the crewmen were eager to find their families. Fortunately most had escaped to the caves, but a few had not been so lucky; among them were Svenheld and Kory. The former had not been located, a victim and now slave. Her son, Vidar's son, was found on the ground outside the burned hall. His little body didn't survive the hot smoke and he was left as refuse by the dark warriors. In all, twenty-five women and children were missing. They had not gotten the word quickly enough and stragglers were easy prey.

If not for the men who held him up, Vidar would have collapsed in despair. Their strength became his, and he was spared the indignity and weakness. They helped him to a nearby crate and he sat, his face vacant and hopeless. No one dared speak to him; none knew what to say, and the shock abated slowly as the crowd dispersed, until Vidar was the only one left on the dock.

By the time he came to his senses everyone was gone and Vidar knew he had to go home. Walking was painful, but didn't compare to the pain he felt in his soul. Picking up the crutch that had been made for him, he began to hobble home when a small, unexpected figure blocked his way.

"I am sorry, Vidar," the small voice said. "I tried to get back with my father but it was too late."

"It is not your fault boy." He tried to walk past him.

"Does it hurt?" the boy asked.

Vidar gave him a quizzical look.

"Your wound, does it hurt? Did you get it in battle? You are an honored warrior." Magnus was enamored with the warriors who went to sea. His father wasn't one of them. He always thought he would go when he was old enough.

"Yes, and it will serve as a reminder of this day." He had a faraway look in his eyes, seeking a horizon that held little meaning for him now. He was neither warrior nor husband, neither sailor nor father. Though grateful for the lad's kindness he excused himself without a word and slowly made his way home. Magnus admired him, and from that point on a bond formed that would last a lifetime.

The Wolf Hunter
754 AD

What is that lamp?
Which lights up men,
But flame engulfs it,
And wargs grasp after it always.
   —King Heidrek in Hervarar saga,

Vargr silently moved through the underbrush. He had been tracking this particular creature for almost seven days. It had taken him over a month of waiting and watching for the female to lead him to her den, and it finally had paid off. Underneath an outcropping on the southern mountain he had discovered the one place she constantly returned to. It was well hidden, a small dugout that led into a larger depression. Big enough for her pups, some food, and herself.

Wolves had fascinated him all his life. They were elusive, and most men kept their distance as long as the wolves kept theirs. Yet there were occasions when a pack hunted close to the village and women scooped up their children lest they be the pack's feast for the night. It was on one of those evenings that Vargr received his name. Like most Vikings his father named him after his own father, and the tradition of the family was passed down from one generation to another. His was Brandt, son of Caldar, son of Brandt, bearer of the sword. They were good, strong names, names that garnered honor and pride.

One evening Caldar, his father, heard screaming and ran from the house brandishing his sword. If any enemy were attempting to lay siege to their home he would dispatch them to the afterlife. The enemy that encircled his home, however, was not men, and he wished it were. Instead, the curse of Fenrir had descended from the mountains to haunt their homes. Fenrir, the son of god Loki, always took the form of a wolf. It was a bad omen for him to visit. It looked as if he had brought his sons Skoll and Hati along.

"Take Brandt and his sister into the house and close the door behind you!" he yelled to his wife. "What do you want, Lord Fenrir? Have you come to test me?"

The wolf's low growl signaled the other wolves and they moved slowly to surround Caldar. He tried to keep an eye on them, but they were masters of the hunt. Slowly they circled, inching him away from the door, until one had come between him and safety.

They were careful not to lunge too soon, but tested Caldar's defenses. One would curl its lip and snarl, pushing forward to see what he would do. Instinctively Caldar swung his sword. As he did, the wolf at his rear quickly moved toward him. He turned and brought his blade around just in time to smack the wolf in the head, forcing a painful yelp from the creature. But instead of frightening him off the wolf became infuriated, shook his head, and advanced again.

The dance fatigued Caldar and each swing of his sword became heavier. Eventually one wolf broke through his defense and nipped his calf, and when he swung around to defend himself another wolf nipped him. Blood dripped from his wounds and his already tired body struggled to stand. Calls from inside the house became distant as Caldar's mind buzzed and dark spots formed on his eyes. He couldn't stand any longer and when all the fight was drained, he fell face first in the dirt. The wolves lunged on their prey and the snarling and tearing of flesh drowned any sound from his lips.

"Mother, I must go and help father!" Brandt cried.

"No, my son, I will not lose two of you to Fenrir."

"I cannot stand here and watch my father die. I must do something!" He looked around and grabbed a log from the fire. Its embers glowed orange, smoke drifting from its smoldering edges. Brandt had taken some animal skins and wrapped them around his hands. Taking hold of the burning log, he raced outside to his mother's protests.

The eyes of the wolves were red and glowed as deeply as the burning torch. Their frenzied meal was interrupted as they curled their lips and growled menacingly; the audacity of this young whelp brandishing his stick set their teeth instinctively on edge. The sight was horrific, each beast holding in its mouth an appendage of his father, but he would not be deterred.

"Away with you!" he yelled. "Leave my father some honor. Take what has filled your stomach and go back to the hell you call home." He slowly approached the wolves, swinging his torch as he went. The air whooshed as the torch moved through the cool air. The wood crackled as the flames lapped at the fuel and burned brighter with each arc. The wolves tugged at their prey, trying to drag Caldar's body into the woods.

"Drop him now!" Brandt continued to berate them with insults and oaths. With every word he moved closer and closer until he could smell the infected breath of the beasts.

But Brandt's approach did not have the affect he wanted; it only made them fiercer. Instead of running into the woods they dropped their prey and stood shoulder-to-shoulder facing him. By this time, however, Brandt was not ready to run, and all the oaths he knew had run their course. The more the wolves growled the deeper Brandt's voice became until his mutterings matched those of the fiends. He was speaking their language, and whatever he was saying became clear to them. They began to walk backwards as Brandt inched forward, their heads lowered as the moon behind his shoulders cast a dark shadow over their bodies. For a split second the whole world stood still and the eyes of wolf and man were held fixed on one another.

In that moment the wind blew hard drowning out the growls of both man and beast. The blood pulsated in Brandt's temples, and its throbbing sound was all he could hear. Rage filled his soul and with one last effort he leaped forward, screaming into the wind, swinging his torch, and turning the predator into prey. The wolves turned on their heels and disappeared into the woods. When his heart slowed and his rage dissipated, he looked down and saw the cold, torn body of his father. No tears were shed, no words were spoken, but Brandt lifted his head and howled into the night.

As the story was told and retold, the boy became man and his name was changed to Vargr—wolf. He was shaped by that night, and the pelts that hung on his wall and across his floor spoke of his fate and fortune. Now, he stood outside the den of the bitch he had tracked for days. Inside were two small pups, eyes closed, and curled together for warmth. Vargr no longer saw the wolf as the enemy he once had been. Years had passed and he grew to respect them as predator and prey. He would not kill the pups, but rather allow them to grow and one day become ornaments of the hunt.

What Vargr did not expect was what awaited him when he turned around. He had gotten so caught up in watching the pups that he wasn't listening for their mother. The wolf that stood a few feet above him was a powerful animal. He had seen her tracks for days and knew that their meeting would not turn out well for one of them. He also knew that if he killed her, the pups would die.

"Steady girl, you don't want to make any quick moves." He spoke softly, hoping for the tone of his voice to set her at ease. Reaching for the knife on his belt he readied himself for to lunge.

Lowering his eyes, Vargr communicated that he was submissive and acknowledged her dominance in this place. For her part, she never took her eyes off him but for a few quick glances toward her pups. They were all she could think of, and they were what she would die for. He realized that he stood between her and the pups and slowly moved to his left, giving her easy access to the den.

"I didn't harm them. You can go in and check. I promise not to hurt you."

She growled and moved cautiously to his right. The pups could smell their mother and they began to whimper, raising her anxiety.

"They are just hungry. They are safe." He stepped back further and a little downhill. "Go ahead, enter the den." Vargr paused, inviting her to trust his presence. He wanted to watch her and the pups interact. There was something primal about the intimacy between mother and pup.

Though he had married, as all good Vikings did, he wasn't in love with his wife. Maybe it stemmed from his relationship with his mother. After his father's death she had become protective and fearful. She nagged him to stay at home, but he was constantly disappearing into the woods. It was a lure that he couldn't resist.

"You will not amount to anything," she would tell him. "Your father died protecting us from those animals and all you can do is follow them into the woods." It was a fascination she couldn't understand. These magnificent animals acted on instinct and the bidding of their master Fenrir. How could he blame them for what was not their choice? Yes, he had become their predator, but what was once done in anger was now an act of honor.

His wife was from an honorable family, but not one with many resources. Vargr's mother had planned their marriage in honor of his father's wishes. He had made arrangements with her clan when they were young and, like the wolves, they had little choice in the matter. She was a fine woman, taller than most other women in the village, and not unattractive. She wore her hair braided and rolled up in a bun, which accentuated her full cheeks, and she could laugh. He would tell her stories and the house would fill with her voice; he loved that about her. However, like his mother, she was not happy about his wanderings.

"Don't you love me?" she queried.

"You know I do, why do you always ask?" he would respond.

"Because you are always gone into the woods. Other men leave their wives for the sea, but you leave me for what, a wolf? I would understand if you snuck around and bedded women, but to be outdone by a big dog!" She would huff and run off, leaving him to himself.

In those moments he was inextricably drawn to the woods, and would find himself standing in the night listening for the wolves' call. When he heard it, a deep impulse to respond ran through his soul. The pups in the den were his as much as the male who bred them. No one understood this about him. They would laugh at him and call him mad if he ever divulged these thoughts and feelings, so he ventured into the forest.

"Take care of our pups," he said to the wolf. She watched him with a wary eye as she nestled down and the pups explored her body until they found her teats and began to suck. Their whimpers subsided as they filled their stomachs and felt safe under the warmth of their mother's body. "I envy you," he said and headed down the hill, through the woods, and home.

The woods were second nature to him. No one in Birka knew them better. Spending his life hunting and trapping gave him an extra sense in the dark underbrush. His familiarity with the woods served him well since the light of day seemed to grow dim sooner. The years had caught up with him and he could no longer hide his ailment any longer. It became apparent to his wife that something was wrong when he stumbled over things she had moved.

"You have become clumsy in your old age," she would say.

"If you would put things where they belonged and kept a tidier house there wouldn't be a problem," he would respond.

"There is nothing wrong with my house or the way I keep it. Maybe you are too used to the dark woods to appreciate what is in the light," she taunted.

"Maybe." One day he finally stopped arguing. "Maybe, I just can't see very well," he said, to which she said nothing. In fact his unexpected honesty compelled her to hover, which he disliked even more than the arguing. "Woman, I am not dying. My eyesight is failing, not my whole body." But for all his bravado he knew that a Viking without sight was as valuable to the community as a dead dog.

It was, however, this turn of events that revealed the depth of his wife's love for him, and since he could no longer venture into the woods by himself she felt her home to be complete. But it wasn't so for Vargr; the draw of the woods, the thrill of the hunt, the companionship of the wolves wasn't something easily shaken. His sight wasn't completely gone and he set about the task of raising a son with an appreciation for wolves and the hunt.

Vargr knew his days as a predator were coming to an end. He was growing blind and no longer trusted his ability to outwit his prey. He had told his story so many times that the line between truth and mythology blurred, and he needed to entrust his legacy to his son. Magnus was a fine young man, strong and brave. He would make a good hunter, but his heart seemed bent in another direction. He spent too much time at the docks, hanging around the scoundrel Vidar. If he weren't careful, he would forsake the destiny of his family.

"Magnus, have you been listening?"

The Father's Way
754 AD

Magnus held in his hand a coiled rope. "That's right, boy," Vidar said. "You keep that up and you will make a fine sailor. That is the heritage of every Viking."

"Not if my father has anything to say about it." He hung his head and his sullen look dampened the mood, which Vidar never liked.

"You make out of life what you want to. If the gods give you a dead fish, use it for bait." He took hold of boy's chin and tilted his head up. "You can spend your life brooding or you can do something with it. So, your father wants you to hunt wolves; is that so bad?"

"I don't want to hunt wolves. I want to sail the sea and see the world." A hint of enthusiasm escaped his lips.

"Ah, I've seen the world and there isn't much to it." He said it, but he didn't believe it and neither did Magnus. "Maybe you shouldn't spend so much time down at the docks. Besides, I will be gone tomorrow and there won't be anyone around to listen to your sad story." Vidar tousled the top of Magnus' head and scooted him home.

As much as Magnus liked Vidar, he wished the older man wouldn't treat him like a child. His father did that and it infuriated him. He was almost old enough to join the community as a man and wanted to be respected as such, but no one else cared. Nonetheless, he had nowhere else to go but home. He took the longest way possible and was distracted by everything that moved. His home was oppressive and the only stories told were of wolves. No stories of honor, no stories of glory, only stories of shaggy creatures.

"Where have you been?" his father asked.

"At the docks." Magnus avoided telling where he went because he knew it would only lead to arguments. But, he couldn't skirt the matter, and every conversation ended the same: no one was talking. He wished it would just start that way.

"What have I told you about the docks?"

"Father, why do you hate them so much? The sea is the heritage of our people. It seems that we are the only family that refuses to see this and people laugh at us." It was the first time Magnus seemed to really care about an answer from his father.

"Not all Vikings are sea farers. Many are farmers, fishermen, and hunters. Fewer scour the seas in search of easy treasure than you think." He spoke with a hint of disdain.

"But are we not all warriors? And are not battles fought on other shores? Why is it wrong for me to desire that kind of life?" He could see his father struggle for an answer. "Father," he continued, "if I may ask and not seem disrespectful. Why do I have to be you?" The hurt in his father's eyes was clear. There was no way around it now, and he steadied himself for an onslaught of angry words. But none came.

"Magnus," he said quietly, "you are almost of age. You and I have argued for too long, and I am too old and sightless to fight you any longer." Vargr took a small pouch sitting next to him. He opened it and emptied the contents on the small table. They weren't ornate, but deeply meaningful. The largest item was a knife fashioned from the bone of a wolf. On the hilt was carved, with surprising clarity, the story of his first encounter with the wolves. The second was a string of wolves' teeth that had been worn by Vargr on special occasions, most significantly his wedding. The final item was a gold coin, old and dented. It was payment from the first wolf pelt Vargr had sold.

"I don't understand, Father. What do these things have to do with anything?" His father was disappointed and the years were showing in the creases that were etched deeper than Magnus had noticed before.

"Why do we fight for honor?" Vargr said to his silent son. "Because it is our heritage, and heritage is about family. Each father passes down to his son something of great value that teaches of their ancestry, their history, what makes being part of their clan special. These items are not trinkets of past wars or battles fought. They are at the core of who I am as a man, as your father." He held the knife in his hand and caressed it as he would a young pup. "When Fenrir came to my father and slew him that day, he could have done the same to me. But deep inside he saw that I was part of him, the part that is wolf. In the moment of my father's death I was more a part of the pack then I was of this community." Vargr could see that Magnus was having difficulty with his explanation.

"The gods play their games, and we don't always know how we fit into their whims," he said, "but there are moments when we come to understand how important we are to their plans. The moment I joined the pack of Fenrir was the moment I understood my true nature, and the beast that beat within my heart."

"Father, are you saying you are the embodiment of Fenrir?"

"No," he laughed. "If that were so I would have wreaked havoc on all the Viking people. We each play a small part in the whole, and my small part has been here, on this island, in this village, with these wolves. It isn't glamorous or glorious, but it has been my fate, a fate I wanted to share with you."

"But father…"

Vargr raised his hand to stop his son from speaking. "I know you believe your heart calls you to the sea, to explore beyond the horizon. I have not become dull enough miss this point. However, I believe that Fenrir is strong in you, and you will find something missing if you do not explore this aspect of your heritage. If you are willing I would like you to seek out Fenrir, to see if the pack lies within you. If it doesn't you are free to explore the world." He sat back and waited for his son to respond.

Magnus let his gaze drop. How could he deny his father this request? Vargr humbled himself to the fate of the gods, and was giving Magnus the choice of his destiny. He could not, would not, dishonor his father by rejecting him. "Father, I accept the challenge."

"Wolves," his father said, "are difficult to track. They can hear you from where the hills begin to rise, and smell you twice as far. When you think you have found their path it disappears as quickly. The male is solitary and travels far. He will call the pack, made up of bitches and whelps, to hunt by his side. Once he is fed, he ventures off until they are needed again. As a pack they have few enemies save man, and even then we are less cunning than we think."

"Why do you hunt them if it is so difficult?" Magnus asked.

"The more difficult the task, the greater the rewards," he explained. "You think there is glory in battle, where men fight and die for honor? I tell you there is more honor in tracking a clever beast and triumphing in your victory than all the wars you could wage. It is wit against wit, not brute strength. Which is easier, sneaking up on an enemy who can't see in the dark or smell past his left hand, or an opponent who lifts both ear and nose to the wind and is gone before you are within a day's walk?"

"You make it sound impossible to track, let alone kill, a wolf. If what you say is true I have no hope in tracking and killing." Magnus would sooner give up than waste his time.

"Difficult, but not impossible. Smell this." Vargr opened a container filled with a yellowish liquid.

"That is awful," Magnus said, moving his head away. "If he smelled that he would definitely run for the hills."

"Not in the least. What you smell is taken from a gland in the female. When the male smells this he thinks one of his kind is nearby. Soaking your clothes in this will mask your sent and lure the male into the open." He smiled at his son's expression.

"That's disgusting. I am not going to wear what might attract a male wolf, and if I smell like that I will never marry."

"Some days I have come home only to find the door barred. Your mother would leave soap on the bench outside and refuse me entrance until I was completely clean. Sometimes it took two days for the odor to pass." They laughed together, easing the tension between them. "You need to follow this practice. Your scent is strong to the wolf and if you do not use this, you will need something to hide it."

"What weapons will I need to kill the wolf?" Magnus asked.

"If you are lucky enough to get close to a wolf a weapon will not be enough. If the male is alone you will have a better chance, but if you are confronted by the pack you may not survive."

"And you want me to face this beast, why?" Magnus was not feeling hopeful about this quest.

"Your best weapon is your cunning. Second to that is the trap. Rope traps have worked, but not often. Wolves are powerful and they will either chew the rope or chew their legs. If the latter he will most likely die of blood loss or starvation. A net trap will keep him from chewing off his leg, but he can still chew through the netting. The most effective trap is the pit. It takes time to dig a hole deep enough, and skill to lure the wolf, but once he is in the pit he can't escape. The key is to know where he will travel so you know where to dig the hole. Wolves are unpredictable and guessing where they will be is almost impossible. That is why tracking them and getting to know their movements is crucial."

"Have you tracked a male lately?" Vargr could see that Magnus hoped to bypass the process by relying in his father's efforts.

"This is your quest, and it can't be made easy. You will spend the better part of your time tracking and observing before you ever see a wolf. You will find evidence before you find presence." He opened up another pouch and told Magnus to pick out its contents and smell it. The odor was as pungent as the first, but the object was solid.

"What is it?" he asked.

"It is scat, droppings of a male wolf. You will see this before you see him. It will tell you where he has been and how long ago he passed that way. Wolves are an enigma: though they are unpredictable, they are still creatures of habit. If nothing has given them caution they will follow very select trails. If they smell or hear something unusual they veer from their routine, but if you are careful you can set your traps and come back to find your prey."

It took a good week for Vargr to go over everything Magnus would need to know in the wild, but he would never be fully prepared. Eventually he would come face to face with Fenrir's spirit. In that moment the man Vargr hoped Magnus to be would be revealed.

The sun had begun to rise, but its rays were still too low to penetrate the trees that lined Vargr's cabin. The shadows cast an ominous haze that didn't bode favorably for Magnus. His mother silently stood by, though her heart wanted to keep her son at home. To display anything other than resolute acceptance of the quest was to bring shame on their house. But she would not let her son go off unprepared.

"This is for you," she said, handing him a pack. "There is some bread and cheese. It won't last long so don't eat it all in one sitting," she cautioned, knowing full well her son was more than capable.

"Thank you." Magnus gave his mother a knowing look that said he would be all right.

"I have something for you as well." Vargr handed Magnus the hilt of his knife. "It has served me well, and it will serve you. Take care of it, clean it, and keep it sharp. Its usefulness is beyond explanation, which will be evident." He gave his son a firm hug, knowing that this would be the last time he saw Magnus as a boy. Whatever happened would be immaterial. He knew his son well enough to have confidence in his abilities and his desire to come home alive.

Magnus turned and walked into the forest canopy. He wanted to look back but he didn't. He wanted his mother to know that he loved her, and that his father had his respect. He knew men didn't show such emotion, but he didn't feel like a man. The shadows of the forest engulfed him and he disappeared from his parents' sight.

Light of the Moon
754 AD

Filling the sky the circle shown
Its light, a beacon to all who see;
Follow the path that leads away,
A light so bright but not its own,
It calls to the beast deep within,
It calls to abandon reason and wit,
It calls to the heart to give away,
It calls for the night to never end.
Under its watch night springs forth strife,
The predator seeks to find its prey,
Terror seizes the very small,
The battle between death and life,
A howl is heard upon the hill,
A word of caution all to heed,
The gathering pack about to stir,
A night to find a meal to kill.

For all their bluster about independence and self-determination, Vikings were a people moored in traditions of honor and glory. The gods dictated the fates of men and they were pawns to their whim. Magnus wanted to be a man in the line of great warriors, sailing the open sea, and seeing new lands. Yet, here he was, trudging through the forest honoring his father's wish, but knowing that wolf hunting wasn't his destiny. But then again, what was his destiny?

The moon hung in the sky, filling the horizon. His father had told him that it is a good omen to have so much light. "You can see danger," he had said, "but beware that danger can see you." That wasn't comforting, but how dangerous could it be? He had spent his life hiking through these hills; all he needed to do was track down a wolf and kill it. His heart sank. He would never get out of the woods. Magnus stopped. Something was drifting in the wind, a sound, low, and then rising. It was a wolf. He was speaking to the moon.

This is good, Magnus thought. He would follow the sound, and even if the wolf wasn't there when he arrived, it would be a starting place to begin his tracking. He turned to the south and made his way up the side of the hill. There were several hills on the island, each separated by a valley, two with small streams and another by a river. It took him a while to reach the peak. The underbrush was denser then he had anticipated, and the bramble cut against his clothing, scratching his hands. He could live with the pain, but the itching was annoying.

He was glad to see the moon as he stepped out on a rock overhang. The moon seemed so large from where he stood that he imagined he could touch it if he reached out far enough. Mesmerized, he might have been pulled over the precipice by this hypnotic sight, if not for the wolf's howl. He turned his head slightly and against the bright background of the moon he could see the silhouette of his prey. His heart began to race, and all of a sudden the excitement of the hunt was swelling inside of him. Something in his throat was trying to escape. He wanted to respond to the wolf's call, but he didn't want to take the chance and spooking his prey.

He hadn't planned to spend the evening traipsing through the woods. His first order of business was to find water and make camp, but the sighting and howl of the wolf made him forget his plans. He wasn't expecting the wolf to be there, because he knew he hadn't prepared his scent or silenced the sound of his advance. Deep down he didn't want the wolf to be there because he wasn't sure if he was properly prepared. It took Magnus an hour and a half to make his way down the hill, and by the time he reached the stream that cut through the valley, the excitement had worn off, the hunt had lost its allure. Even the moon was not so majestic hidden by the leaves and the mountain.

"Herregud!" he cursed. Not paying close enough attention, he had stepped into some thick mud along the bank. *This isn't good*, he thought. The mud was deep enough that the suction held his foot firmly in place. The harder he pulled the tighter it held. At one point he fell back and sat squarely in the wet muck. He swore again. Resigned to the mud, he reached down, untied his boot, and slipped it off his foot. The leather collapsed and he was able to wiggle it back and forth until the black goo released its captive. The boot was all wet and he didn't want to put it back on. He knew he couldn't walk through the woods with only one boot, so he decided to make camp.

His pack was sparsely filled with essential items: fur that could be used for a cape or a blanket, flint, birch bark, and some food. His knife was fastened to his waist by a leather belt. Collecting dry twigs and leaves, he piled them between some rocks to break the wind. When all was in place he took the flint and struck it against his knife, sending small sparks into the air. Leaning closer to the kindling Magnus tried to direct the sparks more effectively until finally one caught the edge of a piece of bark and it burst into a flame. He bent over and blew gently on the small fire until it caught another piece of bark and then another until the flames leaped into the air. The leaves crackled and smoked, which he was sure the wolf would either hear or smell. He hoped that the fire would keep any interested creature of the night at bay, and he laid his head against his pack, pulled the fur over himself, and eventually fell asleep.

> *Sixteen legs and eight eyes*
> *A formidable foe from old tales,*
> *A monster grew from stories told*
> *Of sacred land in which men die,*
> *If one approached it ill forebode.*
> *When two arrived it faltered hearts,*
> *Yet, three proclaimed the loss of hope,*
> *And four confirmed intended kill.*
> *What stirred the heart of noble beasts?*
> *What drove them to collective hunt?*
> *What called them to the dark of night?*
> *An invitation to Fenrir's feast?*
> *They filled their nostrils with their scent,*
> *They sniffed the air before they left.*
> *Upon the wind their prey had called,*
> *To find their victim Fenrir sent.*

Throughout the night Magnus stirred, placed some more wood on the fire, groggily looked around, and then nodded off again. When the morning cold and the sun's irritating light finally bade him rise, there was still fatigue in his muscles and stiffness in his bones. He reached into his pack and pulled out some dried meat his mother had prepared for him. He was thankful, but it merely delayed the hunger that was building. He was torn between the need to find food and the desire to continue the hunt and finish this ordeal, but he knew the latter would not happen until the former was satisfied.

Cutting a small branch from a nearby bush he fashioned a crude spear for catching fish. Making his way back to the stream he hoped he could find some unlucky Löja, a fish common in the area, stuck in a back eddy, under a rotten log. Plenty of decaying foliage lay along the banks and he ventured along the stream's edge until he found a shallow section to straddle the object of his search.

Finally, the small creature poked his head out enough for a clear shot. Magnus threw his spear. The tip hit the branch and glanced off, sending the fish scurrying away. He didn't expect the fish to come back, but it did and positioned itself again under the log. Magnus could see the creature's eyes glaring at him, mocking him, and his mouth moving up and down, laughing at the ineffective fisherman.

I will not give you the satisfaction, he shouted at the fish in his head. After several attempts, however, he decided that there must be a better way to get a meal. Making his way back to his fire he stumbled upon some berry bushes. He frantically picked the delicacies, ignoring the stickers that pulled and scratched his skin. When he was sufficiently filled he opened his pack and filled it with several handfuls. It wasn't his intention to forage for berries this whole trip, but it would tide him over until he was able to trap some small game.

He loved to trap, and he and his friends would often set them to catch rabbits or squirrels. They were fairly successful, so he was confident that he would be this time. Taking the leather laces from his boots he tied them together and fashioned a loop and a long enough tail to reach a small tree. Tapping a stake into the ground under some berry bushes where rabbits liked to forage, he laid the loop off to the side, wrapped the rope around the stake loosely, and then bent the tree down and tied the rope to the top. Once the rabbit stepped into the loop it would dislodge the stake and the tree would sling the animal into the air, closing the loop around its foot. All Magnus had to do was wait. He didn't want to miss out on a fine rabbit dinner, so he found enough vines to build two more traps. Though he didn't expect the vines to produce the same results as the leather rope, he had increased his odds for a meal.

It was best that he wasn't around the traps. Small creatures wouldn't come out with people around. So, in order to give his prey a false sense of security he decided to try to pick up the wolf's trail while the traps did their work. Having eaten the berries, Magnus felt a little more energized. He filled his water pouch from the stream and started up the hill. This side of the hill didn't seem to have as much undergrowth. He didn't know why, but was thankful for the easier path. The trip up was twice as long as the trip down, and as the day moved along so did the heat. He needed to stop and rest.

When he finally stood at the top of the hill he looked out along the horizon at the hills in the distance, and the rock that was surely the wolf's. It was marvelous, and he could imagine how invincible the wolf felt sitting here, talking to the moon. Magnus didn't feel the need to hurry his pursuit; there were traps to check, and as long as he had food, he was enjoying the solitude.

He wondered if this was what his father felt when out on the hunt. Magnus enjoyed its savage allure, but it would get lonely, and the monotony of the woods couldn't compare to the vast opportunities the world had to offer. He was afraid that he wasn't going to be able to convince his father life at sea was better for him, and that in the end he would follow in his father's footsteps.

Looking down he noticed some familiar scat. It was from a wolf—this was where he had stood—and it looked as if he had gone down the hill in the direction of his camp. Magnus was a little unsettled.

When Vargold, the wolf-age, stands,
When evil spreads across the sea,
When worlds crumble and brothers fall,
When blood will wash upon the sand,
Not even Odin, god of war,
Or law giver, Yyr, true;
They will be devoured all,
No more sun, or moon, or star.
Ulfhurgud, his mind does bend
The maddening and woeful fiend,
Ylfskyr, the dangerous wolf
Where treachery has no friend;
All alone, on Fenrir lands
Along with Garmr the son,
The greatest of the wolven heart
Until all that's good no longer stands.

It was late afternoon by the time Magnus wound his way back to his fire. The coals had grown cold, and he approached the site with caution. It had taken him much longer to get back because he had followed what he believed were the wolf's markings, but now he wasn't too sure. Everything looked undisturbed, but he still gave the site a wide berth and went to see if anything was in his traps.

The two made of vines were as he left them, but the third had been sprung. The rabbit had long since stopped its struggling, resigned to an unknown fate. When Magnus approached the trap and touched his catch it jerked alive. He jumped back and almost tripped into the berry bush. If any wolves in the vicinity hadn't known where he was, they did now.

The rabbit thrashed with renewed energy, trying to escape, but it was no use. Magnus knew he had to kill the creature or the leather rope would cut through its leg. He took the rope, untied the knot, and held the rabbit upside down. In shock the animal finally fell still. It took little effort for Magnus to twist its neck, and the creature was relieved of its pain. An eerie feeling sent a shiver through Magnus' body, and, looking up from his kill, he saw the stealthy movement of a large animal in the brush. Slowly he stood and backed away, never taking his eyes off the hidden danger. His breathing quickened and his heart pounded, and the beast's low growl finally revealed its presence.

The wolf was bigger than anything Magnus had ever seen. Its head stood as high as Magnus' chest, and as the wolf lowered his head, ready to pounce, the hair on the nape of its neck added to its ferocious appearance.

Steady, Magnus thought. *Don't let him smell fear.*

But of fear there was plenty. Magnus' natural inclination was to turn and run, but he knew the wolf was faster. He would have to outwit him if he were to survive.

Realizing that he still held the rabbit in his hand, it occurred to him that maybe the wolf would like an easier dinner. "How would you like this tasty little rabbit?" Magnus asked, extending his arm. The wolf's eyes never left him, and when he threw the rabbit into the brush the wolf still didn't move. Two smaller wolves surprised

Magnus as they appeared out of from behind some trees, pouncing on the small morsel, fighting with one another.

If it were possible, Magnus' heart would have burst from the stress. He was glad that the other two were occupied, but he saw little escape from the brute in front of him. He continued to back up until a tree barred his way. *I could climb it*, he thought. He glanced up. The lowest branch was over his head. He would have to jump. If he missed he would be finished; if he grabbed hold of it his dangling legs would still be prime targets.

There is the stream, he thought, his mind scrambling for ideas. If he made it there the wolf might avoid the water, but it was just a stream. The water would hardly reach the wolf's chest. He still held onto hope, until he heard the low growl behind him. Turning sideways, trying to keep one eye in either direction, Magnus saw the fourth wolf: she was as big as the first. The other two must be their pups.

Eyes open, Magnus offered a prayer. "Lord Odin, master of all, protect me from these beasts who threaten me, and I will serve you faithfully all the days of my life."

The dominant wolf slowly walked forward, growling louder, and the she-wolf held her ground to keep him from running. Hearing Magnus' voice the two younger ones looked up, left their dinner, and joined the pack. Seeing a stick lying on the ground, Magnus bent down to pick up the potential weapon. Curling his fingers around the club, he lost his balance and fell backward. His mind whirled with fear, knowing that this would be his last act: a dishonorable Viking, a failed hunter, a meal for the dark creatures of lord Fenrir.

The air suddenly turned cold and Magnus half expected the wings of the Valkyrie to bear down on him, though he knew not to expect them, since his death was not in battle. Unexpectedly, the wolves halted their approach. Their gaze never left their prey, but at least they were no longer advancing. On the wings of the wind a fog swept down from the mountain. It was thick and heavy, and as it moved through the forest, birds flew away and small animals scurried for safety. Magnus' momentary hope of reprieve vanished in a feeling of holy dread, but he would not be undone. If he were to die it would not be as a quivering child, stone cold in fear.

He stood, still holding the stick, and he waved it in the wind; He haltingly lied, "I am not afraid of you. Show yourself or be gone." He hoped nothing would be revealed, but to his dismay a figure formed in the mist, a fearsome man with shaggy strewn hair. What looked like horns sprang from his head, but Magnus could not be sure.

The form became clearer as it stepped out of the fog, not man but beast, not wolf but monster. His eyes glowed red and his teeth looked razor sharp. Chains that had been broken hung from his front legs, reminiscent of his captors' failed attempt. A loud growl that emanated from deep within shook the ground and quaked all but the four wolves.

"Why do you hunt me?"

Magnus understood the voice.

"It is not you I hunt, but these by your side," Magnus said.

"Why do you hunt me?" he asked again, not differentiating himself from the others.

Confused, Magnus decided he could do nothing but tell the truth. "I hunt them to find my destiny. My father wished me to follow his."

The specter, or so it seemed to Magnus, crept closer, sniffing the air around his face. Magnus could feel and smell the stale, putrid odor of his adversary, but with all the self-control he could muster he held his stomach in check. The beast raised his head and howled to the heavens.

"Do you not know me? I am the son of the god Loki, the master of the beast, the slayer at the end of days! Why do you hunt me?"

Magnus didn't know what to say. He was hunting to prove something to his father. He was hunting to find out his destiny. He thought hard; in what seemed like an eternity, only moments passed. Then it hit him and he cried, "I hunt to prove that I am a man!"

Fenrir howled, "You will not be proven today, for this is not your destiny, or that of your family. Your path lies down another way."

"Tell me what path I am to follow, that my way would be clear," Magnus pleaded.

"Should I make your path easy as well? Do you want me to line the way with sweet smelling flower petals?" There was a sinister hiss in his voice.

"If you are not here to guide, why save me from these beasts?"

Fenrir looked the boy over as if to measure his worth. Should he give him a taste of what is to come? What mischief could he cause the gods if he did? That would be worth the trouble. "Yes, I will speak of what is to come. Your destiny is on the sea, but the hunt of a wolf will guide your steps. Fear will not be your companion, but it will set the course of your feet."

"It is a riddle; speak plainly. What will I hunt? Where will the sea take me, and what kind of wolf do I seek?" Magnus asked.

Fenrir had lost interest in this pup, and the low growl of his adversary caused him to hold his tongue. As Magnus stood the mist began to swirl. He hoped the gods would tell him more, but Fenrir disappeared. The fog retreated with haste, and when Magnus turned to face the wolves they were gone, save the hide of one of their kin. It was a gift from Fenrir, for which he was glad. It saved him from having to explain the experience to his father. But what had happened? He just slumped to the ground and thanked Odin for his protection. Covering himself with the new pelt, he fell asleep.

The beast that rides upon the wind
Devours the good of man.
Mischief born to war with gods
To battle Odin in the end.
Fenrir loathes the valiant hall
Where warriors battle dusk to dawn.
Mischief breeds two sons of kind
Until both man and god do fall.
Patiently for Regnarok
In his mouth holds Tyr's hand,
From mischief chained against his will
Bay to the moon upon the rock.
What holds the fortunes of tomorrow?
None on earth can tell.
What lies ahead for this young lad?
Only pain and sorrow.

Trading
769 AD

Magnus' son Arne was on his mind; he had hoped this trip would be his first. Sigrunn was too protective and if she didn't let him go, Arne would wear an effeminate label. He was almost thirteen and his initiation into the clan was imminent. He needed to join his father as a man.

"You are daydreaming again, my friend. You need to keep your eyes on the water or we will be blown into the rocks." Harald was the ship's captain and he didn't relish the idea of losing his vessel. He trusted Magnus' experience as a steersman, but experience was useless if not put into practice.

"Yes sir," Magnus responded. The wind was blowing against them and the crew had to put the oars into the water. Their movement was slow but steady.

"Harald, how old was your son when you took him on his first trade?"

"He was ten. I had to wrestle him away from his mother's apron. He begged me to bring him, and he wasn't too useless," he laughed.

"You must have been very proud of him," Magnus said.

"Yes, I was proud, but he was too young. He spent more time getting in the way than helping. The crew was ready to throw him overboard. I finally had to give him a task that kept him out of the way. I didn't let him come again for another four years." Thinking for a moment he asked, "Your son's name is Arne, is that correct? He is about the age to come on a trade."

"Aye, but I think his mother's apron strings are long and strong. It might take Thor's hammer to break them lose."

They both laughed. The wind was blowing the salt of the sea into their faces, and the low howl made it hard to hear. Magnus loved the sea, the wind, the salt; it made him feel alive and free.

"Port is in view!" the captain bellowed. "Steady with the oars. Prepare to stow them." He was estimating speed and distance. Harald was an accomplished captain and had a keen sense of his ship. "Raise oars."

His men obeyed instantly, lifting their oars straight and clear of the water.

"Secure oars."

They pulled them in quickly, turning them to the side and fastening them to the inside of the hull. It was a complicated maneuver because of their length. If any man wasn't precise he could strike the man behind him in the face. It had happened, and broken noses and lacerations often resulted in oaths and fights. Harald was glad each time there wasn't an incident.

Magnus masterfully directed the ship alongside the dock as it slowed enough for men to jump to the pier and secure it. This wasn't the first time they had used this port, a small inlet with a deep bay. It allowed ships like his to load heavy cargo with no worry of dragging the bottom. The people of this region, capable warriors, spoke a dialect akin to the Germanic people south of the Vikings' home in Birka, yet it was still unintelligible. But he had learned enough of it to trade.

Vidar had told him stories of his first encounter. The residents had seen the sailing vessel, carrying strange people with a strange language, as a threat and approached them with their weapons drawn. Vidar's captain tried to communicate their intention for trade, but the threatening behavior spooked a nervous Viking who threw the first blow. The rest ended with several dead and the inhabitants disappearing into the steppes.

They were able to capture three women and two men, and decided to take them as slaves for their trouble. It ended up being a profitable move: after instructing them in the Norse language, they employed them as interpreters. The next year when they returned the slaves were able to communicate the Vikings' intentions and a trade agreement was established. In a show of good faith the slaves were returned and the Slavic people became good allies.

This time, however, something was different. The village was usually full of people eager to trade, but today it lay silent. Harald saw caution a prudent move and ordered his men to carry weapon and shield. This was a trade vessel but the men were warriors. They would as soon die in battle as barter, and their training and confidence was evident. Staggering their column, they slowly walked down the pier, shields held high to cover their midsections; they were most vulnerable in the open. If the Slavs were to attack, all they had were their shields to protect them. Magnus walked in front with his captain.

"Did you see that? Over to the left, behind the second building?" Magnus didn't divert his gaze; he didn't want to give away what he had seen.

"There are three more to the right. For some reason I don't feel welcome this trip." Harald would rather trade than pillage, but whichever brought him a profit he would use. "When we reach the end of the pier we will move to the center of the village. Create a semicircle to cover our flanks. Don't let anyone get behind us, and whatever you do, don't start a fight. Let's see what the problem is before we destroy our alliance."

When they reached the village center a familiar face met them. It was Bohuslav, the main tradesman who interpreted for them.

"My friend Harald. You have come at a bad time." He was looking around. "Some of our brothers to the south have, uh…come to visit. They are not used to the sight of Vikings and believe the best course of action is to repel your advances."

"Did you tell them that we have come to trade?"

Magnus pointed out armed men at the edge of the village. "Bohuslav, why are we being threatened? Do not hide the truth from me."

"They are not friends. They…" Bohuslav was shot through the throat by an arrow.

"Shield wall!" Harald yelled. With their backs to one another they overlapped their shields and raised them over their heads. Arrows struck them but were unable to penetrate the wall.

"Their main force is to the north. Hold firm until they attack."

Their patience paid off. Frustrated that their arrows could not hit their mark, the Slavs rushed the wall. Securing their feet, the Vikings braced the wall for the onslaught. The charging force struck the wall but could not move it. Only those in front were able to strike, but their swords only met shield. "Swordsmen, strike," the captain called, and the shield parted allowing a Viking sword to stab the closest enemy.

"Archer ready," Magnus commanded. "Now!"

An archer was raised on the shoulder of another man, able to shoot down into the crowd. Before the enemy could counter, he was lowered, disappearing behind the wall. The enemy's frustration mounted as they could only occasionally penetrate the shield wall; even when a man did, he was pulled through and impaled by a waiting sword.

When a sufficient number of enemy warriors lay dead, the Vikings broke formation and engaged the rest man to man. The Norsemen's muscles were sculpted by the oar and ax. They wielded their weapons with the force of three men, and the enemy felt their furor until none were left. When the last man was routed their cry echoed even within the houses of the village. Harald and his men soon found themselves surrounded again, but this time by a grateful crowd.

"Harald has saved us from our enemy. We honor him and his men," the chieftain praised their friends from the north. "Tonight we will feast and drink until we can stand no more."

"Magnus take a few men and station them at the edges of town," Harald instructed. "We don't want to be caught off guard in case others would act treacherously." The captain wouldn't refuse his host, but he also wouldn't chance waking up tomorrow in Valhalla.

Ever the vigilant warrior, Magnus volunteered for the first watch. Something still unsettled him about this whole affair. There wasn't a sufficient force to cause them any real concern. The Slavs they encountered fought well, but they were easily vanquished. He had heard tales of fiercer warriors than these. He felt a little disappointed that there wasn't more blood. Suddenly he heard the snap of a twig.

"Who is there?" Magnus stood and motioned to the two men next to him to spread out and be on guard. "Show yourself or I will slay you where you stand." The usual vibrato echoed into the darkness. Magnus stepped forward holding up a torch he had fashioned from a branch in the fire. He raised it over his head but the flames only danced at the edges of the night. In his periphery, however, he saw movement, and he quickly turned to see men hiding among the brush. Without turning he said to his shipmates, "Go, quickly, before our brothers are too drunk to fight."

The closest to him ran toward the community hall.

Magnus tightened his fingers around his ax and lifted his shield in front of him, and as he did an arrow grazed its edge. He slowly moved backward until he found the corner of a small barn and slipped behind it for cover. As with all Vikings, engagement was preferable to hiding, but one against too many was foolish.

His companion didn't follow Magnus' lead and shouted into the dark. "Show yourselves, you cowards!" The lack of response bolstered his courage. "I and my friend are two, and you cower behind brush in the darkness. Stand and fight like men, or slink back into the darkness where you…"

A guttural sound finished the sentence. The Viking grabbed for the arrow that protruded from his neck and tried to pull it out. Blood ran down his hands and his head whirled as the lack of oxygen buzzed in his ears and spots before his eyes. The last thing he heard was the shouts of an advancing army.

Harald was enjoying himself when the watchman intruded his revelry.

"Captain, we are under attack!"

The warning didn't register at first. He laughed and continued to drink. The watchman was insistent and almost came to blows with his captain before Harald noticed his fidgeting host.

70

"Why do you look so uncomfortable?" He reached out and took hold of his tunic. "Answer me, or by the halls of Valhalla I will slay you."

"Please, my lord." His broken dialect became more difficult to understand though his fear. "We had nothing to do with this. You have freed us and we are grateful, but…" And the words were frozen forever on his lips as Harald's sword slipped through his ribs.

"I was tired of his whining." The captain took another deep drink and then, slamming the mug on the table, yelled, "Kill them all!"

Cries of fear and death filled the room and within minutes only Vikings stood. Nothing is worse than an angry Viking betrayed by allies, nothing that is, than a drunk Viking. The smell of battle cleared their heads and they followed the watchman out of the community hall and down the street.

"Magnus!" the captain yelled. "Are you still alive?"

"The cowards are sneaking in by cloak of night." He pointed to the tall grass and brush in front of them.

"What is he doing?" Harald was pointing at Magnus' companion. "Trying to frighten them with words?" When the arrow pierced the Viking's chest everyone ducked. Harald was totally sober now, every sense keen to what was happening. Looking at the advancing throng he knew they were outnumbered and he didn't relish losing today's victory in the dark. "Head to the ship and put out to sea!" he yelled.

Ten men turned and ran toward the boat but only nine made it, one slumping to the ground. The other fifteen stood their ground and engaged the enemy, giving their comrades time to secure the boat. Slowly they backed their way to the dock, slaying as many of the Slavs as they could before they set sail or died.

"Shield wall!" Magnus shouted. There were too many and he knew they would soon be overrun. The wall would give them some time to breathe under the protection of the gathered shields. "Keep the wall curved and slowly move backward!" he instructed. Even the captain obeyed.

By the time they reached the dock four men had fallen, but fifty of the enemy lay dead. The most dangerous section of the retreat was the dock, but those who had gone before had brandished bows and set loose a volley of arrows. It was just enough for the Vikings to turn and run for the ship. Its hull was already in motion when Magnus' foot cleared the plank, and the arrow that pierced his shoulder propelled him onto the deck.

Home
769 AD

Falling forward, Magnus slumped to the deck. He winced in pain, but was able to sit up and take stock of the situation. The oarsmen were frantically rowing them into the middle of the sound. Those facing the shore lifted their shields and arrows glanced off both shield and hull. Because the warriors were forced to row and hold shields, the ship was veering back and forth, taking longer to reach safety.

Magnus made his way to the aft of the ship and the steersman's station. As he turned the shaft of the arrow scraped one of his shipmates' side, and he raised his hand to protect his face. The arrow's shaft wrenched upward in the wound, and Magnus stifled a cry of pain. He bit hard on his bottom lip as the sound attempted to escape, but he stumbled and fell to the deck of the ship.

Harald stepped to his friend's side and helped him to the steersman's position. He needed Magnus at his station if they were to avoid any more injuries. At the same time, he knew the shaft would be a problem. Grabbing a piece of wood he handed it to Magnus.

"We have to do this my friend." He looked at Magnus, who shook his head yes. Pain wasn't something a Viking invited, and knew it could not be avoided. Magnus was already in pain and knew the halls of Valhalla were lined with the blood of his forefathers. He nodded to his friend and bit down on the wood. Harald, however, didn't break the shaft; he pushed the arrow through the shoulder and when it came out the other side he pulled it the rest of the way.

Magnus passed out for a second as pain shot through his body, and the cold spray of saltwater burned the wound. He woke up to Harald setting him straight next to the rudder. Another crewman was helping to strap Magnus into position so he would not fall into the sea.

"I need you to do this!" Harald slapped Magnus in the face. "You are the best, even injured. Turn into the wind!" he yelled. "Drop the shields and put your back into it." It was Harald's last effort to distance them from their attackers who were preparing another volley of arrows. The ship lurched forward and Magnus' body would have fallen overboard if not for the ropes. Only the adrenaline coursing through his body made the pain tolerable.

Three others were dead or injured by the time they reached a safe distance. The warriors on the shore whooped in victory while the Vikings limping pride carried them to a safety. Once out of the arrows' range, Harald called for the ship to lay anchor. He was concerned with those who were injured, but also with the predicament of those on shore. How could they leave with their honor intact when so many of the crew was dead? He didn't like being run out of town at night. He would rather die than face the shame of this tale, but he needed to let his men heal.

"Harald." One of the crewmen tapped his shoulder. "The keg of fresh water was struck and half is gone." Harald swore and stood, looking toward the town with anger. They couldn't stay long if they ran out of water, but maybe it would be enough.

"Ration it, and give more to the injured." Harald walked the length of his ship to inspect both wood and men. The ship had little damage but his men were a different story. He could let the dead lay on the deck, but by the gods he wasn't going to disallow them a proper burial. "Wrap the dead in some of the furs, tie them well and drop them in the water. The cold will preserve them until we can bury them." Four had been struck by arrows and one wasn't going to live out the night.

"Should we give water to him, captain?" There was no malice in the question.

"No," Harald nodded. "Give it to the living. Soon enough he will drink to his heart's content with his fathers." The Viking life was hard and survival and honor their guide.

When he had inspected his crew, Harald made his way back to Magnus. "How are you doing, friend?"

"I am cold and hungry. Is there anything to eat?"

"Hungry is good. Let me look at your wound." Removing part of Magnus' leather shirt, he could see the wound hadn't been cleaned. Taking some of the salt water from the sea he dribbled it over the wound thinking the stinging would help heal the injury. He then wrapped it back up and helped his friend get comfortable. "There is dried fish to eat. I will cut you some."

Grabbing Harald's arm, Magnus asked, "How bad is it?"

"Not good. We can't stay and fight if we want to live, and we can't live if we have no honor."

"We would rather die with honor then live in shame," Magnus said.

"Yes, but a fool runs toward an unnecessary death and honor is only a word. I would rather your son see you live another day than mourn your death." Harald spoke softly.

To some his words were cowardly, but Magnus knew better. Age tempered the need for war. He thought that smelling the sweet scent of Sigrunn was preferable to the smoky halls of the damned. If they left now they could redeem themselves by returning and taking the village and its inhabitants for booty.

"We can do this another day. Let us return home." Magnus felt horrible and the only thing that tempered the pain was sleep. Unable to keep his eyes open he drifted off, leaving his friend to contemplate their fate.

When Magnus woke the ship had traveled north of the city and around the other side of the mountain. He was lying beside the injured, covered with fur, and all the others were gone. He tried to wake the man next to him, but he was burning up with fever and Magnus knew he wouldn't be of any help. When the fog of sleep cleared his head it dawned on him that Harald had taken the rest and set off over land to exact revenge. He could do nothing but wait.

He hated waiting; there was nothing noble about it. If Harald had asked, he would have stumbled through the woods and faced death with them. Now, he was lying among the dead and one was already attracting flies. It would be his luck that Harald would lead his men to their death and wake up in the halls of Valhalla, and he would die here and be refused at death's gate.

Magnus passed the time, at first, by organizing the ship. His crewmen had left early and the ship was in total disarray. Injured bodies were strewn about the deck, and they groaned on occasion. He hoped they would live, but he soon found that Harald had taken the rations of water with him. Eventually, with parched lips, he talked to the dying for company.

"Well, my friends." He poked one, and, hearing a groan, felt a little less insane. "It looks like we are facing the end like dogs. I don't know what is worse, dying or watching you die. Maybe it would be more merciful for me to put you out of your misery. At least you would die by a sword and not the decay that is eating your insides."

Rolling the groaning man over, Magnus found him drenched with sweat. His forehead was hot to touch and he wasn't long for this life.

"Do you want a quick deliverance to Valhalla?" he asked. "Where is your sword? You must have it in your hands as I slay you or it won't count." He moved some things around and found a sword, but at this point it didn't matter to whom it belonged. Loosening the blankets covering the man, Magnus laid the sword on his chest and wrapped his arms around it, a symbolic gesture of battle.

"There, that is better. You will be ushered proudly into Odin's hall." Looking around for his ax, he continued, "I know this is what I would want, what any true Viking would want." He lifted his ax and brought it down full force, splitting his friend's head in two. For each living and dead crewman he did the same, until he felt the halls of Valhalla were filled.

"But what of me? Who will send me to my father's hall to live with honor the rest of my days? Who, but none are left to send me on my way?" The fever to which the rest had succumbed was now encroaching upon his consciousness. He knew little of what he had just done, but in the best mind would have done the same. Magnus was exhausted and could not move any more. If his friends returned it would be to a corpse. If he didn't, then the grass would grow and cover their bodies, a silent memorial to the fallen. Magnus passed out.

He woke to Harald nudging him. "Magnus what evil has taken over my ship, and how did you survive?"

"You're alive!" Magnus tried to sit up but whatever strength he had was used to keep him this side of death's door. "Where did you go…now I remember…were you successful?"

"We have avenged our honor, yours, and the fallen. My friend, what happened here?"

"I do not know. The last thing I remember is waking to a foul smell, an empty ship, and a lot of pain." Sitting up he could see the bodies of his friends lined up, swords on their breasts, their skulls split open. "By the hammer of Thor, did I do that?"

"Either you or a specter, but my guess the former. Men do strange things when they are wracked with the fever. It is amazing you are still alive." He motioned for one of his men to bring some fresh water. "We will rest here for a couple of days to regain our strength, and then head for home."

Home, thought Magnus. He closed his eyes and slept.

Chapter 10
769 A.D.

There shall be one end for us both; one bond after our vows; nor shall our first love aimlessly perish. Happy am I to have won the joy of such a consort; I shall not go down basely in loneliness to the gods of Tartarus. —Saxo Grammaticus, Gesta Danorum

The early morning water lay as still as glass, and the fowl on the banks sang their songs while foraging for breakfast in the mud and muck. Each day Arne liked to listen to the sounds of the morning filling the air, undisturbed by the hustle of the docks and the noise that sprang to life in Birka. In the quiet he could imagine his future, riding the waves, visiting new lands. The frog's croak was a foreign language that offered opportunities of trade, the seagull flying low warned of an evening storm, and the gentle lapping of water against the docks pushed the hull effortlessly to an unknown destination. He hoped to one-day sail alongside his father in search of great treasure.

His family lived outside the city on a parcel of land handed down to his father by his father's father. Farming and hunting were his heritage, but he would gladly give them up for the sea. It fell to his mother and the children to work the little farm to supplement their rations during the winter months. It wasn't that his father never helped, but the farm came second to his obsession with the sea.

Required to help, Sigrunn, his mother, insisted that he complete his chores before venturing into the city, so before sunrise he slopped the hog, fed the chickens, and made sure enough wood was piled in the box next to the door for his mother to cook the morning meal. But hard work and good food could not satiate his curiosity. This morning was like many others, and no sooner had he set the ax in its place than his feet carried him down the familiar path toward the docks.

As eager as he was to reach his favorite place, his pace slowed to a walk as his attention was drawn to the sights of life beneath the trees. Small game stirred early in search of food before their predators knew they were awake, and Arne would try to sneak up behind without being noticed. Just in front of him a hare stopped and stood perfectly still. It had felt Arne's presence and steadied itself to bolt at a moment's notice. Its nose twitched in the air trying to catch the scent of danger, and its ears pivoted back and forth in search of unusual sounds. The beady black eyes filled with fear struck Arne the most.

Careful, he thought. *Place one foot quietly in front of the other. Breathe slowly; don't let the sound of your exhale be heard.* Arne was no more than five feet away from the hare. He stopped and waited, giving his prey a false sense of security, and the little creature began to nibble on clover. *I will catch you this time,* he thought, and he leaped forward only to find himself face down with nothing but grass and leaves as a prize.

He groaned at the sudden jolt and spit dirt and leaves out of his mouth. From the corner of his eye Arne saw a small *skoggsork* sitting on a tree root inches from his face. The little rodent had seen Arne's failed attempt and didn't even scamper away, adding to his humiliation. But Arne's embarrassment lasted for only a minute because he knew the little devil would never reveal what had just taken place.

The rodents were elusive and as hard as he tried, never caught one. His failure didn't dampen his spirits, but rather gave flight to his imagination. His father told stories of his grandfather's hunts, but they always paled in comparison to Magnus' own stories of faraway lands. Arne wanted to be a great warrior like his father, and sail the seas in search of treasure. These longings brought him to the docks each day.

The wooden pier creaked and groaned against the gentle ebb and flow of the water. The harbor wasn't large, but a series of docks branched out from the shore; in all it could handle five ships. When Arne stepped onto the wooden structure, the bobbing made it difficult to walk and mimicked the ships sailing across the water. Placing his feet squarely beneath him, Arne closed his eyes and pretended to be aboard his father's ship.

Steady as she goes, helmsman. Keep the nose of the dragon pointed to the far shore. Put your backs into your oars. Only speed and courage will get us home safely. A wave splashed against the wood sending a mist into the air and across his face. The motion broke his thoughts as it raised the dock and Arne was caught off-balance. After steadying himself again he made his way to the end and sat, dangling his legs over the edge. The water wasn't high enough for him to dip his toes, but lying on his stomach he stretched enough to reach beneath its surface.

Fish lived beneath the dock and lying there he could see them silently disappear in the silt, but the smaller minnows flicked at the surface in search of food, the little bugs that rested on the top of the water. Arne slipped his hand under the water, without ripple, and the minnows swam between his fingers. Some even nibbled at his skin. It didn't hurt; in fact, it tickled. Just as he was about to close his hand around the unsuspecting creatures his body lurched forward and his face scraped the surface of the water before he was lifted into the air.

"Careful, lad, or the next time you will be neck-deep in the channel." It was Vidar, the old dockhand. He had taken a liking to Arne, and often spent time with him. Setting the boy on his feet he asked, "What has caught your attention this morning? Do you think your father will make it home today?"

Arne shrugged his shoulders. "Maybe."

It had been a week since his father had left, and each day the docks held out hope that he would return. Ships sailed in and out on most days; they came from all over the known world, and their holds were filled with interesting animals, foods, and trinkets that would be sold in the markets, but none of the ships were his father's.

"Give me a hand with this."

Vidar handed him a large rope and instructed him on the proper way of coiling it around a dock post.

"This will help keep the rope from kinking. That way when a ship docks, I can quickly tie it before the waves try to carry it back into the harbor."

Arne took the end of the rope and began to wrap it around the peg, but it wasn't as easy as it looked. It seemed to have a mind of its own and bent in the opposite direction. Instead of a perfectly round coil it was a twisted mess. Vidar patiently stepped behind him and showed him how to extend the rope and allow it to coil in its natural direction.

"It looks like a snake," Arne observed. "Why won't it coil the way I want it to?"

"Everything in life has its own way of coiling. You can fight against it or find its natural path. It is much easier to sail a ship by going with the wind than it is to row against the current."

"But what if the wind blows in a direction you don't want to go?" Arne asked.

Vidar stood stroking his beard. "Well, I guess you pray that the sea god and goddess Aegir and Ran have a fight and the winds begin to blow in your direction." Vidar laughed and gave Arne a slap on the back.

Arne wasn't satisfied with following the winds. His mother was insistent that he stay at home to help with the farm, and Arne was frustrated that his father acquiesced. He was approaching manhood and felt the call of the sea. Other boys his age had stood by their fathers, salt spraying in their faces and the wind howling as it drove the ship, but he only watched them from the shore. He wasn't angry with his father but the siren call left a void in his soul that the comforting words of mother and friends could not fill.

As he stared into the distance the seaboard was filling with people and the noise caught his attention. "The wharf," his mother often exhorted him, "is not a place for a boy. There are dangers and temptations that could bring you harm." She could see the wanderlust rearing its head; he was just like his father and she knew that it was only a matter of time before she lost him to the sea as well. Yet that was the life they were born to; the sea brought forth life, and for a Viking being anchored to port too long was a curse. She could protect him for only so much time.

"Get out of the way, boy." A very large, rough, and unpleasant man was about to kick him aside when Vidar grabbed his shoulder.

"I think it is best you save your anger for a homeless dog and not a boy."

The man turned to stand an inch away from Vidar's face. "What's this mongrel to you?" he growled.

"Useful, which is more than I can say for you." Vidar turned to Arne. "Go to the dock shed and put it in order." Vidar gave a low growl, scowling, and the man walked away as surly as he had come.

The sea was no stranger to Vidar; he had sailed it as Far East as possible, but age had its limitations, and the limp, from a long past battle, kept him tied to the land. Mornings were hardest for him as the cool air stiffened his joints. They served as a reminder that he would never again feel the wind against his face.

Vidar had accepted his role in the community. His responsibility as the dock master was important, and he felt no shame in his job. Yet, he could see his diminished stature among the young. Too many were willing to challenge him, and one of these days he would be forced to defend his honor beyond his ability; his death would be the result. He wasn't afraid to die. He rather relished finding release in the heat of battle. Dying a warrior was more desirous than wasting away in a bed.

Young Arne was a reminder of better times. He had the same lust for the sea, but Vidar's was past while his little friend's lay before him.

"Arne, a ship is approaching. It could be your father's. Do you want to help me secure it when it docks?"

His slim figure raced from the shed and stood as tall as he could to see if the ship had his father's colors. Viking ships didn't fly flags demarking a nation or a king; rather each sail had a distinct color and pattern, and sometimes an image of a serpent was drawn across its width in honor of the goddess of the sea. The closer the ship the longer Arne's face became; it wasn't his father's.

"That's ok, my boy, maybe tomorrow. But you can still help. It will be good practice."

The boy nodded his head and waited patiently.

The wind was light this far inland. Dropping the oars, the men stroked the water in unison. Their strength and precision pushed the heavy vessel through the sea with ease. It was a magnificent sight, the silhouette set against a background of towering green mountains. With each thrust of the oars the ship picked up speed, but the helmsman was precise. At the right moment he gave word to the crew, who lifted their oars and stowed them tightly on the inside of the hull. The ship drifted as the steersman guided it masterfully next to the dock.

"Grab the rope boy."

Arne took a rope from one of the ship's crew.

"Tie it securely; we don't want the ship to float out into the middle of the sound. The crew wouldn't be too happy."

"Is this good enough?" Arne stood back with pride.

Giving his attention to another task Vidar replied, "If you did it like I told you it will hold. If not these men will throw you into the water after their ship."

Arne bent over and took a second look at his work; he was satisfied. Watching the boy stirred in Vidar memories that he had tried to forget, the rope that coiled in its own direction.

Wedding Memories
769 A.D.

Vidar's eyes held that faraway look again; his attention was somewhere else. Arne stepped aside as men began unloading the deck, but he quickly became bored. Turning to make his way back to the farm, he realized that the sun was at its highest and his mother would be furious. He set his sail for home and pretended the wind carried him with great speed.

"You're late." She was disappointed, and Arne hated disappointing his mother. "You need to wash up and assist me. You've forgotten that I'm helping with your cousin's wedding."

Of course he had forgotten. Who cared about a silly wedding when men set out to sea?

"Ragnhild's mother expected me an hour ago." She gave him a slap on the back of the head and whisked him off to fulfill his promise.

After rushing her son off to finish his chores, a smile spread across Sigrunn's face as she remembered her own wedding, seventeen years earlier.

761 AD

Magnus was so proper, or properly scared, she thought. He came with his father and two uncles and sat before her father. Magnus would declare his intentions as the family delegates negotiated the bride price and a settlement of dowry. She and her sisters waited outside trying to suppress their giddiness.

"He is so handsome," her youngest sister giggled.

"That is not important," Sigrunn said, craning her neck to see out the door.

"You would rather marry an ugly man, fat and old?" Her other sister pushed out her stomach and scrunched her face.

"I would rather it be the young man who has entered our house. And if you two are as lucky as I am, the goddess will allow you a man as honorable as Magnus."

"I don't know. He doesn't look much like a man, more of a boy if you ask me," her sister teased.

"If all boys were like him, we would be in Valhalla," the youngest sighed. The boys she knew were immature and thought only of games. Sigrunn was a woman at sixteen, and she and Magnus had known each other all their lives. This was the formal proposal to a lifetime of childhood negotiations.

"Master Yngve." Magnus cleared his throat. "I have come to propose a union of our two families, an offer to marry your daughter, Sigrunn."

Yngve looked the boy up and down. "Magnus, I have known you all your life, but what makes you think I want to give you my daughter?" He had a twinkle in his eye, but Magnus would not be undone.

"I believe, sir, that our union would be beneficial for both our houses. I want to offer you the bride price of twenty ounces of silver and two cows to secure our alliance." He was sitting tall, sure that his offer was generous.

"Indeed, you do bring a fair amount, if I thought my allegiance could be bought at such a low price." Yngve held out his hand to one of his family, who placed a bag of coins in his palm. "I have here thirty pieces of silver and a fine horse, bridle, and shield outside. Surely, you can match my generosity."

Magnus looked at his father. He didn't know if they had more to give, but his father had come prepared and handed his son another pouch. He opened it and counted out fifteen more coins. "I believe that this will be sufficient to assuage any dishonor caused by my first offer."

Yngve laughed, stood, and shook the boy's hand in agreement.

"It is settled. The wedding will take place in a week, next Friday. I do believe the goddess Frigga will be honored, and that the festivities will be in keeping with your status."

The week couldn't go any faster for Sigrunn. Her mother, aunts, and sisters wouldn't let her out of their sight. Whenever she tried to leave their home they would scoot her back until they were sure the way was clear, and Magnus couldn't see her. They weren't taking any chances with her purity. What Sigrunn enjoyed the most were the new clothes. Her mother had gone through her belongings and packed away her childhood attire and dressed her in the more appropriate apparel of a woman. As they walked through the town everyone knew that she was marked for marriage.

Sigrunn was nervous as they arrived at the bathhouse. It was usually reserved for the men, but when a young woman was being prepared for matrimony it was vacated for the cleansing ritual. Once they were inside, the door was secured and the fire under the rocks lit and fanned until they were sufficiently heated. Water was poured over them to steam the room. She could feel sweat beading on her forehead as her aunts helped her undress.

Standing naked in the center, surrounded by her attendants, Sigrunn waited as her mother dipped a ladle into a bucket of warm water. Pouring the water over Sigrunn's head she said, "May the water of purification wash away the old life of a maiden and purify you for your husband." More steam was created and they sat on the benches. The rest of the afternoon brought a blush to her face as she was instructed in the duties of a wife.

When they were finished, Sigrunn was led to a small room adjacent to the bathhouse. There, cold water was poured over her body, and a special mixture of magical herbs and flowers was rubbed on her skin. Her mother recited, "May the cold water close your skin to protect you from sickness, and the aroma of sweet herbs and flowers make you attractive to your husband and ward off evil from your home."

"Mother," Sigrunn asked, "do you think our life will be plagued with evil?"

She comforted her daughter's concerns replying, "Fate and the gods can play tricks on our lives. It is always best to be prepared for what might come. Evil comes to those who seek it, but sometimes it sneaks into our lives when we least expect it.

"Has there been unexpected evil in your life?"

A dark cloud momentarily fell across her mother's face. "You know that your father isn't my first husband. One before him was killed in battle during the first year of our marriage. His death was noble, but it left a deep hole I thought would never be filled." Her countenance brightened. "But your father rescued me from my despair and has given me a wonderful life, and a lovely daughter, who is now a bride herself. Let's not worry about what we can't control.

For now these flowers will make you smell sweet for your husband, and your night will be filled with bliss."

After drying off, Sigrunn dressed in a brand new set of cloths, colorful and festive. Her hair was brushed out to lie gently on her shoulders with a wreath of flowers decoratively woven into her hair. Her mother stepped back and began to cry. Sigrunn put her arms around her and they both wept.

Magnus had also been busy with wedding preparations. According to tradition he was required to obtain an ancestral sword belonging to a dead forbearer. He had no idea where to get one. His father just smiled and took him out to the city's edge, where their family burial mound was dug.

"Magnus, like me before you, you must ask your ancestors for direction, that they will lead you to the sword of their choosing." He handed him a shovel and stood back.

Looking around, Magnus tentatively began to dig. The shovel's blade struck its first bone, sending a shiver up his spine. He gently removed the dirt to reveal some bones neatly lying with a shield and spear, but no sword. It took two more tries before he found a grave that held a sword, and after reverently replacing the dirt on the mound he quickly, and proudly, strode back into town wearing the decorative scabbard. Men nodded in affirmation and some slapped him on his back in congratulations.

His father met him at the bathhouse, and it was his time to go through the ceremony of purification. He was stripped and bathed, water was poured over his head, and he was instructed in the ways of women. "Son, don't think for a moment you can understand a woman. It is safer to fight in battle than to wage war with your wife. If you take care of her she will defend you against every adversary, but if you cross her she will cause you more grief than you can imagine."

"Father," Magnus asked, "has mother ever given you such grief?"

He laughed. "Grief is just the other side of pleasure. Worry less about what your bride might do, and give attention to how you will win her love. If you do the latter, the former is easier to bear."

Magnus' uncles chimed in and all gave him advice on how to woo his bride. When all was said and done he was dressed in clean clothes and the sword was strapped to his waist.

As they walked outside his father said, "Wait, Magnus. I have one more thing to give you. Like my father before me, I give you the hammer of Thor. It is a symbol of your mastery in this union and surety of fruit in your marriage."

Magnus beamed as he took the hammer. Tomorrow could not come soon enough.

Yngve opened the evening by presenting the appropriate sacrifices. "To Thor I offer this goat to be sacrificed, that he might look favorably on this union."

The chieftain of the city took the goat to the center of the procession and slit its throat, catching some of the blood in a bowl. The mixture was placed on the altar's fire and heated, and a bundle of sticks was dipped in the liquid. Magnus and Sigrunn stood in front of the altar and the chieftain sprinkled them with the blood as her father, making the Hammer-sign—a gentle downward movement followed by a swift movement to the right and left—conferred a blessing. The rest of the goat was taken away and roasted for the feast.

"To the goddess Freyr," he continued, "We dedicate this horse to gain favor and fertility." The horse was committed to the care of the chieftain.

When the sacrifices were finished Magnus turned to his bride. Nervous, he looked intently into her eyes while fumbling for his sword. Holding it in the air he said, "I give you this sword as a symbol of my protection for you and our children. It is to pass from you to our first born and to his first born after him as a constant testimony of this promise."

Sigrunn had a sword as well, and it felt clumsy and heavy in her hand. She drew it from the scabbard and held it in the air. "With this sword I transfer my father's role of guardian to you, for my protection and the protection of our children." After she had spoken these words they each tilted the hilt of their swords revealing the finger rings that would bind them. They pronounced their undying commitment to one another, and after receiving each other's swords they were officially wed.

The festivities began, and taking the bridal ale, the first symbol of service to her new husband, Sigrunn said:

> Ale I bring you, you oak-of-battle,
> With strength blended and brightest honor;
> 'Tis mixed with magic and mighty sons,
> With goodly spells, wish-speeding runes.

Magnus took his cup and, making the sign of Thor, recited:

> Bring the Hammer the bride to bless
> On the maiden's lap lay you Mjolnir;
> In Vor's name then our wedlock hallow!

By the time the evening was finished most of the guests were drunk, but it couldn't be complete until the six witnesses performed their duty. Escorting the new bride and groom, they led Sigrunn and Magnus by torchlight to their new home and bridal chamber. After ensuring that the correct couple entered the room, Magnus' friends stood guard for the whole evening, occasionally shouting encouragement.

The sun rose early, its rays filtering through the cracks in the wooden window shutter. Magnus had his arm around his new bride, and he lay for a while watching her sleep. Sigrunn was beautiful and the morning light lit her soft skin. He traced his hand along the contours of her body, and she stirred awake.

"Good morning, my love," she said, smiling as he leaned over and kissed her. "Last night doesn't seem to have filled your appetite."

"I could never get my fill of you." Magnus was trying to remember the advice of his uncles on wooing his new bride. "Are you as satisfied with me, as I am with you?"

She playfully pushed him away. "I am not so easily conquered. You will have to give more than a night of passion to win over my heart."

"Then how about two." He wrapped her in his strong arms and pulled her close to his body.

Allowing him this consolation she began to whisper something when they were interrupted by a knock on the door. Before they could answer it opened, and Sigrunn's attendants rushed her out of bed into an adjoining room. The girls giggled as they glimpsed Magnus lying in bed with a dumbfounded look on his face.

"Couldn't you have waited a while longer?" he pleaded unsuccessfully.

"This is so beautiful." Sigrunn was looking at the *hustrulinet* her attendants had brought. It was a long, finely pleated, snow-white linen cloth veil that symbolized her new status as a wife. She sat admiring it as they braided her hair and bound it in the coiffure reserved for married women. Once they were finished with her hair the *hustrulinet* was fastened to her braids with six pins along the sides of her temple.

Magnus was gone by the time they came through the house. The witnesses from the night before had swept him away to the community hall. Accompanied by her attendants, Sigrunn arrived minutes later to find him standing at the center surrounded by the members of both families. She walked up to him and stood by his side.

"Sigrunn," he said, turning to look into her eyes. "If I have pleased you, and you are willing to be my wife, I give you this gift to solidify the union of our two families."

His father handed him a box filled with coins and other household items. This was the morning gift and it was the final act to complete the legal requirements of their marriage.

"It is my honor and privilege to accept these gifts and bind myself to you before the gods and these witnesses." She could barely keep a straight face. The formality was necessary, but she would have rather stayed in bed.

Magnus took a ring from his belt where three keys were fastened. Handing them to her he said, "This key is the key to our house, where you are welcomed as the mistress of the household. This key is for the trunk in the shed. It is filled with household items that will make your work easier, and this key unlocks my heart. I entrust it to you for safe keeping in hope of many children." When he finished he bent over and kissed her to the cheers of all the witnesses.

With great celebration they were carried away for another day of feasting and jubilation. The couple, however, couldn't wait for the day to end so they could be in each other's arms once again. When evening came, and the last reveler went home, Sigrunn pulled Magnus close and finished the sentence she had begun to whisper that morning, and nine months later Arne was born.

769 AD

As time passed Sigrunn came to miss those simpler days when they were first married. Magnus tended the farm his father had left, but it had fallen into disrepair. He loved his father. They were close, but his father's obsession with mountain wolves caused a rift between father and son. Magnus had a different call, one that carried him far from home. Sigrunn stood at the door and looked toward town. There the docks filled with people, women who waited for their husbands to return. An unknown force led Magnus away from Birka, and Sigrunn longed for his return.

Docks
769 AD

"Vidar, is this how the knot is supposed to look?" Arne was helping the dockhand straighten his ropes. Vidar was teaching him skills necessary to be a ship's crewman.

"You have done a fine job. Next time, however, leave more room at the end of the rope. That way you can take out the slack when needed."

Vidar was one of the most patient men Arne had met. He looked up to him the same way he did his father. Learning ship craft should have been a skill passed down from father to son, but Arne always felt his father was too busy for him. He had asked to accompany him on this latest voyage, but as usual his mother protested and Arne was left on the dock watching his father's ship sail away. He didn't want to resent his mother, so it fell to his father, because he believed his mother led the family, which made his father look weak.

"Vidar, why do you help me?" Arne asked.

The question caught Vidar off guard and took him back to an earlier time.

A pebble hit the side of Vidar's head. He turned and shot an angry look at the boy. "Why did you do that?" He scowled.

"You didn't answer the question. Why do you teach me these things?"

"What do you mean?"

"Every day I come to the docks and most people see me as a nuisance, but you don't." Arne looked at Vidar, but the old Viking never took his eyes off his task.

"How do you know that I don't?" He let a small smile peak through his beard. "Maybe your father paid me to look after you."

Arne thought about it for a minute, and wasn't sure whether to believe him or not. "I don't think so, my father wouldn't hire someone so clumsy." Arne ducked in time so that the deck peg Vidar tossed at him just missed his head. "And with such bad aim."

They laughed and the moment passed.

"You didn't answer my question; why do you teach me?"

"Because it needs to be done, and we are here." Vidar was pulling a rope that extended far into the cove. Crustaceans foraged at its bottom. Vidar tended the traps while the other men were away on trade. "A community is only as strong as its weakest member. I can no longer contribute on board ship or in battle, so I do my part around the docks. When I have opportunity I pass on what little knowledge I have."

"Have you taught other boys?" Arne asked.

"Only the slow ones," he responded, and Arne scowled at him. "Sometimes fathers leave their sons home too long. Like you, they naturally make their way to the docks and their hearts long for the sea. If their mothers aren't too controlling they are allowed to help me and they learn enough to be ready when their time comes."

"My mom doesn't like me down here."

"Your mother loves you, boy. Never forget that!" He said it more harshly then he meant to—the surprise on Arne's face told him so.

"Do you think you are here because you have decided so? Sigrunn allows it. She is a strong woman, and if she did not give consent you would be home baking bread."

"I didn't mean any disrespect," Arne apologized.

"Then don't give it. Your word is who you are. Don't throw words around carelessly. You are better off saying nothing than saying something you will regret."

"Is that why you don't talk much?" Arne teased, and Vidar just smiled.

Silence fell between the two, and Arne's mind raced with questions and thoughts. Then he spoke what was deepest in his heart. "It's been five weeks. I'm worried that my father will never return." He kept working, but his voice quivered.

"He will return, but if he doesn't you will meet him in Valhalla." Vidar had hoped to die in battle, or at sea.

"I know that is what we should desire, but I want my father to come home."

"See the fog over the water? Our lives are like that. We wish we could see through it and know what is coming. We think it would be safer. But we can't and it isn't. Fate and the gods keep us in silence; otherwise we would not choose to face the difficult things in life. Since we don't know what is ahead we have to face good and bad with the courage that is ours by birth." Speaking as much to himself as to Arne, he continued, "Accept today's blessings and prepare for tomorrow's sorrow."

"But the fog burns off with the afternoon heat, and I can see to the horizon. Should life be that clear as well?"

"You have an old man's mind. Why do you care about tomorrow? Doesn't today's worries occupy your time? But then again you are young and the whole world is at your grasp. At my age I am content to enjoy the day. Tomorrow may never come."

"The problem," Arne said, "*is* that tomorrow never comes. My father says he will be back tomorrow, I can go on trade with him tomorrow, I will be a man tomorrow…I hate tomorrow!"

Vidar pulled up another trap and it was empty. "Maybe tomorrow."

Arne furrowed his brow.

"Eventually," Vidar continued, "a crab will crawl into the trap and we will enjoy a succulent meal. In the meantime we must be patient. Patience tempers passion. Patience builds self-control. Patience allows tomorrow time to bring about its greatest rewards. The impatient will almost always have empty hands."

Arne was listening while looking over the fog-hidden water. Impatience was a mark of his personality, his mother often told him so. But why did the gods keep so much from them? Why couldn't they reveal the future? It would make life less complicated. Arne didn't agree with Vidar that the hidden future made life more exciting. He would rather know what he was sailing into; it was less dangerous.

Mulling these things over he thought he saw something disturb the distant fog and ran to the pier's edge. Straining his sight as far as he could he let out a gasp. "It's a ship! It's a ship with my father's colors!" He could hardly contain himself.

"Steady yourself boy or you're going to fall into the water," Vidar said. "Arne, instead of running to your father as soon as the ship docks, why not show him you're a man by helping me secure it, and helping with the cargo?" Arne agreed.

Magnus waved when he saw his son, and Arne returned the welcome, but when his father jumped to shore he was not met with the greeting he expected. Instead his son tied the ship to its moorings, and quickly climbed aboard to help the rest of the crew.

"A very fine young man you have there, Magnus." Vidar stepped up behind the steersman.

"Not what I expected. But you are right, he is a fine young man." Magnus was proud of his son, and knew he had Vidar to thank. He placed a hand on his shoulder and gave him a look of gratitude. Rubbing his own shoulder and looking toward the village he said, "It's good to be home."

Coming of Age
776 AD

Setting his feet evenly beneath his body, about the same width as his shoulders, Arne raised the ax high over his head, and with all his strength brought it to bear against the log. It glanced off the edge and pulled him toward the ground, but he caught his balance and swore. Two out of three times he seemed to miss the mark, and frustrated he placed the log back on the chopping stump to try again.

"You're not going to get the better of me," he muttered to himself. "Keep your eye on the wood, raise the ax high…" He brought it forcefully down and this time the log split in two.

Magnus was standing by the barn, watching his son. Arne's muscles were already showing definition, and the workout with the wood helped to add tone and strength. He was proud of his boy, and knew the time was coming when he would be a man, accepted into the community as an adult. But there was more to being a man than splitting logs. He would have to contribute to the community by helping to provide for its physical needs, and participating in civic decisions and protection. A time could come when his ax would be wielded against an enemy much deadlier than a piece of wood.

"Arne," he said approaching his son. "You are getting better each day."

"No I'm not. I keep missing. A couple of times I thought I was going to chop off my leg."

"It comes with practice." Magnus took the ax and with one swift movement brought it down into the log and sent the two halves flying. "It isn't always about force. You have to let the weight of the ax head do the work. Your job is to keep an eye on the mark; the metal against wood will do its job. Here, try it again."

Arne grabbed the ax and took another swipe; this time he didn't think about the ax but rather the object of his aim.

"I did it!" he yelled, almost hitting his father.

Magnus grabbed the handle with one hand and rumpled Arne's shaggy head of hair with the other. After they stacked the split wood next to the house Arne started to run off when his father grabbed the back of his shirt.

"Chopping wood isn't enough to make you a warrior. We need to spend some time practicing combat. Defending the clan is an essential part of being an adult and contributing to the community." Magnus tossed Arne one of the practice swords that lay next to the house. "Take your stand, boy."

Arne walked sideways keeping his eyes on his father. Finally he stopped and squared off, placing his feet firmly underneath his shoulders, just like when he was chopping wood. Magnus looked him up and down, moving closer with every step. He was within arm's length when he reached out and pushed Arne in the chest and sent the boy falling backward into the dirt.

"Balance, son. If you can be easily knocked over you won't have time to swing your sword. Now get up and set your stance like mine."

Arne stood and watched his father. Magnus placed one foot at shoulder-width from the other, and slightly to the rear.

"Proper balance will allow you to focus on your sword. That's right; keep your feet to shoulder-width as much as possible. Now watch how I move." He slid his foot about an inch from the ground in case he was caught off guard and needed to plant it again quickly. "Careful, don't cross your feet or bring them together."

"This is hard. Why can't we just fight?" Arne was impatient and his thoughts elsewhere.

"Practice today, and you will live tomorrow." Magnus knew it was more fun to strike wood against wood, but that would do Arne little good if he couldn't master some basic techniques. "Notice how I am holding my grip. This allows me the most movement when I strike my target. You want the strength of your wrist behind the hilt, not your thumb." He stepped closer to Arne, looking more closely. "See how my thumb is pointing to the left? If your thumb is pointing up, your sword could be knocked from your hand."

"How is that?" Arne pointed his sword toward his father, and when he thought Magnus was not paying attention he lunged forward to stab him. Magnus, the experienced soldier, was not caught off-guard. He merely sidestepped the thrust and with the flat of his sword smacked his son on the hindquarters, sending him again into the dirt.

Magnus laughed. "Always be aware of your opponent and what your next move will be, because he may react in ways you weren't expecting." He held out his hand and helped Arne to his feet. "I want you to practice with your friend over here." Magnus had set up a practice dummy. "Thrusting your sword is only one of eight different moves you can attack with. There are seven slashing moves, and the more you practice, the better your body will react without thinking."

Striking the dummy, Magnus showed Arne the left and right on a horizontal slash, the up or down moves on both diagonals and overhead strike, and one of the most difficult moves: the backward strike if your enemy gets past the point of the sword.

The wooden dummy didn't fight back, which added to Arne's dissatisfaction. "Are we finished yet?"

"Not yet. I want you to practice this a while longer; then we will work on defensive moves." His son's shoulders sagged and Arne sighed, but he continued to instruct him, stopping him on occasion and correcting his technique.

"Son, turn and face me. You are doing a good job, and will make a fine warrior. But a good fighter knows as much about defense as he does offense. A sturdier enemy will come at you quickly and with strength. You need to be able to fend off his attack so that you will be in a position to counter." As he spoke Magnus moved his body. "Hold the sword in front of you, that's right. Keep the blade pointing up. Now rotate your arms and body to move the hilt to the left and right. This will defend against attacks to your upper body and midsection. Thrust your sword at me."

Arne obliged his father and each time Magnus smartly deflected his son's blade.

"Now to protect your lower body dip the point of the sword toward the ground, either to your right or left," he continued.

"Always block with the third of the sword closest to the hilt or your opponent might overpower your defense. And finally, if your attacker is slow, dodge him instead of blocking. This will give you a better chance of counterattacking because your sword will be free."

They had worked hard enough for one day, and Arne was ready to quit.

"I think that is sufficient for today," his father conceded.

They had a lot more to work on besides the sword. Arne would need instruction on using the spear, the ax, and the shield, especially the shield. Fighting as a unit was essential, and the use of the shield wall was the core of their strength, but that would have to wait for another day.

"We've practiced enough for a whole week," his son said with a sigh and a smile.

"Do you have all your chores finished?"

"Yes. May I meet Eirik down by Salvik?"

"What will the two of you be doing, or is trouble on the rise?" He could see some mischief in his son's eyes.

"We are just going to fish, maybe lay some traps for small game."

"That's fine. Just make sure you are home before the evening meal. And if that young Eirik starts any mischief, don't let him get you into trouble." He didn't want to dampen the boy's fun, but he knew Eirik and his father. They had a mean streak in them, and could be found in the middle of many bad situations in Birka.

"I'll be careful," he said, rolling his eyes. Eirik had his shortcomings, but Arne saw good in him, and they were best friends. His father was overly concerned and protective, which frustrated Arne. He knew his dad meant well, but he was almost a man; at thirteen he didn't need his father telling him what to do all of the time.

"I'll be home late afternoon," he yelled into the wind as he ran down the path and out of sight.

Friends
776 AD

Salvik was only a couple of miles through the forest. It was a small port used for lighter vessels with shallow drafts. Most of the time it was empty and made a great place for fishing. Arne was supposed to meet Eirik there thirty minutes ago. He hoped he had waited.

Few paths ran through this part of the woods, but the deer trails proved wide enough for Arne. He knew them well, having played in this area often with his friend. He pretended to be on an expedition that required him to move stealthily through the underbrush. Each footfall was practiced and even the leaves didn't rustle under his feet. Stopping, he would listen for birds singing or watch for a fox and her pups foraging for food.

He loved being in the wild, but his father was always cautioning him. "Arne, the woods can be dangerous. There are as many wolves as there are foxes." At least he didn't forbid going into the woods.

Arne stopped suddenly. He heard something unusual—it didn't sound like a small animal, and when he saw five red deer rush past him he knew something bigger was on its way. It could be a bear, but they only crossed over the sea on rare occasions. He wasn't taking any chances though and decided to climb a tree. Most of the trees on the island were birch, not good for climbing. The occasional oak, with its low branches proved a sturdy tower against larger predators, and Arne climbed the nearest one as high as he could to see what was approaching. There was no bear, or even a wolf, just the noisy creature Eirik and a couple of boys from town.

"I thought you said he would be here by now?" a boy slightly taller than Eirik asked.

"He's probably late. His dad always has him doing something. He will be here." Eirik was impatient and irritated. Just as Arne was about to call out to them and reveal his perch high in the tree, Eirik continued, "He will be surprised, don't worry, he won't know what hit him."

Arne didn't understand his statement. What would he be surprised by, and why had Eirik brought these boys with him? All he could think of was his father's warning. "If Eirik starts any mischief…"

His kind heart couldn't believe that Eirik, his friend, would plan something hurtful. Yet instead of calling out to the boys, or going home, he decided to follow from a distance, which proved to be easier than he expected. They were not trying to be quiet as they walked, so even if Arne stepped on a twig they would never have noticed.

Their path led straight to Salvik. Maybe his fears were premature. Eirik's statement must presage something less insidious than his father's warning warranted. Arne was so caught up in his thoughts that he hadn't noticed Eirik and his friends swerve off the path and back again. Before their movements registered he stepped onto a thatched piece of ground. He wasn't able to keep his balance and fell through, into the pit below. As hard as he tried not to cry out, the air escaped his lungs and was easily heard.

The pit wasn't very big and Arne was surprised when he fell through its camouflaged opening. Several trapping pits—each thirteen feet deep and lined with wooden planks—were strewn throughout the island, but this one was freshly dug. A few roots crawled along the edge of the hole, and he used them to climb out. At the top Eirik and his friends met him. They hadn't expected him to escape.

"Eirik, how did you miss stepping in the hole?" Arne still didn't realize who had dug it.

"We dug the hole." He looked at his friends as if to solicit approval.

"Why did you dig a boar hole in the middle of the path, and though I'm glad, why was it so shallow?" He waited for an answer.

"Arne you're so stupid!" Eirik seemed nervous and his voice cracked as he spoke. "The hole was meant to catch you, and it worked, except you climbed out."

He wasn't making any sense, "But why were you trying…"

"We're not friends anymore. I'm tired of hanging out with a little kid." Eirik was two years older, but that had never been a problem before. "Gunnar and Ivar are my friends now, and they don't like you." Before Arne could say another word Eirik had stepped up to him and pushed him to the dirt.

"Eirik," Gunnar said. He was the tallest of the three. "Leave him alone."

Eirik looked at him in confusion. They had been planning this all week.

Gunnar reached a hand out to help Arne up. "It's a little crowded in the woods; let's talk about this out in the open." His cordial attitude didn't fool Arne. He knew nothing good would come of this, and as they walked he looked for something to use as a weapon. They were only fifty yards to the edge of the woods when he saw a stick suitable to fend off his attackers. Eirik was in front of him, the other two behind. He reached out and grabbed the stick. Pushing Eirik in the back to throw him off balance Arne turned and struck Ivar in the neck. Ivar let out a loud cry and fell to the ground, but before Arne could swing again, Gunnar grabbed his arm.

"Eirik, get over here and help me."

Arne was stronger than the boy had anticipated, and with a swift movement he brought his knee up and kicked Gunnar in the groin. His assailant fell over, doubled up on the ground. Eirik was still behind him, however, and hit Arne in the back of the head. Before he could recover the others were on top of him hitting and punching.

"This will teach you." Gunnar's tone was venomous. "You and your father think you are so smart, walking around town as if you own the place." Arne couldn't make any sense of what he was saying. "Well, now you're a nobody, with no friends." Arne pulled his knees to his chest and covered his head with his hands. All he could do at this point was try to protect himself. Finally they tired of their sport and stood back panting.

"I think that is enough," Eirik said.

Giving him a cold look, Gunnar retorted, "I say when it is enough," and he kicked Arne one more time. "Now it is enough." He spat at him and the three boys walked off.

Arne's eye was swelling and his whole body ached. A sharp pain stabbed in his ribs, making it hard to breathe. None of this made sense. Why were they so angry with him? And why was Eirik hanging out with such mean kids? He had recognized them, but he didn't know them or why they would want to hurt him. Arne lay on the ground for a while longer hoping that the pain would subside, and when it didn't he knew he had to get up and make his way home.

The hour trip through the forest took him two and a half. It was past the evening meal and almost dark when he stumbled into the house.

Magnus was angry with Arne for being late, but when he saw his son he felt guilty. As Sigrunn tended to his wounds, his father paced the room, his anger now turned toward those who had beaten his son. This was no childhood scuffle; it was an intentional assault, and their family honor was at stake. He knew he could do nothing until morning, and his wife's caution only infuriated him more.

Going outside, Magnus slammed the door. It took him a while, but he allowed the cool evening to assuage his boiling rage. "I will get to the bottom of this," he told himself. He knew all the boys' fathers and none of this would end well.

Tempers
776 AD

"Open the door and come out and face me!" Magnus was standing outside Trygve's house. He knocked on the doorframe harder. "You and your son are cowards! Come and face me like a man."

"Leave us alone, he is not here." The voice of a woman spoke through the door.

"Then where is he? Answer me or I will break the door down to find him cowering in a corner." Magnus was not in a mood to trifle with a woman.

"They went into town. Now leave us alone." The fear in her voice was evident, but Magnus couldn't tell if it was of him or her own husband.

"You have a scoundrel for a husband, and you will be better off without him." His threat was not empty, but even he knew it was a little overstated. He turned and headed for town. The farms around Birka weren't far away and surrounded the town for protection, so the distance Magnus had to travel was not too gst. It was not long before he found Trygve and Eirik; they were standing with two other men and their sons, Ivar and Gunnar. They heard him before they saw him.

"I am not surprised to see a pack of dogs cowering together."

The men looked confused while the boys' faces turned white. Trygve stood straight and faced Magnus. "Why is my brother throwing insults so freely?" There wasn't any love lost between these men. They had often been at odds during the gathering of freemen called the Thing, but their squabbles had never deteriorated into the streets.

"Don't tell me you are unaware of your boys' actions?" He stepped forward and pointed at Eirik in particular.

Trygve countered the move and placed himself between his son and Magnus. "Speak plainly, Magnus. What actions are you alluding to?"

"These three mongrels trapped my Arne, and then beat him half to death, and I demand satisfaction!" Magnus could feel the heat rise in his neck. He hadn't meant to become so angry, but just the sight of these men and their boys infuriated him.

"What kind of satisfaction are you looking for? You spout accusations and threats, but where is your boy? Why isn't he here with you?" Trygve's smirk added to his consternation. "Why isn't Arne defending his own honor?"

"What do you know of honor? Your son and theirs ambushed him and left him to die. Honor demands satisfaction, and I am here to collect." He instinctively reached for his sword.

"Are you challenging my son to personal combat? He is barely a man." Trygve's face flickered with concern.

"If you worry about your son, maybe you should stand in his place. Will you defend the misdeeds of your family?" This wasn't the direction Magnus had expected to take; he really hadn't been sure what to expect. He wanted satisfaction, but he didn't know what it would be. He definitely wasn't looking to fight a child, but he would take it out on the boy's father.

"What is this commotion?" Sigurd asked. Sigurd was the *lovsigemann*, or law reader. The laws of Birka were not written, so it was the responsibility of the *lovsigemann* to speak the law during the Thing and help the Earl rule according to their precepts. Two large warriors accompanied him.

"You are disrupting the peace of the community. What disagreement is there that needs to be judged?" He was directing his comments to Magnus, who reiterated the events that had led to their altercation. After a moment of consideration the *lovsigemann* replied, "The Earl is in the community hall. We will take this off the streets and before him." He turned and walked away with a company of people in his wake.

The community hall was the largest building in Birka. Under its roof people were married, gods were honored, and civil matters were judged. Evenly spaced poles supported the oblong building. A raised chair stood off-center, and on it sat the Earl, Torstein.

"Magnus and Trygve, why have you disrupted the peace of our town?" he asked.

Sigurd recited the inciting events as the hall continued to fill with curious men.

"Trygve, what do you have to say for your son?"

"My lord, Earl, this is a matter between boys. Magnus and his son have overreacted to the natural order of youth establishing dominance. Surely if he cannot endure some minor pain he will never become a man." Trygve was appealing well to the Earl's sense of honor among men.

"If it were just between Trygve's son and mine it would be a simple matter. But three against one is not an honorable act. They built a trap as if he were an animal instead of challenging him face to face. A boy learns these traits from his father!"

The room erupted in shouts, some for and some against the statement. It was a direct challenge to Trygve, one that could not be ignored.

To regain order the *lovsigemann* stamped the rod in his hand. "Order, order," he yelled. "Listen to your Earl!"

When everyone calmed down and the last voice quieted, the Earl spoke, "Trygve, your son is two years older than Arne, and has been accepted into the community as a man. Arne is yet to receive his ring and pledge his life. Sigurd, what is the law in regard to a man's treatment of a boy?"

"It is the law of our community that a man who mistreats the boy of another member is to pay restitution or meet the boy's father in personal combat."

"This is an unusual case," the Earl continued. "What restitution is required?"

"According to Magnus' report of the health of his son, restitution would be in the amount of 25 pieces of silver," Sigurd said.

"My son doesn't have that kind of money!" Trygve responded.

"Then the law says," Sigurd continued, "that he is to meet Magnus in personal combat."

The room again burst into noise. Sigurd stamped his staff again until all was quiet.

All eyes darted between Magnus and the Earl. The consensus was against the idea of personal combat between Eirik and Magnus, even though the people stood firmly behind Magnus.

"This is a most unusual case. Eirik is responsible as a man in our community, but is no match for you, my friend." The Earl was speaking directly to Magnus. "It serves no one's honor to sentence the boy to sure death at your hands." He paused and stood. "My judgment is for personal combat."

The room exploded, but quieted when the Earl finally raised his hand. "The combat will be between Eirik and Arne, and will not be to death. The two will engage in combat using training sticks and shields. The boy who is knocked down three times will be considered vanquished." Looking at Magnus and Trygve, he continued, "Is this agreeable?"

Trygve puffed out his chest and answered yes. His boy was taller and older, and definitely had the advantage. Magnus, on the other hand was stuck. If he turned down the offer his family would face dishonor, but accepting it would pit his son against unfavorable odds. He nodded his head.

"Is this agreeable to the assembly?"

To a man they yelled yes with raised hands. Their Earl had judged wisely and in the process provided the community some exciting entertainment.

Magnus pushed passed Trygve and left the hall dissatisfied with the outcome, even though it was the best decision. He was angry with himself for putting his son in this situation. Arne was no match for Eirik; he had little training and was smaller. This was the only answer; if he had done nothing Arne would become a target for bullying, Magnus would have to prepare his son.

Son's Honor
776 AD

Sigrunn was livid. "How could you let this happen? Your temper has put your son in danger. You didn't even talk to me about it before going off hot-headed." She was almost shouting.

Magnus tried to interrupt occasionally, but he knew she had to speak her mind.

"What do you think is going to happen?"

"Sigrunn, they will be using practice swords, and it isn't to death."

"Only practice swords! They can deliver severe damage. I have even seen people killed by them." She was adamant.

"You are overreacting."

"You mean like when you went into town?" she countered.

"Quiet, wife." Magnus put up his hand and said in a firm tone, "The decision has been made. Now we must prepare Arne. Eirik is taller and older, but he isn't as smart as our son. A good warrior is strong, but a better warrior is smart. This match will be as much about wit and skill as it is about strength. Trygve will be overconfident, and he spends little time with his son's training. I would bet all we have on Arne." His son was sitting up and through the pain he beamed with pride.

"Mother, I am ready. Eirik is slow and thoughtless. If there hadn't been three of them I would have beat him."

She gave her son a stern look, and Magnus responded, "You are not ready. First you need to heal, and then sharpen your skills. You have the sympathy of the crowd. If you win you will be esteemed, if you fail you will be considered a boy who is not yet ready to be a man."

The rest of the evening was quiet. Sigrunn was not happy and her mood was a stifling cloud over the house.

Arne's injuries took some time to heal and after three weeks of rest he was ready to train. However, once the town learned he was up and about, Magnus was pressured to set the date for combat. He was stalling to give his son more time. Word came from the Earl that Arne must be ready in four weeks, and Magnus made use of the opportunity.

He set up a training course consisting of three practice dummies. Each one was designed to help Arne hone a specific skill. The first dummy was for strengthening his arms. Arne spent hours hacking and thrusting. The second was a pole with rods sticking out at different levels and distances around the radius. This one taught Arne to move his sword in and out and around quickly. The third dummy was unusual. Magnus made it so it could move back and forth on a cart. Arne was to use his shield to deflect the force of the dummy thrust. Each week centered on a specific skill though each skill was constantly practiced. During the fourth week Magnus replaced the dummy so that Arne practiced with a real target.

"Arne you are doing well, but you must anticipate your opponent's move. All he has to do is step out of the way and knock you off balance to the ground. Three times and you're out. Rush me with your sword."

Arne did as he was instructed and his father deflected the sword with his shield, pivoted, stuck out his leg, and sent his son sprawling to the ground. "That is what I am talking about. Undisciplined attacks are easy to deflect. In a real combat, I would have struck you in the back with my sword." The rest of the day they worked on balance, defense, and tactics. Occasionally Sigrunn brought them something to drink, and as she watched she couldn't help admiring her son's improvement, and she was proud.

The day came and Magnus and his family walked to the center of Birka. A crowd had already assembled and a circle formed. The Earl and Sigurd were standing at its edge near the great hall. Trygve and Eirik were waiting, and when Magnus and Arne stepped close to the Earl the circle closed behind them.

"We have come to witness personal combat between Eirik, son of Trygve, and Arne, son of Magnus. The rules are as follows. Each can use a practice sword and a shield. Attacks will halt when a combatant falls to the ground. If he stands the combat will continue. If he chooses to remain down, it will end. The match will be complete when a combatant has fallen three times, and the honor will go to the victor."

Magnus and Arne stood opposite of Eirik and Trygve. "Arne, don't be overconfident. You are ready. If you put into practice what you have learned you will do well. Don't attack first. He will taunt you and try to draw you out. Let his frustration cause him to make the first move. Choose your moves carefully and strike when you have the advantage." He gave Arne a little nudge into the circle.

Magnus was right, and Eirik began his taunts. "You were a boy yesterday and you're a boy today. You have no honor and your disgrace will soon be made clear."

If his battle technique was as practiced as his taunts, Arne was in trouble. But Arne stood his ground; he circled when Eirik moved, and didn't rush forward.

"You are a coward, and you walk around trying to avoid combat." Eirik was frustrated and when his patience couldn't be contained any longer he rushed Arne.

Arne was prepared and did exactly what his father had done in practice. He deflected the sword with his shield, pivoted, and swept his leg around and sent Eirik to the ground. The crowd went wild and Eirik's father screamed. "Get up, you idiot. Don't let that insolent child get the best of you."

Eirik jumped up, fueled by his anger. He rushed Arne again, but this time he held his body straight and didn't let his momentum carry him forward. Instead his greater weight fell full force on Arne and knocked him to the ground. The crowd again yelled and Eirik stood over his opponent. "You were lucky, and you are weak."

Sigurd pushed him aside and reminded him to allow Arne the opportunity to stand. He turned to the crowd. "It stands at one knockdown apiece. Are the combatants ready to reengage?" He stepped aside to allow the contest to continue.

They were both more cautious, and it was Arne who made the first move this time. Unlike Eirik he didn't rush forward, but instead made several offensive slashes with his sword. Eirik deflected them reflexively, but each slash pushed him backward. Arne felt good about his tactic, but when Eirik set his feet and pushed back with his shield Arne felt his opponent's strength and had to move backward. Stepping into one of the strokes, Arne deflected Eirik's sword and pushed him to the side. He was going to pivot and push him off balance, but before he had the chance Eirik's sword swung around and caught him in the back. He felt a stinging pain spread over his skin and wasn't able to regain his balance when Eirik smashed his shield hard against his head.

His skull buzzed, and when the fog cleared he was looking into Eirik's smiling face. "You might as well stay down. You are no match for me. Save yourself further humiliation and go home, boy."

Arne refused to return his barbs; he had to concentrate. The buzzing didn't go away as he stood. He felt a little wobbly but was able to keep his balance. His tactics weren't working. Eirik had longer arms and greater strength. If he were to win, he would need to change his strategy. Two things could work against Eirik: overconfidence and blind rage. His confidence was not misplaced, but could he control his anger? Arne decided words were his best weapon.

"You're right, I am just a boy." Magnus looked at his son perplexed. "I am sure you will be proud at the end of the day knowing you have beaten someone smaller. It will be the same look you had when it took three of you to beat me in the woods."

Eirik looked around at the men in the circle. They were smiling and laughing. Arne continued, "I won't give up; what choice do I have but to fight someone who is bigger and better?" With these words Arne weakly struck at him, leaving himself exposed.

At first Eirik was annoyed, but his annoyance soon turned to humiliation. As he felt the crowd stare his humiliation turned to anger, and in his anger he rushed at what he thought was Arne's weakness. But as soon as Eirik was towering over his crouching body, Arne set his hands against the back of his shield and pushed firmly up, catching Eirik under the chin. The force and pain sent him flying back.

Arne pressed the attack and swung repeatedly, hitting Eirik's flailing shield and landing a blow against his chest. Eirik fell to one knee. He tried to stand, stunned and confused, but before he could set his feet squarely Arne was already on top him; he struck Eirik's shield, then swung around and struck him in the back. Pain shot through Eirik's back and he let out a cry. When he looked around he saw his father's anger and disappointment. His confidence waned and when he turned to face his opponent all he felt was the force of Arne's shield against his face, and everything went black.

Arne stood over Eirik breathing heavily. He had won and the crowd was chanting his name. Magnus ran to his son and lifted him triumphantly in the air, while Trygve glared and picked up his son with the help of friends and carried him home.

"A little unconventional son, but you did it!"

Sigurd called for order and after a few minutes the crowd became silent. The Earl moved to the center and put his hand on Arne's shoulder. "You have been tested today and found both brave and competent as a warrior. This is an unusual situation and I am making an exception." The Earl took a ring armband from his arm and placed it on Arne's wrist. "Arne, son of Magnus, do you swear loyalty to me and my family?"

Arne was speechless. He looked at his father who smiled broadly. Looking back to the Earl he said, "Yes, I swear."

"Then I welcome you into the community of men with all of its rights and responsibilities." The chants from the crowd rose again as Magnus and Sigrunn wrapped their arms around their son, and the three of them walked through the crowd and then home.

Adulthood
776 AD

Today was important for Arne; it was the first time that he would accompany his father to the Thing as an accepted adult in the community. The Thing was held outside during the summer months and good weather, or at the community hall when necessary. Taking advantage of the gathering, the community set up markets and festivals. The Earl made judgment over disputes and decisions for the community. He wasn't a king and didn't hold absolute power, but he was of great influence.

At a settlement meeting he decided disputes between families who couldn't reconcile their differences. Seldom did anyone vote against the Earl, but on occasions it happened. Wise Earls knew the mood of the community, and if opposition was strong against a position that he held, it was in his best interest to revise his plans. He needed them as much, if not more, than they needed him.

All men who participated in the Thing were freemen who farmed, hunted, and traded. They were tied to the land and the sea. Land, cattle, slaves, silver, and gold gauged the status of wealth and prosperity for freemen, and the Earl had obtained more of these than any other. He often owned the ships the traders sailed, and consolidated the better lands for himself. His right to lead was passed from generation to generation, and all who wanted to be a part of the community pledged their loyalty to both him and his family.

However, his office could easily be wrested from his hand by *holmgang*, a duel to the death, but because of the people's high regard for oaths sworn, few broke theirs unless matters with the Earl became grave.

The Thing was a necessary part of life, Magnus explained to his son. "People always disagree with each other, and if there aren't common laws, then we would always be fighting. As Freemen we have a part in making the laws, and the Earl enforces them, and keeps us accountable."

"Does he have to obey the laws?" Arne asked.

"Of course; he is not above the law. If he is caught disobeying the law he is subject to the community, and his right as Earl can be challenged." Magnus enjoyed their conversations.

They were almost into town and they began to join others who were making their way to the Thing. Sigrunn was with them; she had brought some produce and cheese to sell at the market. She loved coming into town and seeing the rest of her family. Though they didn't live far away the daily routine kept them from seeing each other often.

"How long will the Thing last today?" she asked Magnus.

"I don't know. Several disagreements between families haven't been settled, and I think Brynhild has an accusation against her husband."

"Really? I will have to be sure and attend." The Thing could be entertainment as much as a place of justice.

Birka had swelled to almost 500 people for the event. Tents were set up to ward off the summer heat, and the smell and noise of animals filled the air. The men were gathering around a raised platform on which the Earl would sit and pass judgment. After he took his seat, the *lovsigemann* stepped forward and banged his staff on the platform.

"Attention, please, attention." His voice carried over the crowd. "Let us begin this month's Thing with a recitation of the law." It was his job to set to memory the laws, which they all agreed to obey, but because they were not written down, it was important for them to be recited at each meeting. If an alteration or an addition to the canon had occurred, the community could question it. The men in Birka were a lively group and as the law was recited there were often vocal affirmations to energize the moment. As the *lovsigemann* wound down he asked the crowd, "And to these laws and ordinances do we agree?"

Everyone raised their hands in the air and yelled, "We agree!"

"Then," the *lovsigemann* concluded, "We will begin. The first dispute is between the families of Geir and Knut. Bring in the twelve who will judge."

Each time an irreconcilable dispute was brought before the Thing, the Earl would select twelve to thirty-six peers to judge the situation. The number depended on the case's importance.

The *lovsigemann* looked at the men and said, "Freedman Geir has accused Freedman Knut of stealing one of his pigs. Geir step forward and bring your case."

Geir was the average height of his brethren, and he was animated as he spoke. "My sow gave birth to eight healthy piglets. We were fattening them up for sale. Three weeks ago one of them was missing; the pen was secure, and there were footprints leading away from my farm in the direction of my neighbor Knut." Geir was waving his arms and pointing at the accused, who stood still and silent. "I went to his house and asked him if he had seen my pig."

"And what did the accused say?" asked the *lovsigemann*.

"He told me to get off his property and was offended that I would allege such thievery, and then he closed the door in my face. I could smell my pig in his house."

The community of men laughed at the thought.

"Did you see the pig with your eyes?" the *lovsigemann* continued.

"The evidence was clear; I didn't need to see it. Knut's behavior condemns him. Why would he treat his neighbor in such a way if he were innocent?

"Do you have anything else to say at this time?"

Geir shook his head no.

"Then we will allow Knut to speak."

He glared at Geir, "You say that you saw footprints leading away from your farm? Has no one else walked that path besides me, you, or your family? It is a common trail and I am sure any number of my brothers here could have left their prints behind. Did you see me with your pig?" The question was rhetorical and he paused for emphasis. "Of course not, but you say you smelled him in my house. I would suggest that it was your own foul odor you smelled, along with the rest of your brood." His insult roused the crowd to laughter. "As far as my behavior, I don't entertain anyone in my home who falsely accuses me of theft. You are lucky I didn't step out and slay you where you stood."

Geir stepped forward at the affront, but two men blocked his path.

The *lovsigemann* addressed Knut. "So, my brother, where do you think the pig went?"

"How should I know? Maybe he sold it or ate it himself. Maybe his son left the pen unlatched and closed it later to cover his tracks." Frustrated he turned to the twelve jurors. "This whole thing has been a waste of my time and yours. Unless he has a witness or proof let's finish this business today."

Looking at Geir the *lovsigemann* asked, "Do you have any witnesses?"

He said no.

"Then we will leave it to the jurors to render a judgment."

Decisions of this sort never took very long, partly because there was no obvious verdict, and they would rather leave it up to the fate of the gods. This way they didn't offend a brother and the disputers would fight it out. One of the jurors stepped forward. "We call for the *holmgang* of first blood." The *holmgang* was a duel, and first blood referred to the extent of the combat. The two parties would meet on the beach of the lagoon and fight with sword and shield. The person whose blood first touched the ground would be declared loser by the gods. It was a common verdict for this kind of case so didn't come as a surprise to either Geir or Knut. They had brought their swords and shields just in case.

Justice
776 AD

"The duel will take place later this afternoon after the last case is heard," said the *lovsigemann*. He continued, "An accusation has been brought forward by Brynhild against her legal husband, Ulf. Brynhild, will you please step forward and plead your case." Everyone knew the situation between Brynhild and Ulf. He was not an easy man to befriend, let alone live with. But she had accepted his offer to marry, and without a solid case against him this might be a waste of time.

"On the day of my marriage, Ulf took me into his bed chamber and promised to care, protect, and honor me as his wife. Over the first two years he proved to be an honorable man and kept his promise." The men's eyes seemed to penetrate her soul. "But he has changed, and times on our farm have been hard. Ulf sailed with the traders and tried to support our family as best he could. But life is always hard, and the gods bless at their own pleasure." She was interrupted.

"Brynhild," the *lovsigemann* interjected, "you are giving us a glowing picture of your husband. What accusations do you bring before us?"

"As I was saying," she continued, "Ulf changed. He has treated our children and me with dishonor in front of others. He has called me a whore and has struck me on no less than three public occasions." Murmurs whispered among the crowd. "I have endured the humiliation for the last time and call for a judgment of divorce."

"That is a strong request, Brynhild. Are you sure that is the course you want to take?" the *lovsigemann* asked. "Are there any witnesses?"

She looked around the room and pointed at three men and said, "These men, their wives, and many more among you have seen his behavior. This assembly stands as my testimony. Which one of you will step forward and speak?" Four men stepped forward, and there was no need for them to say a word.

"Ulf, do you want to give a response?" the *lovsigemann* asked.

His dishonor was evident, and his anger rose as he felt betrayed by his brothers. "It seems that I am accused and judged already." Turning and looking at the crowd, he continued, "Which one of you who have been mistreated by the gods as I, have not taken your frustration out on your wife? Do you dare judge me for the same actions of which you are guilty?"

"Father," Arne whispered, "I have never seen you strike my mother. Is what he claims true?"

"It is true that wives receive the brunt of their husbands' frustration. That is the natural course of married people, but few ever lay a hand on their wives, and I have never touched your mother in anger."

Arne returned his attention to the scene that was unfolding.

"And what do you expect from me?" Ulf continued his tirade. "She has been unfaithful. While I was away on trade, she took advantage of my absence to engage in all sorts of whoring. I have put up with it because of my deep love for her."

Brynhild interrupted. "That is a lie, and I challenge him to produce any testimony to the contrary."

"See, she lashes out to illicit sympathy from the community!"

"Your charge, Ulf, is egregious. If you are correct, Brynhild could be sentenced to death." The *lovsigemann* was careful to explain the consequence of Ulf's accusation. "Have you caught her in the act, and if so, why is this the first we have heard of it?"

"You have not heard of it before, because it isn't true." Brynhild was angry. "He is trying to deceive you and take your eyes off of his own actions."

"What am I to prove? A wife who turns away from my touch, hours of silence between her and her husband… If not for the love of another man, why would she treat me in such a way?" His attempt at diverting the community cast doubt in the minds of some.

"There is no need for another man to turn my heart cold toward you. What woman would want to be touched by a man who would strike her and humiliate her in front of friends and family? I have testimony of witnesses to your deeds, and I call for a judgment in this matter." She stood her ground, and the strength of her conviction was compelling.

"Ulf, do you have any more to say, or any witnesses to produce?"

Ulf stood silent.

"Then the judgment is in favor of Brynhild and her petition for divorce. She will retain her dowry, and in addition, Ulf will compensate her for her public humiliation the price of two silver armbands and three cows." Sigurd stamped his staff three times in summation.

Ulf had known before the meeting that Brynhild was going to win the judgment. He had hoped to escape any further penalty, but his obnoxious display had cost him. He dropped the two armbands on the ground in front of his now former wife, and quickly left, promising to deliver the cattle to her father's house.

Brynhild stood tall and proud, but the tear that ran down her cheek displayed her aching heart. She had not wanted this, but the alternative of living with a violent husband was worse. Ulf wasn't the only one who had lost, for even though she would take her two daughters with her, their son would remain with his father. She hoped in time he would understand and forgive her.

Tug of War
776 AD

A break was called, with the Thing to resume in two hours. Arne was disappointed because he had been enjoying himself, but he was encouraged when Magnus took him to compete in some of the afternoon activities. Not only was the market busy with people selling their wares, but men gathered to compete in a display of strength and skill. The one that Magnus enjoyed the most was the family tug-of-war. His was the undefeated champion of Birka, and this would be Arne's first chance to participate. Five main clans made up the people of Birka and each sent a delegation to defend their honor. As Arne and his father made their way through the crowd they caught up with their old friend, Vidar.

"Are you going to the tug-of-war?" Arne asked him.

"I would never miss it. My family hasn't won a match since I was as tall as you, but today will be different," he said, looking at Magnus with a playful smile. "We are going to bring down the house of Magnus. Prepare yourself to be dragged through the mud."

On the edge of town was a large dirt pit that had been filled with water. Across its center lay a long thick rope. Each team sported five contestants whose goal was to pull the opposing team into the pit. The team with the last man standing outside of the pit won. The family selected team members according to their strength, but this year Magnus had negotiated for his son to participate. He hoped that the strength of the other four would carry the day.

"There are two key positions when pulling on the rope, the first and the last." Magnus was walking Arne around the pit. "The first person plants his feet and tries to keep the group from being pulled in on the first tug. We like to place our heaviest family member in that position. The last person is the anchor and the final hope. If everyone else is pulled in, he has to have the strength of ten men."

"Where will I stand?" Arne wasn't sure about this. "Maybe I shouldn't be on the team. If we lose everyone will blame me."

Magnus tousled his hair. "It is all in fun, and we won't lose. Most teams include someone young. We will make the best of it and have a good time."

The other family members had arrived, and they greeted one another as warriors ready for battle. Because there were five teams, the winner from the previous year sat out the first round. That always gave Magnus' family the advantage of scouting the competition. This year only one other team had a young man—Eirik's family looked to avenge their earlier dishonor.

"Don't worry, Arne. This is much less important than your personal combat with Eirik. If we lose here we have lost nothing."

The matches were ferocious. The crowds cheered on their clans and teams chided and harassed their opponents. When it came to the final round it was between the families of Magnus and Trygve. Before each match the opposing teams met face to face in a show of intimidation.

"You have a strong team, Trygve." Magnus was trying to be polite.

"And we will beat you. I hope you can find enough water to wash off the filth you are about to swallow." Trygve was less congenial, and he turned and walked away.

The contestants picked up their respective ropes, and when the field judge dropped the stone the game began. As soon as the stone hit the ground a collective grunt sounded from both sides as they dug in their heels and strained every fiber of their muscles. Team Magnus was not budging either way and that meant neither was Trygve's. This wouldn't last long. Both teams were tired from previous bouts and the moment of truth was coming; the lead man on Magnus' team slipped and the whole team was dragged forward.

The second in line caught his balance and dug into the dirt, while the man in front of him slipped, trying to get out of the mud. The shift in weight, however, caught Trygve's team off guard and Eirik lost his balance. He was fourth in line, the same as Arne. It was enough for the team to lose momentum and Magnus yelled for his team to pull. The initial tug did its job and Magnus pulled their first man into the mud. The teams again evenly matched, the rope came to a standstill, and the team leaders accosted their own team members, hurling insults of womanly strength if they lost. In the end Magnus' team couldn't hold the line and before they could recover they were sliding forward. When the second in line fell into the mud they could do no more. When Arne was at the pit's edge and the team's weight was carrying the rest forward, Magnus gripped his son and they flew into the mud together, laughing.

Fun was the purpose of these events, but a few with highly competitive spirits saw every event as a life or death struggle. Magnus tried to teach Arne the difference, but as he saw Trygve's haughty spirit and Eirik's approach he knew there would be words. Magnus spoke first. Sticking out his hand he said, "Well done, Trygve. You fought hard and won. Congratulations."

Magnus' conciliatory tone softened Trygve. "Thank you," he sputtered. "You did well too." Puffing up his chest, "We have unseated the clan Magnus for the first time. It is a cause for celebration." He grabbed Magnus by the shoulder and yelled, "I will buy you the first drink!"

Eirik was not as gracious; he walked past Arne, bumping his shoulder, but Arne didn't make a big deal about it. He remembered what his father had said and knew that this game was not worth fighting over. Running past his father, Arne slapped him on the back and then disappeared into the crowd in search of his mother and cousins. He would leave his father at the mercy of their "enemy."

Witness
776 AD

They were late for the resumption of the Thing, but not by much. The Earl, seeing the fierce tug-of-war was over, called the Thing back to order. By the time Magnus had found Arne and made it back to the assembly, the *lovsigemann* had just begun to call the twelve jurors to order.

"Today we will be judging Valdemar for the murder of his long time neighbor, Leif. Both are members in good standing in the community."

Valdemar was pushed in front of the Earl's chair, arms tied behind his back.

"Valdemar, son of Gunnar, what do you have to say for yourself?"

Valdemar was a fisherman, who spent most of his days on his boat throwing his net into the sound. He preferred the silence of his boat to the bustle of community life. His wife was as unkempt as he and had not bore him any children. The circumstances of his neighbor's death were suspicious, and his wife's involvement was unknown.

"I did not murder Leif. I barely talked to him. Why would I want to hurt him?'

"We have a witness who says he saw you come from his farm." Sigurd motioned for the witness to step forward. "What did you see?"

Arne was surprised when his father stepped to the center stage.

"Two weeks ago I was in the forest to the northeast hunting red deer when I saw Valdemar running from the direction of Leif's home."

"Did you see him and Leif fighting?"

"No, but since I was in the area I went to Leif's house and found him dead."

"Was there anything to show how Leif had died?"

"There was an ax lodged in his back." Magnus didn't look at Valdemar and continued, "I found Leif's wife huddled in the barn sobbing."

"Thank you. Vigdis, could you please step forward? I am sorry about your husband. What can you tell us about his death?" Sigurd asked.

"I was in the barn collecting eggs when I heard arguing. I came outside to see what was happening and Leif yelled for me to go back into the barn. I hesitated because the children were in the house, but Leif insisted so I obeyed." Tears filled her eyes.

"Did you see the man your husband was arguing with?" Sigurd questioned.

"Not his face. His back was to me, but he was carrying a fish basket. Leif was telling him he wasn't interested. The man wouldn't listen. That is all I saw before going into the barn."

"There are other fisherman in the community. Couldn't one of them have been with your husband?" It was Sigurd's job to investigate every possibility.

"Yes, my lord. The man could have been someone other than Valdemar, but Magnus says that he saw him coming from our farm," Vigdis petitioned.

"That is true, but you didn't see him. All you can confirm is that there was an argument between two men. Did you come out of the barn at any time before Magnus found you?"

"No," she answered.

"How long was it before he left?" Sigurd asked.

"I don't know. When everything became quiet I was afraid to come out. I didn't want to bring attention to me or the children, so I stayed hidden in the barn."

"Even if it were Valdemar with your husband, could someone else have killed him between the time he left and the time that Magnus arrived at your farm?"

"Yes…No…I mean, I am not sure. Are you trying to excuse what this man did to my Leif? Are you trying to deny me justice?" Vigdis was almost screaming.

Sigurd stood silent until Vigdis calmed herself. "I merely want the truth. Vigdis you have been very helpful. You may step away."

Family in the crowd swarmed around her to give her comfort.

"Are there any others who can give testimony for or against Valdemar?"

No one spoke up and Sigurd turned again to Valdemar. "I want to be clear in regard to the penalty of perjury. If you are found guilty of both murder and lying, the consequences will be most egregious for you and your family. So before I hand this matter over to the jury for their verdict, would you like to amend your testimony?"

Valdemar wasn't a brave man, but he tried hard not to be intimidated by the community. They had never been receptive to him or his family. Some people bought his fish, but they turned their nose up at him.

"I said I didn't murder him. That doesn't mean I wasn't there when he died." He had everyone's attention now. "Yes, I was there, and I had a fish basket just as she said. All I wanted to do was trade for some other kind of meat. I had seen the chickens and cows, and I knew Leif was a good hunter. But he told me he wasn't interested. He said that I should get off his property, but I just wanted him to see that it was a good trade." He fell quiet.

Sigurd waited, though the rest of the Thing was impatient with his silence. "Valdemar, how did Leif die?"

"When he wouldn't listen I opened the basket and stuck it in his face so he could see the quality of the fish. That's when Vigdis came out. When she went back into the barn Leif turned to me and pushed me to the ground. I wasn't thinking straight. I was so angry because he wouldn't listen; he wouldn't trade with me. Before I could get up Leif kicked me a couple of times and told me to get off his property or he would kick me all the way down the hill like a dog. The last time he tried to kick me I grabbed his foot and pushed back as hard as I could. He stumbled backward, and before he could catch his balance I jumped up and pushed him in the chest as hard as I could. He fell against the house and then to the ground." Valdemar's eyes looked pleadingly at the crowd. "I didn't mean to kill him. When I turned him over I realized he had fallen against his ax. I panicked and ran away."

When Sigurd was satisfied that Valdemar had said all he was going to say, he turned to the jury. "His fate is in your hands. You know the law, now judge him and dispense justice."

"Father, do you think they will find him guilty?" Arne asked.

"He is guilty, the question is what punishment he will get. The law is pretty clear; what he did may not have been intentional, but he is still responsible." Viking law was specific and swift in its judgment. It didn't take long for the jurors to reach a decision.

Once they had reassembled, Sigurd asked for their judgment. "We find Valdemar guilty of killing Leif and leaving Vigdis a widow, their children orphans, and his parents without a son. As punishment we call for the confiscation of his land, boat, and any possessions to pay the restitution to the family. In addition he will be subject to *skoggangur* and banished from the community. No one is to feed or shelter him, and his wife will be given to Vigdis as a slave. If Leif's family pursues him and kills him they will not be found guilty of his death."

All eyes fell on Valdemar. He was astonished and frightened. How could he survive outside the community? Even though he had little contact they were his people and would have come to his aid in time of need. Now he was their enemy.

"You can't do this; I have nowhere to go. The island is small and I will have no way to leave it. Please, there must be another way." His pleading only added to the community's disdain for his weakness.

In an unusual act of compassion the Earl stood and said, "Because Valdemar's act was not intentional, I ask the community to give him safe passage off the island. What say you?" Conversation buzzed momentarily among the men, and they saw the justness of the Earl's wisdom. With one accord they agreed. Two men took Valdemar away and he was never seen again.

Regaining order, Sigurd reminded them, "We have one matter to finish before the end of the Thing. Geir and Knut must settle their difference in accordance with the fate of the gods. Let's accompany them to the lagoon."

Fate
776 AD

Knut and Geir headed the procession, and were determined to put an end to this disagreement, once and for all. They were glad, however, that their fate was not the same as Valdemar's. They would rather enter into a duel of blood than be excommunicated from the community. Once they arrived on the beach the men of the community formed a circle to mark the boundary of their combat.

"An accusation of theft has been brought with no solid evidence to corroborate the story. It has been decided that a duel of blood will allow the gods to determine guilt or innocence. Remember, the first man's blood to touch the sand is the guilty party, and punishment will be administered accordingly." Sigurd raised his hand as the two men prepared to fight.

Geir was about an inch taller than Knut, and both seemed awkward as they anticipated the fall of Sigurd's hand.

"You are nothing but a thief, and the god's will give me victory," Geir taunted.

"You are a mad man. You imagined more pigs than you had, and now you blame me for your stupidity." Knut was carefully circling, looking for the right moment to strike. He wanted the first blow to be his, and when Sigurd dropped his arm Knut rushed forward bringing his sword downward with a powerful blow, but

Geir was ready. He raised his shield over his head and took the full force of the strike, which almost knocked him to the ground.

"You will have to do better than that or the women will think you easy prey." Geir breathed heavily.

"Then maybe this will prove a better blow." Knut struck again, and then again, driving Geir backward, but this time Geir deflected the last blow and turned just enough for Knut to slide by. As he did, Knut gave his opponent a push that knocked him into the sand. If Geir had been thinking clearly, he could have attacked and drawn first blood, but Knut's onslaught took the wind out of him and he staggered away lungs heaving.

"I have to hand it to you Knut, you are stronger than you look, and you look like one of my pigs." The crowd laughed. "Pay me the price of the pig and we can go home."

"Words of a desperate man. Are you having difficulty breathing? Maybe you are afraid you will lose and the community will know just what you are, a liar and a thief!" Knut rushed again, expecting Geir to stand his ground as before, but this time his opponent deflected the sword with his own, and then followed with his own volley.

The crowd was cheering them on to engage faster and harder. They loved a good fight, but it had been a long day and many wanted to return home. With his last move, Geir had the advantage, and with a quick upward motion he drew Knut's attention to the sword. Dropping his shield, he struck Knut in the jaw with his fist, knocking him backward. Geir dropped his sword and began punching Knut in the face until finally blood flew from his mouth on to the sand. The crowd erupted into a roar of delight.

Rushing in to break up the fight, Sigurd declared the contest over and Geir the winner. "It has been settled. The gods have determined that Geir's testimony is true, and that sentence must be judged against Knut."

Two men stood next to Knut to ensure his compliance to the decree.

"Since there is no evidence that a pig was in the possession of the accused he will not forfeit his home, but will pay restitution in the amount three times the value of the pig. This concludes the session of the Thing. Are all in agreement?"

The dismissal was met with enthusiastic approval, and the crowd thinned as men collected their families and went home.

Magnus had been standing with Arne, and they waited a while before leaving to find Sigrunn. He hated walking through crowds, so they spent time skipping pebbles across the water. Finally they found Sigrunn packing up the remainder of the produce. Little was left, but she had done some trading and was going home with as much as she had brought.

That evening after their meal, they sat around the hearth's the low burning fire. It had been a long day and Sigrunn was ready to go to bed, but when she suggested that everyone retire, she knew from Arne's silence that he wanted to talk with his father privately. She left them alone.

"Something seems to be weighing on your mind," Magnus finally said to his son.

"I know that the law is important, but why was Valdemar judged so harshly? He didn't mean to kill Leif; it was an accident."

"The law maintains order. It helps keep the community from falling into chaos. If Valdemar were to escape punishment it would encourage others to do the same."

"I understand that, but why was he cast out of the community?" Arne's inquisitiveness overshadowed his compassion.

"Valdemar's carelessness didn't just affect Leif, but his family and clan as well. If he had no family, a wife, or parents, then maybe another punishment would have been chosen. But Leif had people who were dependent on him, and Valdemar's actions caused them great harm. The price of restitution was far more than a man like Valdemar could ever repay. Staying in the community with that kind of debt would have caused hardship on all and resentment would follow. This way, the family receives what they are due and Valdemar escapes with his life."

"But what about the right of revenge? If he had not been excommunicated, Leif's family would not have been able to hurt him." Arne had listened well to the *lovsigemann*.

"Excommunication liberates the criminal and the victims. The criminal is free to run, and the victims are free to exact revenge. There is also a cost. The victim has lost someone they love and care for, and the criminal loses his family and community. There are no winners in these matters, only losers. Harsh punishment is about justice. Mercy is left to the gods, and they rarely show any to those who cross them. We are better served in following their example. Honor is upheld when men maintain their oaths and live disciplined lives."

They sat quietly for a while, but Arne's eyes fluttered closed, then open. His father scooped him up in his arms and laid him in his bed. The young man was his father's son, and he loved him deeply. Slipping into bed, he watched his wife sleep for a while. Magnus thought about the day and Arne's questions about law and justice. They lived hard and sometimes harsh lives, but they were not animals, and the laws gave them a framework for living. He couldn't imagine what it would be like if everyone did what was right in their own eyes, without caring what other people thought. They were a community of people who loved, cared, and supported one another. It was what made life worthwhile, and one day Arne would understand this great gift that the gods had given them.

An Uncertain Place
776 AD

"Magnus." Yngve pounded on the door. "Magnus open up."

"Father," Sigrunn answered. "What is the matter?"

"Where is Magnus?" was his only reply. "Send Arne to get his father."

Sigrunn called for Arne and told him to go into the fields and find Magnus. "What has gotten you so excited?" she asked, but Yngve wouldn't speak of it until her husband had come. It didn't take Arne long to fetch his father.

"Yngve, tell me, why are you so agitated?" Magnus had barely gotten through the door. His father's unexpected visit and Arne's excitement piqued Magnus' interest.

"You must come at once. Torstein's ships have returned."

Nothing was new about returning ships, but the ones he was talking about were raiders. Magnus didn't mind a good fight, but he was a trader and not keen on the idea of raids. They were bad for business. People who were afraid of you didn't want to trade; instead they hid when they heard you coming. There was also a high toll on life.

"What is the hurry? I am sure there will be time enough to glory in the bounty of their ventures."

145

"Torstein's son is dead." Yngve's face was grave. Steinar was the Earl's only son and was to take his father's place; this was not a good omen.

"Arne, come with me." Looking at Sigrunn he said, "We will be back later."

"I am going with you." Her eyes were adamant. "His wife, as well as any others who have become widows, will need the comfort of the community." There was no arguing with her and they left for town.

When they reached Birka the whole town was in mourning. Two other men had lost their lives and their widows could be heard wailing from the town's edge. A procession of men carried the slain to a small building off of the community hall called "the place of the dead." There they prepared the bodies for burial and their journey to the next life. When Magnus and Arne entered the hall men were already drinking and retelling the stories of the departed's glory.

"Steinar fought bravely," one man said. "We had formed the shield wall and were holding off fifty men. Finally we broke their offense and drove them back into their village. Steinar led the charge and dispatched ten men before he was struck down." A howl of cheers rang through the hall, horns filled with ale extolling the event.

"I saw with my own eyes the Valkyries descend and carry his soul to Valhalla," another man intoned, and men nodded their heads in approval. "As well as the other two who died with him. They fought and died with honor." The hall fell silent in honor of the dead, and it was only broken when Torstein stood, lifted his horn, and took a deep draught of ale. It was their custom to bury bodies within a day of their return because the corpses began to decay and smell.

Steinar was of royal blood; therefore, his burial would be more elaborate than his comrades'. While the warriors were celebrating, slaves were digging the graves outside of town, and wives were collecting items that their fallen husbands would need in the afterlife. Torstein ordered one of his smaller boats pulled on shore. Steinar's body was cleaned, dressed in warrior's clothing and weapons, and then laid on the ship. His slaves brought colorful cushions, tools, weapons, spices, and various other prestigious items that he would need in Valhalla. Steinar had three slave girls. As per their custom, the women were asked if they would like to accompany their master on his journey to Valhalla. Only one did, and she was taken away and ritually cleansed and dressed.

Chessa had been a slave for ten years, and was the same age as her master. She was brought from the east after a raiding party had attacked her village. Torstein assigned her to his young son, and she was loyal to him his whole life. She knew her life was uncertain now, and though she didn't look forward to the rituals leading to her death, she would be treated with honor for her decision. After her bath she was adorned with jewelry and led to the tents surrounding the city. There she engaged in sexual intercourse with the owner of the tent, asking him what he wanted her to do for him, in honor of her master, when he entered Valhalla.

After the ritual intercourse Chessa was led to a doorframe and raised three times and when she was set down she said, "I see my master sitting in paradise, and it is beautiful and green and with him are men and slaves and he calls me. Lead me to him." Her escorts handed her a chicken and she killed it as a sacrifice. They removed her jewelry, drank two flasks of ale, and sang. The Angel of Death, an old woman of the village, led her to the tent of her dead master, where six of his closest friends had intercourse with her, and then slit her throat. These same six men carried her body to the boat and laid her on the cushions at the foot of Steinar. Those who were assembled stood silent in honor of the fallen dead, and the six men set the boat on fire.

Magnus and Arne stood quietly as they watched the black smoke rise into the sky. It smelled of sweet oak, but soon began to mix with the stench of burning flesh. It was a reminder that death was a mixture of sorrow and joy, sorrow for those who remained but joy for the warrior entering into the Hall of Odin.

"It is a pity," said Olaf.

Magnus looked perplexed. "Why do you pity him? He died in battle and has won a place in Valhalla."

"You and I have traveled to distant lands, Magnus, and you know that I was baptized a Christian. It is a pity to know that Steinar and his comrades have died without being saved by the Christian God." Olaf wasn't being judgmental; he was just stating what he believed.

Few Vikings embraced the foreign god of the Christians, but some who had been exposed to the teachings in far away lands had embraced this new faith. Their understanding was rudimentary but they accepted that paradise was not obtained through valor, honor, or even noble deeds. Instead paradise was open to all who believed in the Christian leader, Jesus.

"I have heard the stories, too, Olaf. A weak god who couldn't even save his son too easily sways you. I prefer Odin and Thor, gods of strength and glory. They have protected us so far and will lead us into the glorious halls when we pass from this life. Add your Jesus if you wish, but don't forget who owns the skies." Magnus put his arm around Arne and led him toward home; he had had enough mortality for one day.

The ceremonies of death didn't end with the burning of the ship. Once the flames died out the bones were collected and laid to rest beneath the earth. The warrior was buried in a sitting position with his treasure close so he could use it with ease in Valhalla. As the final shovel of dirt was thrown on Steinar's grave, Torstein spoke, "To the winds you sought adventure and spoil. To the winds you fought for honor and glory. To the winds you sailed to distant lands. To the winds that blow you to Valhalla." He turned and went home and the crowd followed.

"Do all who die go to Valhalla?" Arne asked as they walked home. Sigrunn joined them as they passed the community hall.

"Only those who die in battle are the chosen warriors who enter Odin's Great Hall."

"Then where do the rest go, and what about mother?"

"It depends on how you live your life. Those who die of old age or disease, and are not killed in battle are led to the gloom and murky Helheim, ruled by Hel, the sister of the World Serpent and the wolf Fenrir, and the daughter of Loki and his wife Angrboda. But those whose lives are marked by dishonor awaken in the Hall of Hiflheim. It is a vast and cold region and lies underneath the third roots of Yggdrasil, close to the spring-roaring cauldron. It is there that the serpent Nidhoog eats corpses and gnaws on the roots of Yggdrasil."

"Is there no place that is warm and accepting for those who are not warriors and who do not die in battle?" Arne asked.

"It is not for us to decide our fates. They lie in the hands of the gods. If we live with honor and die with honor, then in the next life we will do the same." They had reached the house and it was late. Magnus shooed Arne off to bed, and he and Sigrunn settled in for a good night's sleep.

The wind blew from the north and the weather was turning cold. Soon the earth would be covered with snow, and the cycle of life and death would continue. Arne's dreams were filled with specters of the dead and rotting corpses. He woke suddenly in the night, sweating. The world was an uncertain place, and he was determined to live his life with honor and courage.

Harvest Feast
776 AD

"Tie the sheaves in tight bundles, and stack them in the barn." Arne was helping Sigrunn bring in the last of the harvest. Much of it would be used to make bread throughout the winter months; the rest would be fed to the cattle. Magnus was bringing in one of the nine cows that they owned.

"Will we have enough for all the cattle this year?"

"No." She seemed a little surly. "I think it will only stretch out for seven." Brightening up, she added, "We will at least have two to offer as sacrifices during Vetrnaetr." Magnus always looked forward to Vetrnaetr. It marked the end of the year's harvest and work, and the celebration of Winternights was filled with festivities and stories.

"Will you have everything ready? There are only two days before Vetrnaetr." Magnus teased her because Sigrunn was always ready. She worked hard and kept their home in order, plus she loved leading the house in the celebration.

Arne was coming back into the yard.

"Did you leave the last stalk in the field?"

He nodded yes, and she motioned for him to sit next to her for their noon meal. It wasn't much—a couple of slices of bread and some cheese.

"Do you know why we leave the sheaf in the field?"

Arne sat next to her; he loved hearing his mother tell the story.

"The gods have blessed the land, and we have received its bounty with thanksgiving. Vetrnaetr is the celebration of those gifts. We bring before the god Freyr a sacrifice to honor him for bringing success to our fields, to our fighting, and to our beds." She put her hand to her stomach and smiled at Magnus. She was pregnant and felt doubly blessed this year. "The stalk is left in the field because when the sun goes down on the eve of Vetrnaetr, and all the celebration is finished, Odin begins his Wild Hunt." She looked at Magnus and he picked up the story.

"The warriors of old rise to meet Odin, and specters ride through the woods killing everything in their path. The nights belong to the hunters and their hounds, and any human found in their wake is either killed, driven mad, or cursed with his impending doom. The sheaf is left to feed the hunters and fill their stomachs so that they will leave our home untouched."

"What are the hounds like?" Arne asked.

"The most ferocious beasts that could ever be summoned from hell. They howl to the sound of Odin's horn, as if the sound itself was the cause of their pain. Their ghostlike appearance fades in and out of the darkness as they hurry along the wind. Sitting astride his eight-legged horse, Sleipnir, Odin oversees the Valkyries who accompany the hunt and whisk away all who have died. The days are shortened and the nights long, and it is a bad omen for any man to see the horsemen storm through the sky."

There was a rustling in the trees near the edge of the woods. Magnus motioned for them to sit silently and watch. They heard a low grunt and the flat nose of a boar poked out of the brush. When he saw the humans staring at him he quickly disappeared into the forest.

"Shall we go hunt him, Father?" Arne was motivated by the story of the wild hunt.

"No, seeing the boar is a good omen. He is the companion of Freyr and has come as a blessing to our home." Magnus could tell his son was disappointed. "There will be time for hunting before the winter snows come. Right now we need to prepare for the upcoming festivities." Looking at his wife, he smiled. "What do you require from your humble servants?"

The next two days flew by as food was prepared, the house cleaned, and the stores put up for the winter months. Magnus chose two of the thinnest cows to sacrifice. The others would need to be fattened to survive the long season. The two he chose weren't bony by any means, and after the sacrifice they were butchered and cured. Their deaths would be honored for providing a year of nourishment.

The eve of Vetrnaetr marks the beginning of the Winternights, and the day's festival is a celebration of the year's hard work and bounty. Sigrunn was excited because it was a time when the women of the Birka extolled their role as masters of their homes. It was true that the men ruled, but women were strong and competent, and partners with their husbands in providing for the family. Sigrunn also had the honor of being with child; she was already three months pregnant and beginning to show. She would be the envy of the celebration. Trying on the dress that she had worked on all summer for this event, she soon found that some alterations were needed to accommodate the baby. When she was finished, she slipped it over the top of her head and let it drape to the floor. She added a chain of flowers that hung from her neck, and braided some into her hair. Magnus was standing behind her, watching her preen, and when she turned and saw him Sigrunn's face turned a rich shade of red.

"You are the most beautiful woman in Birka." He wrapped his arms around her and placed his hand on her stomach. "Do you think it will be another boy?"

"Would you be disappointed if it were a girl?" Boys were more prized, but she wouldn't mind having another girl in the house.

"I pray that he is a boy, but a little girl will be loved just as much." In true Viking spirit he would rather have ten boys, but without girls, whom would they marry? "How much longer until we join the festivities?"

"Give me another hour, then we can head into town. Do you have the wagon loaded?" She cocked her head and gave him a look. She loved Magnus with all her heart and she knew he loved her, and she looked forward to the festival and offering a sacrifice to Freyr for the health of their baby. Over the last three years she had two miscarriages, and she longed to hold a baby in her arms and remove the dishonor.

Wild Hunt
776 AD

Arne fidgeted and Magnus fiddled with the horses harness as they waited for Sigrunn to finally come out of the house. Jumping off the wagon Arne said, "Mother why don't you ride in the wagon?" It was more of a cart than a wagon, and the pony that pulled it wouldn't be any worse with her as a passenger. She smilingly obliged his offer and relished not having to walk into town, feeling like a queen.

As they approached Birka they joined with other families. The woman of the house led each family, and every woman was dressed in her finest clothing. They were colorfully adorned and carried wreaths and flowers to celebrate the event. Arne was not unaware of the brightly adorned females. As he had hoped, they merged with the family of Bjorn. He had two sons and three daughters, the oldest of which had caught his eye.

Walking up beside her Arne stammered, "Hello, Torunn." Her name meant love, and she must have been its goddess because she had bewitched him. She giggled and they walked together quietly. Her younger brother asked Arne if he thought his sister was pretty.

She gave him a dirty look. "Leave Arne alone." He didn't.

"Mother, tell Inge to leave Arne alone." He was scolded, but her words fell on deaf ears.

"Of a truth, he doesn't bother me." All Arne cared about was walking next to Torunn.

When they entered Birka everyone was gathered around the community hall, where tables spilled out onto the courtyard laden with an abundance of food. In the center of the town an altar stood, where families sacrificed their cattle to the god of their choosing, and honored their long dead ancestors. Musicians were practicing next to the fire, men who were proficient with the cow-horn, the Jorvik panpipe, the lyre, and the drum. But all fell silent when Sigurd took the stage and stamped his staff. When he had everyone's attention he offered a prayer:

> *Lord Odin and lady Freya,*
> *We give our greetings to thee.*
> *Please bless this bounty set here before us*
> *And enjoy this good food with us*
> *As we do enjoy it.*
> *Hail and love to Thee.*

When he was finished the music played, and people danced, ate, and drank till their hearts were content. Sigrunn gathered the wives into a circle, where the men stood in the center. They watched their wives dance around them, enticing them to join in their song.

> *Ahti dwelt upon an island,*
> *By the bay near Kauko's headland,*
> *And his fields he tilled industriously,*
> *And the fields he trenched with ploughing,*
> *And his ears were of the finest,*
> *And his hearing of the keenest.*
> *Heard he shouting in the village,*

From the lake came sounds of hammering,
On the ice the sound of footsteps,
On the heath a sledge was rattling.
Therefore in his mind he fancied,
In his brain the notion entered,
That at Pohjola was a wedding,
And a drinking-bout in secret.

After each refrain the men responded, until they could not stand under the weight of their ale. Magnus tripped his way to the end of the table where food was plentiful, and he filled his stomach once again. Unaffected by the revelry of the old, young couples sat at the edge of the festivities in the familiar air of romance.

The sun was setting and soon evening would call for the hunters of Odin to ride, the sobering moment upon them. As the last ray cast its light over the trees and the fire's embers rose in the wind, it was time for the warriors to march. Magnus rallied the men and the line between the spirits and the earth sobered their drunken hearts. Olaf brought a bucket of dark paint and set it on the table. Each warrior dipped his hand into the bucket and pulled out a glob to smear on his face so that he faded into the darkness. When the last man had donned his color, each picked up his spear and shield. Silently they marched in order until they had surrounded the communal fire. The women, who had been dancing stood still, the musicians fell silent, and all moved to the side.

In silence they stood until the sky was ready to listen. Magnus spoke and after each refrain the company of men slapped their spears against black shields and spoke in a low grunt,

Odin, the Hunter and Father of us all,
You rise tonight on the winds of fall.

157

With hounds from Hel, and horns forlorn
On your eight-legged steed the hunt is born.

A ghostly army marches at your word,
Their blackened shields and specter's sword.

No warrior can stand against such foe,
Terrifying shadows and eyes that glow.

Attend your hearths; keep the night at bay
And pray your soul is kept till day.

At the end of the ritual, the assemblage left everything in its place and quietly headed home. In the silence they hoped the hunter and his party would not notice them; and the embers of the fire remained lit to ward off demons in their midst. As the last person left nocturnal creatures moved in to scavenge the leftover food, filling their bellies in preparation for a long hibernation.

Their pace toward home was quicker than when they went to Winternights celebration. Shadows grew longer and darkness was upon them before they all reached their thresholds safely. Magnus scooted his family into the security of their home and proceeded to light the pile of wood that he and Arne had prepared for this evening's fire. The Wild Hunt unleashed an army of demons whose presence in the shadows would be dispelled by the fire's light. To keep his home safe, Magnus would tend the fire throughout the evening and keep watch over his family.

The kindling ignited, the flames lapped at the dry wood. As they rose Magnus' heart beat a little slower, the light revealing nothing but the familiar surroundings of his farm. As the evening progressed, however, so did the winds. They steadily blew harder, and the leaves of the trees rustled together, taunting the flames so they ran from an unknown presence. Grabbing his shield and sword, Magnus beat against it, hoping the noise would chase the specters away. He bellowed into the wind,

Fly from me you hounds of hell!
Take not your vengeance on me and mine!
Sleipnir carry your master far
Take not my soul before its time!

Protect me, fathers long past dead
Who entered into Valhalla's hall!
Take me not in tonight's Wild Hunt!
But slain with honor in a battle fall!

Magnus' dog lay next to him, the nape of his neck standing straight, teeth bared, a low growl emanating from deep within his throat. He too saw the unseen and it did not bode well. Magnus continued to strike spear against shield and repeated his prayer. With the passing hours the weight of his shield grew heavy, but he stood, a sentinel against the unseen world that threatened his home. He could sense the spirits trying to lull him to sleep, wanting to enter his dreams and entice him away. But with the strength and courage of a warrior he beat back his tempters and held the weight of his eyelids at bay, until the sun's rays rose over the trees and the light of day chased the specters away.

Stumbling into the house, he woke Arne and told him to get water and quench the fire. The boy rubbed his eyes and asked, "Did you see the hunt?" But the expression on his father's face stifled any more questions, and he obediently went and tended the fire.

Magnus undressed, washed his hands and face, and curled up next to his wife. Her gentle breathing soothed him into sleep, but it wasn't peaceful. The snarling teeth of howling hounds, the horn of Odin calling to his hunters, and the hoof beats of Sleipnir and his kin haunted his dreams. No peaceful rest would come this day, and his tossing forced Sigrunn to rise earlier than she would have liked. Taking some embers Arne had saved from the fire, she started her own fire for cooking. At least she could prepare a hot meal for her husband after his grueling night's watch.

"Father looked…"—Arne paused before saying his next words—"frightened. What do you think he saw, Mother?"

"Don't mistake exhaustion for fear. Your father is a brave man, and he spent a long night tending the fire to keep us safe. In all the years that he has watched over us there has been nothing to fear, and I am sure that last night was no different." She had Arne collect eggs from the chickens as she took some pork from the curing house. The smell permeated their small home, and eventually Magnus could resist the lure of food no longer. It not only filled his empty stomach but it rescued him from the darkness of his dream.

.

Volur
776 AD

All day Magnus moved from one thing to another, having difficulty concentrating. Sigrunn asked, "Are you well, my husband?"

"I am fine." But clearly he wasn't.

Carefully she persisted, "Has something about last night upset you?"

He looked off into the woods. He could still hear the howling and the hoof beats, the hunter and his horn. "It was nothing I could not handle. The fire protected us and kept the hunt at bay." He put down his armful of wood and walked away. All Sigrunn could do was watch her husband's turmoil and pray. "Odin, far-wanderer, grant my husband wisdom, courage, and victory. Friend Thor, grant him your strength, and both be with him."

Magnus walked for hours through the woods, trying to clear the images from his head, but the effort was futile. Finally he broke through the tree line just north of Birka. His path was no longer random as he approached the Earl's home. Unsure of how to broach the subject he paced outside for thirty minutes. The Earl, seeing his distraught friend, came up from behind and asked, "Magnus, you have been here for a while. What is it that you want?"

Nervously he answered, "I have seen the Hunter."

The Earl put his hand on Magnus' shoulder and led him to a nearby bench. "What did you see? Are you sure it was Odin?"

"I am sure. The air was filled with hunters and Odin's horn was as loud as thunder. I kept my fire lit to keep them at bay, but my dreams have been disturbing ever since. I must speak to the Volur."

The Volur was the seer and had attached her fortune to the fortune of Torstein. She spoke prophecies and omens to direct him in victory and save him from defeat. Rarely did she speak on behalf of common men and when she did the price was high.

"Magnus, my friend, I am not sure that is a good idea. The Volur is a crafty lady and she has peered into the darkness so much that her riddles are difficult to interpret and costly as well."

"I have seen the Hunt, and it is not a good omen. I need to know. I will pay her demands." Magnus and the Earl had been friends for a long time. Magnus was a faithful and loyal member of the community. He didn't participate in the raids, for his was a life of trade, but he was always willing and able to pick up an ax and shield to defend his lord and the community. If he were willing to pay the price, then what harm would there be?

"Give me a few minutes to call her from her meditations. Meet us in the back room of the great hall. There she divines the will of the gods."

The hall was dark and the darkness seemed thicker than usual. It took a few minutes for his eyes to adjust, and then Magnus made his way to the rear chamber. His wait was only twenty minutes but it seemed like hours. When the Volur walked into the room a chill blew across his face; it seemed as if death had entered. She was dressed in a white gown, and her face was wrinkled. Her features seemed timeless. Silently she sat before a metal cauldron filled with a liquid unfamiliar to Magnus. She motioned for him to sit and he did.

"What do you see?" he asked, but she said nothing. A few minutes went by and he asked again, "What do you see? What does my future hold?" Magnus was becoming frustrated with her silence, and right before he was ready to get up and walk out she began to sway back and forth. She started beating a drum lying at her side. The Volur's body swayed to its rhythm as a low hum filled the room and smoke rose from the cauldron.

"You have seen the hunt and the Hunter," she said, but that was no new revelation; the Earl could have told her that. "His hounds and hunters disturbed your home. It is not a good omen to have seen Odin ride." The Volur continued to sway and became more animated as she chanted,

> Now awful it is to be without,
> As blood-red rack races overhead;
> Is the welkin gory with warriors' blood,
> As we Valkyries war-songs chanted?
> Your eyes have seen the wild Hunt
> And gruesome cry of honored dead;
> What lies ahead in warriors' blood
> That lies beneath your wounded head?

The Volur fell silent and stopped moving. Her breathing was so shallow that Magnus wasn't sure whether she was alive or dead.

"What does this mean? Are you saying that I will die? Will it be in battle? Will the Valkyries come for me and take me to Valhalla? When will this battle take place?" Like the Earl had said, the riddle was difficult to understand, but Magnus knew the bottom line; he would die in battle from a head wound. He could take comfort that the winter months separated them from any battle. He would spend these next months with his family, preparing them for his impending departure.

The Earl met him outside, and Magnus' face said it all.

"I am sure that it will not be as bad as she predicted. She has been wrong at times, though she usually twists it to fit her own purposes. Don't fret over her words."

"My lord." Magnus became formal. "Everyone knows that seeing the Hunt is a bad omen and causes death, madness, or impending doom. I am neither dead nor mad; therefore the prophecy spells out my demise. I take comfort knowing that I will die in battle and will see my father again in Odin's Hall." He looked intently into the Earl's eyes. "I have enough to leave Arne and Sigrunn provided for, but humbly ask that when my death comes the community will watch over them."

The Earl slapped him on the back and assured him of their sworn duty to his unyielding loyalty.

When Magnus stepped through the door Sigrunn could see in his eyes the anguish of his soul. "What worries you, Magnus?"

"Sigrunn, I need you to sit down." She didn't like the sound of this. He told her of the hunt and going to see the Volur. He believed that telling her everything was the best way to prepare her for the future. "But we have the winter together. After that there is no guarantee. What I do know is that I will fall in battle, and that is honorable. You will be provided for and Arne is a man, capable of running the farm."

They hadn't noticed Arne standing at the door. When they turned and saw him, he was stoic, trying to understand and absorb what he had heard. His youthful misgivings taunted him to turn and run, but he was a man now and would not cry. Magnus held out his arm, instinctively drawing Arne in, and the three of them hugged.

"We will no longer speak of this. Life is precious and short. We will make the best of our time and prepare for the coming of our new child. We will celebrate, and pray that Odin will call me to battle at the right time and for the honor of our family."

Sigrunn threw her arms around his neck. Cheeks softened by tears, he let the warmth of her body comfort his tortured soul. And it was so; they never spoke of it again.

Entr'acte

Between the veils that hide heaven and hell lays the land of Midgard. Between the crest of hill and sky lay the aspirations of man. Between the heart and soul, glory and greed, lay siege. Between innocence and guile is the spirit of ambition.

The winds of the north eventually touch the winds of the south, and they clash in thunder and storm. What touches the soul of one will stir the heart of another, until somewhere they meet and at that moment all is won and lost.

What speaks from the darkness, but the voice of reason? What calls to the soul but heart and emotion? What dances to the music of ardor and passion? What drives a man to the edge? What causes him to abandon all?

Out of the Hunt, a destiny is told and beyond the horizon another is called. Two lives, one destiny: both wrestle with the beast within.

The Wolf King

Their barking was loud and their burning blood fueled them all the more. They had caught the scent and were released to run down their prey. These dogs were bred for this purpose, with long bodies and legs to match. Thin and lean, they could run as fast as horses, and loved the thrill of the hunt more than food. Their masters rode upon steeds, strong and anxious as they pulled against their reins. They too would follow the hunt until they could run no more, and who sat upon the largest and most majestic steed of all? Who else but the King!

"Your majesty, the wolves have been spotted. The dogs are on their trail as we speak. Shall we follow closely, or allow them to corner the pack?"

"We can't let the dogs have all the fun. Let's catch them before they tear apart the beasts and we are left with nothing but the carcasses." The King buried his spurs into the sides of his horse, which neighed loudly and, lurching forward, carried the King with all haste.

Pointing into the distance the Duke cried loudly, "Over there! The dogs are off and up the side of the mountain!" Turning his horse he leaned forward, signaling his beast to charge up the hill. The horse complied without any hesitation and breathed heavily under his master's weight, bearing him gladly.

The King wasn't far behind and had to duck in order to avoid being struck by a low hanging-branch. If he had been wearing his crown its height would have borne the brunt of the blow. Fortunately only strands of hair were left behind.

Without warning his horse stopped, and the King's weight carried him forward, almost over the stallion's neck. "By all that is good, why have we stopped?" he exclaimed. To his relief his horse had halted before heading over a cliff. In their hurry to follow the dogs, the men had missed the precipice hidden by trees and bushes. The Duke had barely stopped as well and regretted his inability to warn the king in time and spare him the terrifying experience.

"My apologies sire. I should have warned you, but…" the Duke stammered.

"Forget about it, my friend. A little fear strengthens the heart." He sat back as the echo of the dogs disappeared in the ravine below, but another sound caught his ear. In the distance a howl so forlorn spoke of a heart in pain. What sorrow did this wolf know that he would speak it each night to the moon? But he was not alone: as soon as he called out another spoke in return, and then another until the evening's twilight was a canine cacophony so piercing that the hunting dogs stopped and shivered. Giving heed to the night, they returned to their masters and cowered around the legs of the horses, at risk of being stepped on.

"As far as you can see, who owns this vast land?" The King was contemplative as he deeply inhaled the cool mountain air. "Truly Duke, to whom does this belong?"

"To you, my lord. Who else commands the allegiance of all the people?" Like the people of this realm he held the king in high esteem.

"Yes, it is true that I have subdued those who would dare stand against me, but who owns the land? I am but a humble steward. No, this land belongs to them." He pointed into the distance. "It belongs to the wolves, the creatures to whom God gave dominion." He waited as the thought sank in, and when he could bear it no more he concluded, "But God has given me free range. Shall we continue the hunt in the morning?"

They turned their horses toward a small stream that flowed between the hills, and found the spot where their servants had set up camp. A knave approached and took the reins from the king with assurances that he would take good care of His Majesty's prized stallion. Another young man assisted in taking his sword and helped him find a level place to remove his light mail. He had not wanted to wear armor on the hunt this morning, but the captain of the guard had insisted. "You never know what danger lies in the dark. Better safe than sorry," the captain had said. Sorry is how the king felt under the weight of its chains. No matter how hard he tried, he could not talk his blacksmith into making any lighter. He wished an elf, with his magic, could make a mail as light as a feather. But, alas, that was make-believe.

Sitting at the fire, he felt as alive as ever. War was constantly around him, but in these moments during the hunt he felt the weight of the crown less. Stories were told and songs were sung. Though the servants were not allowed to associate with royalty at court, here in the woods those lines were often crossed. The King saw his servants as his children, and who would not want their children to experience the gracious nature of their father? He ordered food to be cooked and drink to be drunk until the night slipped away as quietly as the stars.

"Tell us the story of the she-wolf," a servant had requested.

"Please, please," the others enjoined.

After several false attempts to stave off their request, the King consented to retell the tale of the glory of Rome. He cleared his throat and looked into the fire.

"There was a mighty king named Numitor, whose brother Amulius was jealous of his power. He worked hard behind the scenes, bolstering his position and gathering a following that would stand against the king. Eventually he revolted and seized power from his brother. Having slain his brother, Amulius proceeded to slaughter all male heirs to the throne, solidifying his claim for generations.

"In an act of compassion he spared the beautiful daughter of his brother, but forced Rhea Silvia to become a Vestal Virgin and swore her to chastity in service to the temple. Her beauty did not go unnoticed among the gods, one in particular. Mars, the god of war, took pity on her state and came to her and she conceived the twins Romulus and Remus.

"When Amulius found out, he had the twins taken from their mother and left the infants to die in the river Tiber. The gods would not have them die, and ordered the river to carry them to safety, deep in the woods. Their cries were heard by a she-wolf, who took them in as her pups, and they suckled at her teats until they were full. She would soon realize that the twins needed others like themselves to survive. She led them near a farm where a shepherd and his wife heard their cries, rescued them, and raised them as their own.

"Their natural abilities as leaders were evident early and they acquired their own following. Many years later they learned their true identities and gathered a force of men who were willing to overthrow the tyrant Amulius and establish once again the kingdom of their father."

He had the audience's rapt attention, and took the opportunity to remind them of their duty. "The moral of the story is to forsake false gods and serve faithfully the true God and his anointed king." His statement was met with a rousing round of "Hear! Hear!" and "Long live the King!"

As the night wore on and bellies were filled, the sentinel's howl could still be heard. The moon rose high and lit the landscape so that torches were not necessary to light the way. The light called to the wolves and they answered back; the King was mesmerized by their sound.

"Why are you so drawn to the sound of the wolf?" the Duke inquired.

"Listen."

They both tilted their heads.

"Do you not understand what they say?"

The Duke shook his head no.

"The she-wolf has always represented the birth and strength of Rome. In her bosom the greatest empire to have existed had its origins. She suckled and nurtured, and even knew when to let go. I admire the birth and rebirth she represents." He paused and picked at the fire with a stick. "Then there is the male. He is a lone figure standing on the mountain howling at the moon. He picks the largest object in the sky and defiantly dares it to howl back. He is alone and master of his domain."

He looked at his friend. "Being king must seem to some a glorious position. There are servants, castles, land, and wealth beyond measure. But it is a lonely place. I see the world and it is daunting and without a shepherd. I take to it the cross of Christ that it may find peace, but it fights me at every turn. Some say I should stay home and be satisfied. But how can I be satisfied until all kneel before the King of Kings? So, I fight those within and those without and I howl at the moon. I cannot do this on my own or in my own strength. I am suckled by the Spirit and nurtured by his presence. I have been called by my savior and given responsibilities beyond measure. I have not asked for this, but I will not shrink from it. I am the Emperor of the new Rome, not for my own glory, but for God's."

The Duke couldn't help but be moved and silently resolved to follow this man unto death. In that same instant an idea was also forged in his mind. The King excused himself and his servants helped him retire for the evening. In the morning the Duke sent a message to some prominent friends in Rome. He hoped to surprise the King on his birthday.

The morning brought a new freshness: crisp air, damp leaves, and birds singing to the undisturbed glory of their creator. The King relished this time, before servants and knights fussed over his every move. He slipped on his robe and boots and walked along the edge of the river as it laughed its way down the banks. Stooping, he carefully cupped his hands to lift the cold liquid to his lips, ever watchful of his surroundings. Fish played in the water, and he could see one hiding under a decaying log trapped beneath the surface. Its mouth opened and closed as if to warn him away, but he fixed his eyes on the scaly creature in hopes of snatching him from its perch. Slowly he stepped into the cold water and breathed deeply to stifle a gasp at the chill. He was careful not to cause a ripple and chase his breakfast away, but just as he was about to reach for his prize a twig snapped behind him.

The king froze, every muscle in his body tensing with the full awareness that his life could be in danger. If it were an enemy, an arrow would have already pierced his back, but a servant would have already spoken. The deep breathing and heavy grunt spoke of another possibility—a bear! He would gladly give the animal his fish if the bear would let him pass, but he had only two options: face the creature or dive into the water. Bears were large but quick, and if he didn't act soon its sharp claws would be upon him. Without further consideration he quickly jumped into the river. The ice-cold water drenched his already numb feet. Struggling, he flipped onto his back just in time to see the large bear stand on its hind legs and roar laughingly at the King's humiliation.

The King was swept away by the current. It was stronger than he had anticipated and his leather coat and boots made maneuvering difficult. His arms grew tired as he fought against the water, and he thought he was all right until he realized that the current had increased in speed. Once again flipping onto his back he could see the waves capped in white as they lapped against large rocks. He knew he couldn't fight the current and decided that the best strategy was to go with the flow. He used his feet to push off oncoming rocks, and his hands fought to keep his head above the surface. It was working and all he had to do was outlast the river.

Praying, he asked God for favor, that this would not be the end to a lifetime of service. If he was spared, the King vowed to redouble his efforts to bring salvation to the pagan north. Just as he was about to utter the word "amen," he was spun around and his leg struck a rock. If it was God's will for him to survive it wasn't going to come about without some effort by the King. Pain shot through his leg, and the numbness seemed, for a moment, to leave it. He didn't think it was broken, but it hurt too much to push with.

He wasn't going to make it, and he released himself to his watery grave and the good grace of God. His head went under the water for a third time and his mind went to sleep. Fowls, watching from their perch above saw the royal man of God float downstream in a most undignified manner.

Who are you? a voice said.

I am the King, he said incredulously, astonished that someone would not recognize him. *Is that not apparent?*

What is a king? the voice asked.

Well, the king thought, *a king is a steward of God's kingdom.*

And God has sent you?

He has, but I believe I have lost my way.

The king was not sure where he was. The last thing he remembered was water splashing on his face. As he thought about it, everything was dark and all he felt was a floating sensation.

Who are you?

I am not a king, the voice responded.

But who are you? The King repeated.

I am the maker of kings. Do you not recognize me?

I am sorry, but I cannot see you. Are you God, for He is the only anointer of Kings? The King responded.

So you say. No, I am the mother of the powerful, the nurturer of the twins, she said, as the darkness was filled with the glow of her eyes.

I recognize you, but I do not fear you. You are the she-wolf, the mother of Rome.

The King's feeling bordered on awe, but he felt guilty, for only God deserved such adoration.

Why are you here? Will you usher me to the throne of God?

I am to warn you, she said.

Warn me about what? His voice intensified.

I am here to warn you of the hunter of wolves. Your ambition will destroy you, and the work of your hand will have been for naught. Seek another path before he rides in on the winds of the north.

The eyes dimmed, and in a puff of smoke the she-wolf disappeared.

It all seemed a waste since he was already passing from this life, but at that very moment the King's eyes opened and he realized his body had washed ashore. Barely breathing he pulled himself along the sandy riverbank away from the water. Fortunately he had washed up on the same side as his camp, but he knew that if he didn't keep moving the cold would take over his body and he would certainly stand before his Maker today.

The cold and hunger and an injured leg made his return to camp take longer than he had hoped. As he approached, the familiar commotion of soldiers and servants bustling about felt good, and he knew he was home.

Breaking through the tree line he was met with a hundred questions and gentle reprimands from the Duke about the dangers of wandering off alone. And how did he get all wet? The King brushed the mothering aside with a wave of his hand and accepted gratefully the plate of food offered by his servant. "Thank you," he said, and the servant walked away pleased with the king's appreciation.

He had stood at death's door many times before, but this was the first time he had come close enough to touch the other side. What did it all mean? Was the she-wolf a good omen or the temptation of the evil one, who wanders the earth seeking whom he can devour? The King would not be devoured, and he decided the warning was a distraction to keep him from his true calling. He rubbed his leg and wished he had stayed in bed.

Ogier, the Dane
768 A.D

"Come here boy," Sigfred, King of the Danes, commanded his grandson.

Being royalty seemed to distance grandfather and grandson, and the former never was impressed with the latter. Ogier tried to honor his grandfather and sought his approval. All he desired was a kind word or moment of tenderness. The King's son, Gudfred, invested little effort in the boy's training or rearing. After the loss of his wife he spent his days sulking. If Sigfred's grandson were to take the throne one day he would need to build a stronger personality.

"Let me take a look at you." He motioned for the boy to come closer and stand before him. Stroking his long beard, the king stood and walked around the boy as if inspecting his guard. "Don't slouch, it isn't becoming of a prince." Sitting once again, he motioned for his grandson to take the chair next to him. "Tell me what you have learned today."

Ogier spent every day in the company of tutors and soldiers. He loved learning and the academics and languages came easily. "I have been learning to speak the language of the Franks." Ogier ignored the sigh of displeasure from his grandfather. The King's dislike was less about the language than the people. He had been at war with the arrogant Charlemagne for years and loathed even the thought of him.

Ogier continued, "It is a difficult language, but I think I am getting used to it." He beamed with pride.

"It will serve you well, I am sure, but what of your other studies?" By this the King meant combat training. He had instructed his grandson to give as much, if not more, attention to warfare.

"The prince is improving, my King," a rather lanky, balding man said as he bowed. "He has been spending some time each day with the sword." His explanation of weaponry was as awkward as the King's ability to speak French.

"Let the boy speak for himself. Better yet, let's have a demonstration," said the King, motioning to one of the guards. Slapping his grandson on the back, the King pushed Ogier forward and directed him to take one of the proffered swords. "If your work with the blade is comparable to your progress with languages, we should have some fun.

Ogier took hold of the sword. It was heavier than the practice ones, and felt thick in his hand. The crooked smile on his grandfather's face hinted at his impending humiliation; there was no way to avoid it. If he couldn't escape the outcome he might as well diminish it by making his grandfather work. "To warn you, grandfather, your age will slow you down despite your experience." Ogier lunged forward and with a quick step surprised the King.

The King would not be undone and at the last minute deflected the sword with his own and stepped to the side. "You are brazen before your King. But a sharp tongue is cut off by a sharper sword." The King twirled as he moved forward. His action disoriented the boy and by the time he could react the King swung around and smacked the flat of the sword against his behind. It stung and flung Ogier awkwardly toward the wall, but he was able to steady himself.

"I am glad my inexperience gives the King delight." He was walking in a circle, trying to find some weakness, but it eluded him. "My teachers seem deficient in their ability to instruct me. Maybe the King should kindly stoop to training his own grandson." He meant the taunts to elicit an emotional response that would show him a weakness in his opponent. Taunts, however, worked both ways.

"Maybe," the King said, "if the gods had given me a grandson I would."

The words provoked the desired response and Ogier felt the heat rise in his body, generated by anger at his grandfather's words. His face flushed and he clenched his jaws. The smirk on his grandfather's lips beckoned him to lose all self-control and lunge perilously at the king. Through his gritted teeth he said, "I will not be bullied into a false step." But he threw himself forward, and what he dreaded came to pass.

Ogier's lack of control was easy to avoid. The King simply stepped sideways, and as the boy passed he gave him a hard push to the floor. Ogier didn't move and his humiliation was complete. The King knelt beside him and took hold of his arm to help him up. "Don't mistake my actions for a lack of love. It is my love for you that demands more. When you become king only those who respect your sword will listen to you. Only those who fear your authority will obey." He brushed the dust off his grandson and gave his teacher instructions for the boy to spend more time with the sword.

The boy dared not look at his grandfather and he heard none of his grandfather's words. All that rang in his ears was his increasing disdain and contempt. *How could he be so cruel?* he thought. He dreaded even more the pity on his teacher's face.

"I don't need your pity." He glared.

"I do not pity you, my lord. I was merely concerned about your next step in training. Do you wish me to select a new trainer?"

"It doesn't matter. Do what needs to be done." At that moment Ogier decided that he would become the warrior his grandfather always wanted.

King Sigfred had already forgotten his grandson. The pressing business of the monarchy took precedence over everything, and this continual war with the Franks was going to be his end. He had barely sat down on his throne when his lieutenants came into his chambers. They stood in his presence and did not speak until he addressed them. He wore power with ease and liked to make his warriors feel its strength. He had coalesced the fragmented clans and submitted them to his rule, and though the Earls of each clan had a say the King's word was law.

"How have our forces fared this year?" He had three divisions equaling 7,000 men. They had never faced the full strength of Charlemagne's army because of the division between the Frankish princes. He rather liked it that way, but word had come that Charlemagne was becoming more assertive and his appetite for conquest had set his eyes to the north once again. King Sigfred knew that a lax king was a dead king, which is why he pushed his grandson so hard.

"My King, the Franks have left a small contingent of cavalry and footmen along our border. Word has come that trouble lies at his southern border and he has left to give his attention elsewhere. With this reprieve I suggest that we fortify our positions and reclaim some of the land lost at the beginning of the summer."

"My King," interjected another lieutenant, "I humbly disagree. While fortifying our positions we lose a valuable opportunity to strike at our enemy. We have several weeks of good weather to advance a campaign to reclaim more than we have lost. Charlemagne is counting on us to run and lick our wounds because the summer is almost over. I say we muster our troops and advance, take no prisoners, and display the might and power of our King. We can use the winter months to rebuild."

The King looked between the two. He liked having his lieutenants argue; it gave him options and allowed for the best ideas to float to the top. But something was missing from both plans. The first seemed too cautious and the second was not ambitious enough. "Do we have sufficient forces to pin down the northern army while striking at the heart of the Franks?

The first lieutenant was confused. "If you are speaking of the king of the Franks, he has gone to the borders of Spain."

"That is our opportunity. While his forces are engaged in the south, we keep his northern army, as is, trapped in small skirmishes on our border. We take the larger part of our army and lay siege at Aachen."

A smile crossed all their lips; the thought of destroying his city, the heart of Charlemagne, was ingenious. Ever since Pippin's death, Charlemagne had trained his eye on the town of Aachen, as its central location would be ideal for ruling the Empire. To destroy it would be a victory in itself.

The southern border of Denmark was narrow and easily defended. The opposite was true as well; it was hard to cross unnoticed with an army. However, small raiding parties designed to antagonize Charlemagne's army like gnats could keep them busy for months. King Sigfred would then sail around the peninsula, land at Antwerp, and march on the city of Aachen. The plan was ambitious and for it to work they would have to sail soon and in utmost secrecy.

Ogier was called to his grandfather's war room. "Grandson, it is time for you to take your place over the army on the border. The captain of the guard will serve as your guide and confidant." He motioned for Arwin to approach. "Arwin is a brave and capable master of the troops, and I am confident that he will teach you everything that you need to know." Taking his grandson's shoulders into his hands he continued. "You will have the final say, but listen to him and you will not fail. Can you do this?"

What *this* was wasn't exactly clear. But he could not let his grandfather down.

"I won't disappoint you."

"Good. Come, we have much to discuss." The officers gathered and his plan's final touches were ready to be implemented. He would sail to Antwerp and then on to Aachen with his army, while his grandson, under the tutelage of Arwin, provided the diversion he needed. *This*, he thought, *will either make him a man or kill him*. He would leave his grandson's fate in the hands of the gods.

Ancestors
768 AD

"Why have you brought me here?" Ogier asked.

"You will see." Arwin was leading him down a dark hallway. It twisted and turned, steadily heading deeper into the earth. Ogier surmised that it led outside the castle walls, but he could not guess much beyond that.

"It's dark and smells. How much further?"

Ogier was tired. They had spent the day running through weapon drills and lessons on strategy. All he wanted to do was go to his bedchamber and sleep for two days.

"We are almost there." The elevation began to ascend and the cold air slowly grew a little warmer. A slight breeze blew in from somewhere and pushed the musty smell around. The stifling odor made it difficult to breathe.

"Ouch!" Ogier swore.

"Watch your head, Prince. The ceiling gets lower as we come to the end." Arwin was tasked with continuing the Prince's training and advising him if any conflicts arose. The problem was that Ogier didn't understand the responsibility of the crown. He was two generations from the throne, and like all children who had not fought for their position he took it for granted. What he needed was perspective, and Arwin hoped their excursion would provide what was lacking. "Just through this door."

The source of the air became apparent when they stepped through the door. It was still musty but less stifling. It took a moment as Arwin lit torches distributed throughout the dark cave, but as he finished the light revealed an unexpected wonder. The hall was made from African Black Stone Granite. Each stone measured four feet square and was polished to a mirror's gleam. Though each stone was square it was precisely placed to create a circular room with twelve alcoves.

The pattern was simple but elegant, and at the corner of each stone a brilliant jewel shone. Some were diamonds, others were emerald and rubies, but a few Ogier did not recognize. In each alcove a large sarcophagus stood, along with a warrior engraved from a single stone. Across his chest he held ax, shield, and sword, and each statue carried a misshapen piece of stone on his shoulders.

"Why do the warriors lack faces?" Ogier asked.

"Because there are no warriors lying inside. These are the tombs of generations to come—Kings who served their people well and died for the honor of their gods." Arwin drew Ogier's attention to the center of the room where a large sarcophagus lay horizontally. It was made of the same stone, but the warrior bore an image. "This is the resting place of your great-grandfather, Ongendus, the first King of the Danes."

"I have heard stories of him and his noble deeds to bring together the warring tribes." Ogier ran his hand across the smooth but dusty coffin. There was reverence in his touch and awe in his voice. "What was he like, do you know?"

"I know only the stories passed down from warrior to warrior. He was ruthless and feared by all his enemies. He brought the tribes together through intimidation instead of negotiation. But he was also a masterful statesman and won the hearts of his loyal subjects." He grew quiet as Ogier slowly walked around the room.

"Why have I not seen this before?" Ogier asked.

"No one comes here except for the funeral of a king. Your grandfather will be next, then your father, and then you. After the funeral the door is sealed and a guard placed at its entrance."

"But there was no guard when we came in," Ogier puzzled.

"No, we have come in through a back tunnel, one that was built in the event an escape from the castle was necessary," Arwin answered.

"Why, then, have we not come through the front door?" Ogier looked at his mentor, a feeling of reticence dawning slowly upon him.

"I have brought you here for a purpose, one that should not reach the ears of the King. My cause is not nefarious, but it is out of the ordinary." Directing his apprentice to sit on a stone bench near the entrance to the tomb, he continued. "You question everything and worry about a great deal more. As you watch your grandfather and father go off to war, I can see doubt in your eyes. You wanted to go with them, not because you are in support of their cause, but because you are a young man of honor and duty. Am I wrong in anything I have surmised?"

Ogier shook his head. "Why must they challenge Charlemagne? It seems to me a fool's errand. Would we not be better to remain in our own lands and rule our own people?"

"Yes, and that is why I have brought you here. Nobility always seeks to extend its reign, either through force, commerce, or religion." He stood and walked over to the wall, touching two of its corners. A hidden door opened and Arwin pulled out a small box.

"What is that?" Ogier asked.

"A battle wages in the heavens, one that is unseen, but fierce. It is a war between our gods and the god of Charlemagne. Your great-grandfather, in a moment of weak-mindedness, allowed a priest named Saint Willibord to visit our country. In the process he tried to convert the King to his own religion. King Ongendus was amused at the teachings and paid them little mind, but he allowed the priest to spread his message. Charlemagne has used the priest's influence to rally those converts to his cause and your father's kingdom has been shaken."

"Has this been the cause of our wars?" Ogier asked.

"The cause of war is never so simple, but it has played its part. We all sacrifice for what we believe. What do you believe, my young prince?"

Arwin's question was penetrating. Ogier had never thought about what he believed; only what everyone had told him to believe.

He contemplated for a moment and then declared, "I believe in father Odin and his son Thor. I believe in the sacred halls of Valhalla. I believe in the destiny of my grandfather's kingdom. This is what I have been taught and will always believe. Do you doubt my faith? Is this why you ask?"

"It is not my doubt that is tested, Prince." He placed his hand on Ogier's shoulder. "It is my responsibility to teach you the ways of war. When you lead men into battle you must know the reason for which you call them to die. Rally them for treasure and they will fail you. Rally them for power and they will change sides. Rally them for heart and home and they will scale the three levels of hell for you, but you must believe."

"But what of the box?" Ogier's attention was brought back to the container at their feet.

"The box holds the remains of the last priest to have stood before King Ongendus. He presented to the King the evidence for his god and declared that he was mightier than father Odin. Upon the challenge, it is said, your great-grandfather stood and took a spear from the guard and yelled, 'If your god is mightier than Odin he will surely save you from my spear,' and with an action as quick as the wind he threw the spear, piercing the priest's heart. The body was burned and the ashes displayed on the mantle of the king, a reminder to his honor and belief: no god can stand before the Viking gods. When the King was buried the ashes were stored alongside of him, a trophy to show in the afterlife."

"Is the war with Charlemagne a continuation of this conflict?"

"The apprentice learns quickly. When you stand in battle you battle not only men, but the unseen war of the heavens."

Ogier didn't speak again until they were back in the castle. He wondered about his great-grandfather, and worried that his own courage would falter in the face of war. He knew that what was untested was untrue, and he couldn't wait for his first kill.

Time of Rejoicing
776 AD

"Your grandfather and father have gone to wage a great battle, to break once and for all Charlemagne's hold on our borders. They have tasked us with keeping the northern troops occupied. We have seldom attacked them toe-to-toe because their forces have always been larger, but we have skirmished with them and been successful."

Arwin was helping the young prince dress as they prepared to take a squad of warriors to the border between Jutland and the Franks

Standing back the Prince asked, "Well, how do I look?"

Arwin laughed out loud.

"What is so funny? Dare you make fun of the Prince?"

"Sorry my Lord, but how you look matters little on the field of battle. Your handsome smile will lay frozen on your face while the life in your eyes dims. Vanity does not win battles," Arwin said solemnly. He quickly continued, "But the Prince has worked hard and your sword is as keen to kill your enemy as the next."

"Yes," Ogier said, "but there is nothing wrong with looking good either."

They both laughed and walked through the castle, bodyguards flanking the young prince as they headed for his first test in battle.

"Remember, Your Majesty, you are the commander that they are following. Your order is law—for them to disobey is death—so don't command them to do anything on a whim." Arwin was helping Ogier mount his horse.

When his first knight was firmly in his saddle, the Prince gave the signal and they rode to the south.

"Arwin," Ogier said so that no one would overhear, "I am nervous."

"Good," was his response.

"Doesn't that worry you?"

"Not in the least. All warriors are nervous when they go into battle. Channel it so that it becomes strength. Depend on your training and let instinct guide your movements. If fear grips your heart you will be lost."

Arwin was a good instructor and Ogier felt more confident with him at his side. Yet, it was his word that would send the men into battle, and he would make sure that he gave them the right orders. The next couple of days were boring. All they did was ride, eat, and sleep. Ogier was getting a little impatient, and he could feel the blood lust creeping into his throat.

On the third sunrise Ogier found that the soldiers had already broken camp and were waiting for him. "Arwin… Where is Arwin?" he commanded.

His faithful servant stepped out of the woods to his rear. "I am here, my lord. How can I serve you this morning?" Arwin knew Ogier was confused.

"Why did you not wake me? Were you planning to leave me behind?" His anger was showing, and the men sat on their horses looking perplexedly at Arwin.

"I am sorry, my prince. I was leaving three men to guard you. I was merely taking the rest to scout the area. We are not far from the

Franks' camp. I thought it best to find out as much information as possible before risking your life."

"That is not your decision. Hold your place."

Ogier quickly dressed as his mount was prepared, and Arwin stewed in his annoyance that his decision had been challenged publicly. When the Prince was finally ready, he mounted his horse and instructed Arwin to lead the way.

"Yes, my lord." Though he was irritated, he was proud that the young prince had asserted himself; it was a good omen. They had reached the summit when Arwin put up his hand. "Beyond those trees, see the small wisp of smoke? Those are not our fires." He pointed them out to the Prince.

"Dismount," he ordered. Pulling Ogier to his side, he asked the Prince what he would like to do. "Remember what we talked about."

When Ogier and Arwin had discussed tactics in his training it had been aimed at strike and retreat. He motioned to two soldiers. "We don't want to attack any position without knowing how many will be on our tail. Go get me a count." They nodded and stole away into the trees.

They were gone the better part of an hour, but when they returned the news was both good and bad. The bad news was that over a hundred soldiers were in the camp. The good news was that these were only a fraction of what they had expected. Breaking his squad of twenty men into groups of five, Ogier showed them where he wanted them to take up position.

"I want to deploy four groups: one to the north, south, east and west. When the sun stands at its zenith, the team to the north will engage first. Draw them out, but don't get too close. When the Franks begin to mobilize and make chase the team to the south will engage. There will be momentary confusion before they divide into two to defend their rear. Once that happens both east and west will engage their flanks. This will happen quickly; we are not here to wage a full-on assault. Once the Franks deploy, disappear into the hills. We will reconvene at the rendezvous point." Looking at Arwin he instructed, "You will take the final group."

"My lord, if I may. The last group will have the least engagement, and I would suggest that you be on that squad. The first group will be engaged the longest and I…well, I am more experienced." Arwin was treading lightly to avoid offending the Prince.

"Live or die, it is my command to make." Ogier didn't wait for a reply. "You have your orders. Let's head out."

It didn't take them long to set their positions and as the sun climbed Ogier readied for a fight. They had approached from the northern road, so it was easy to spot the Franks' camp. The Franks didn't seem to worry, their defenses obviously lax. Ogier's squad strung their bows and launched a volley of arrows into the middle of the camp. They could hear the painful cry of a soldier and the run to arms and horses. They continued to launch arrows until they could see horses heading in their direction. They melted into the woods.

While the horses bounded down the road, more painful cries arose from the southern part of the camp. In the melee the northern pursuers hesitated and another volley of arrows rained from overhead, piercing the throat of one soldier whose rearing horse fell into another.

As Ogier had said the attack lasted less than thirty minutes, and the Franks never knew who had hit them. By the time they were able to order their troops, Ogier and his men were three miles into the woods resting at a hidden spring.

"Excellent job, my lord." Arwin was generous with his praise and the others cheered him on as well. "You have proven yourself an apt tactician and a formidable warrior. It is a great honor for me to serve you." He bowed before the young prince and the others did as well.

"Thank you for your words, but I fear that we are not as protected as we would like. Might we save the reprieve until we are safely beyond our borders?" He was smiling but he felt uneasy until they were mounted and further down the road.

That evening they rested in the camp of a greater force. Theirs was not the only raiding group, and the returning warriors brought stories of success and glory. What they also brought was news of Charlemagne's troop strength, and Arwin was apprehensive.

"What dampens my mentor's mood?" Ogier inquired. "This is a time of rejoicing."

"It is but I am concerned that it is premature," Arwin replied.

"Do tell how our aim was not achieved?" the Prince requested.

"We were made to believe that Charlemagne had left a full army to fend off our armies, but we have not engaged any notable strength. My fear is that we have been deceived and that a greater army awaits your grandfather."

"Today we have fought and killed hundreds," Ogier said.

"Yes, but we should have fought thousands," Arwin cautioned. "We are gnats bothering the cub, when the mother is hunting another."

"And what do you suggest?" Ogier was young and the wine was affecting his head.

"Give me leave to bring word to your father and grandfather." He waited for Ogier to gather his wits.

"Yes, yes," the drunk prince said. "Take whoever you need. I will be fine until you return."

"Thank you, my Prince." Arwin selected three of his best men and made tomorrow a near companion.

Late Summer
768 AD

When King Sigfred was satisfied that Charlemagne's forces were adequately distracted, he set sail with 75 ships and 6,000 warriors. The sight of such an armada struck fear into the hearts of Antwerp's citizens. Word arrived a day in advance and the city was evacuated. Few were left when King Sigfred landed. It bolstered his confidence—he felt he could devour all who stood in his way. They marched on the city, taking whatever they found of value. The inhabitants didn't have time to take all their possessions, and the king completely plundered the city. Anyone left was put to the sword. Antwerp, however, wasn't their prize; word of their coming would arrive at Aachen days before them, and that fortress would not fall without a fight.

As King Sigfred approached Aachen the palace was an imposing sight. He had seen it before, but its appearance always struck awe and wonder into his heart. The natural protection of the river required less fortification, and Sigfred would have to concentrate his forces to the west, east, and north walls, but even then the walls were twenty-five feet thick. The northern section of the palace was the residence of the King. It was there he imagined Charlemagne cowering during times of battle. The King of the Franks liked to bring the royalty of his conquered lands here to see its splendor. It was a majestic structure rising one story higher than the chapel. It consisted of a four-story entrance that ran the width of its southern exterior with a turret sitting at its center.

It was between the King's quarters and the chapel that would prove to be most difficult. The wall turned another ninety degrees, dipping to three stories, and continued north for another one-hundred feet, connecting to a four-story structure that ran perpendicularly twenty-five feet on each side of the wall. This was the servants' quarters as well as the main entrance for the King's. The configuration would catch his warrior in a cross fire if the tower guards were not killed first.

The last time he was here he was made to grovel, this time he would raze it to the ground, and he came prepared to accomplish the task. Antwerp served as a good source of not only food, but also of wood to construct the war machines necessary to protect his men and penetrate the palace defenses. There was little resistance as his army approached the city; his massive force encamped around the city dwarfed any hope for those in the castle.

King Charlemagne had left a small garrison to protect the castle, and their apprehension grew as they watched King Sigfred swarm the surrounding countryside. They met daily in the chapel and prayed for God's deliverance. As they waited, their commander was not idle. He knew that if help did not arrive all would perish. When news of King Sigfred's advance reached the castle, the commander of the guard dispatched four couriers, two to deliver a message to the King in the south and two to the army in the north. They sped away in different directions in hope that one would reach his destination. The King of the Danes wasn't a fool and had sent men to the north and south of the city, in case the commander took such an action.

The race to penetrate the Vikings' wall of warriors was on, and only the swift feet of their horses gave them any chance to survive.

"What are your orders, my king?" Sigfred's men were ready to fight and would have flung themselves against the castle if there were asked.

"In time, my friend. We must be patient." Sigfred stepped to the opening of his tent and looked toward the castle wall. "There may not be many of them, but from within that fortress they could hold off our army long enough for help to arrive." Turning to Pailfi, one of his lieutenants, the King asked, "Any word on the messengers they sent?"

"None, my lord. We don't think they have broken our line; it is only a matter of time before we find them." He wasn't as confident as he forced himself to sound.

"Good." The King walked to a table at the center of his tent. In the middle stood a small-scale model of the fortress and around it were wooden structures made of twigs. "These need to be built before we attack the castle. They are war machines invented by the Romans. They used them to scale large walls and launch rocks to beat down their foes." His men looked doubtful.

"You are willing to die for glory, and rightly so. To die in battle is to enter the sacred halls of Valhalla, but to be victorious over our enemy is more glorious. We will not waste lives for a losing cause when the means to victory is in our hands."

Next to him was an elderly man, stooped over and grey. He evidently wasn't a warrior, and his presence seemed out of place among the others. "This is Nasi. He is skilled in making these machines. His ancestors are from our people, but he spent many years among the Franks. His love for them and their brutality is the same as ours. You are to give him whatever he asks to build our machines.

We have three days, so put your backs to the task and motivate your men to do the same."

"Three days, my king!" Pailfi's cautioned. "It does not seem possible to build five of these structures in so little time; the men have little experience."

"All they need is patience and an ear to obedience." Sigfred understood their reluctance to do battle in a new way, but time was of the essence and hesitation could be the end of them all. "Your attitude will lead the way. If they see your doubts they will doubt. If you are confident they will follow." Looking Pailfi in the eyes he asked, "Are you confident that I know what I am doing?" There was no need for an answer. Anything but yes meant death, and Pailfi bowed, turned, and left the tent.

Pailfi was a good soldier and wanted nothing more than to see the Franks dead. He gathered the clan leaders and broke them into teams that would work around the clock until the job was finished. He couldn't fathom how they were going to accomplish such a great task, but as Nasi explained how each part could be built separately then brought together at the end, it started to make sense. None knew the true origins of the device, passed down from civilization to civilization, beginning with the ancient Greeks, and no one cared to know. Each structure would consist of five levels with each level surrounded by walls. The walls would stop short of the next floor so warriors could launch arrows through the gap. Wheels at the base would allow the men to maneuver it into position. It would take his warriors every hour and then some to complete the five monstrous towers in three days. But the towers weren't the only structures ordered by the king. He wanted two catapults as well. They were not as large but would take time.

Pailfi had ten men under him who were leaders of their clans. They knew what was at stake and pledged their lives to the King and his cause. Vidfari, an eleventh, was not included in the clan leadership. His role had diminished because of an indiscretion in another battle. He had taken it upon himself to prematurely lead his men against Charlemagne's forces in the north, against King Sigfred's command. It was a risk he thought would bring him glory, but in the end it rained disgrace on his family and meant the loss of honor for himself. The gods had smiled on him, for the King could have had him killed. He stood outside Pailfi's tent as the plans were laid out, his resentment growing as his humiliation festered. To add to his discomfort it began to rain.

When all had been said the clan leaders left Pailfi's tent and began to organize their men for the task ahead. When the last warrior stepped across the threshold and disappeared into the night, Vidfari took the opportunity to approach Pailfi, and cleared his throat to get his attention.

Surprised to see the object of the King's disfavor, Pailfi called for the guard.

"Please, my lord, don't cast me aside."

Pailfi thought better of it, pulled his brother into the tent and said, "Why have you dragged yourself out from under the rock of your dishonor to disturb my presence? I have nothing to say to you or anything to offer."

"You could offer me kindness, brother." The words stuck in his throat, the thought of groveling repulsive to both of them.

"Do not speak to me of kindness, you who brought shame on our house," Pailfi said, raising his voice.

"Can you not show me kindness, just as the King showed you? Instead of turning his back on our family altogether he has taken you into his confidence."

"His mercy on me was because of my innocence in your treacherous act."

"I have been falsely accused. Is it treasonous to fight against the master's enemies? I may have been foolish to think that an independent act wouldn't be seen as such a heinous crime, when all I wanted was to bring honor to my King."

Pailfi approached his brother and stood menacingly over him, the heat of his breath falling ominously into his face. "You know nothing of honor. Your actions brought death to your men and embarrassment to your King. He was not ready for war and your actions brought it knocking on our door." He was half yelling as he tried to control his temper. "Now you come here for who knows what purpose, to scheme against the power of the King."

"No, my brother, on the contrary. I have come to offer my service, to redeem myself in the eyes of family and king."

It was the slight smirk crossing his brother's lips that pushed Pailfi over the line. He struck Vidfari across the face and knocked him to the ground. Before his brother could regain his senses, Pailfi kicked him out of the tent and told him never to return.

What humiliation Vidfari felt soon turned and fueled his anger toward both brother and crown. The winds of misfortune and the silence of the gods sped him further down the road of revenge. What he had hoped to be his redemption now fed his anger. He slinked away and stole a horse to ride south.

Desertion
768 AD

Vidfari fled with nothing but the intensity of his hatred to keep him warm. He knew his time was limited; if he were to make true his brother's accusations he would have to make haste his companion. Reflection did not temper his rage, and with each pound of his steed's hooves his determination was sealed. What he did not anticipated were the sentries, which had been dispatched to find and capture the messengers sent from the castle. As he rushed down the road he spotted the Viking warriors.

"Friend or foe?" cried the voice ahead.

Steadying his nerve he spoke. "I am…" He stopped midsentence. His dishonor was known throughout the army, though his face was not. He could possibly talk his way past if they did not know his identity. "I am on an errand for the King's right hand." It was more believable than an errand for the King himself.

"What nightly errand could be more pressing than our own?" The guards had been told nothing was more important than stopping the messengers.

"Have you accomplished your goal, or do you waste the night interfering with my mission?" Vidfari countered.

"What have you that proves your word? You look familiar… Have we met?"

The dim moonlight was bright enough for simple identification. If this man recognized his face it could quickly put an end to his quest before it had even begun.

"I am Pailfi, and often confused with my brother, Vidfari. This emblem is our clan's and should be proof enough." He hoped his lie would put them at ease. There was silence as the guards contemplated the situation.

Vidfari quickly spoke. "Our orders are not at cross purposes. I was sent to gather information on your progress and return to my brother with good news... you do have good news?" He could see their discomfort. "If this is all you have for me, then I will take my leave and make contact with the other parties."

The incongruity of Vidfari's answer with his initial response to their meeting had begun to sink in, and he knew he only had a moment to move past and flee. "Vidfari," the one in charge said. In panic Vidfari's heart beat faster. "Stand down." the sentry continued, "You are lying to us, what treachery do you intend? You seem to be well-acquainted with them."

With his right hand Vidfari slowly grasped the hilt of a small dagger in his belt, and before any of the guards could make a move, he threw it at the leader. The knife pierced his throat, releasing both blood and breath. In the confusion he kicked his horse while drawing his sword. In one quick motion he moved forward and hacked at an adjoining soldier while driving his horse into another. The commotion caught the guards off balance, physically and mentally.

Darkness closed around him before the warriors regained their wits, but they soon sped into the black after him. The road, wide enough for three horses, allowed for a swift pursuit, and the sound of their horses' hooves filled the night.

There was no turning back now; Vidfari drove his horse forward for fear as much as his mission of revenge. If he did not either break free or stand and fight, all would be lost. He preferred to flee, but the latter could prove to be his only choice; they were catching up with him.

To his right a low-hanging branch crossed the path—it could be his salvation. Testing his balance he let go of the horse's mane until he was sure he would not fall off, and when the opportunity came he reached up, grabbed the branch and swung up and over it until the horse was running down the road on its own. If his pursuers saw him he would be an easy target in the tree; if they didn't the opposite would be true. To his relief they passed under him. As the last of the four warriors sped by, Vidfari dropped on his horse, drew his enemy's dagger, and slit his throat before the man knew what had happened. Shoving the body to the side, Vidfari fell in line behind the others as the warrior vanished into the dark brush.

He did not attempt another kill, for an upfront assault might prove fatal. Instead he gradually slowed his horse until he was sufficiently behind to take another, smaller path that fortune provided. The night's activities wore on him, and when he was at a safe distance fatigue began to set in. As his adrenaline subsided the weight on his eyes tempted him to stop and rest, but he couldn't if he was to fulfill his destined path. What had begun as an act of revenge swelled into a mission of passion, and he pressed on to complete his task.

Regret
768 AD

The Viking guard was not his only concern; his northern attire would stand out among the Franks. He would have to find different clothes if he was to avoid drawing attention to himself. Breaking through the tree line Vidfari came upon a small farm. He approached the house slowly. Its occupants were still asleep, and he hoped he would not have to force himself on them, not because he had an aversion to killing Franks, but the mess and distraction was more than he needed. He found little in the barn, though he allowed his horse to feed on the hay while he searched for anything that would be useful. But his attempt at stealth was for naught as the farmer's early morning routine woke the household; when he turned around, he was face to face with a small boy.

The boy froze before the giant Norseman, who loomed as large and frightening as a dragon. Vidfari was on him in an instant, and placed his hand over the boy's mouth. "Don't speak or I will slit your throat." The boy didn't understand the words, but he understood the threatening intent. "I do not want to hurt you, but if you give me away I will kill you. Do you understand me?" Vidfari used hand gestures to emphasize his point and the boy was well aware of the consequences.

Pointing to the house the child tried to communicate that his parents would expect him and would come for him if he didn't return soon. Of course all Vidfari understood was that someone was in the house, which meant only two possible outcomes. He would either have to leave without the clothes, or kill the family and take what he needed. Weighing his options he decided the latter was the better course of action. Turning the boy around, he pushed him out of the barn and toward the house. The door flew open and the boy fell to the floor, while Vidfari shouted at a young man sitting at a table and a woman tending a fire. In the corner a handmade cradle rocked back and forth, and the baby inside began crying at the loud, harsh sounds.

Without hesitation Vidfari swung his sword across the father's throat and his body slumped to the ground. Then he silenced the scream of the wife, who instinctively reached for the baby. He felt no malice as he slew the mother, and standing over the crying baby he hesitated in a momentary twinge of compassion. But in that split second he knew he could not leave alive anyone who could exact future revenge. When Vidfari walked out the door with his new set of clothes he left the house silent.

His course was set; both traitor and enemy, he was a man marked for death. As he drove himself to warn the King of the Franks, the burning embers of revenge began to dim and thoughts of his actions' consequences slowed his pace.

What am I doing, he thought. *I am a Viking; how can I betray my people? But haven't they betrayed me? Haven't they dismissed me as no better than a dog?* He had no love for the Franks, and even if he was just in his actions helping the Franks was becoming a distasteful thought. They would accept his help, but they would never accept him, and King Charlemagne's reputation of conversion or death would leave his body nothing more than worm food. Lost in his thoughts Vidfari stopped at the edge of a river. The sound of water rushing below the bridge reminded him of home—no amount of water could wash away his regret.

Vidfari could do nothing more than build a fire and figure out his next steps. He couldn't go back and he couldn't go forward, so he decided to set his course to the east, away from both family and Franks. He sat silently, allowing the river to drown out his heavy heart, but what the river's sounds had hidden the darkness revealed.

To the south and across the river a glow ascended above the trees. His curiosity overrode caution and he doused the flames, slipping into the dark. The roaring river was an advantage, hiding the sound of his approach, and what he found threw off his feelings of despair and revenge, for as far as he could see small fires dotted the landscape. The silent discipline of an advancing army struck him with fear.

Return of the King
768 AD

"My lord, here is the report you requested." The soldier handed the folded pouch to the King's attaché, bowed slightly, and was dismissed.

The King was standing over a map of the city of Aachen. His expression was a mixture of sadness and determination. His suspicions had come to pass and he knew their outcome would leave the streets of his favorite town filled with the blood of both enemy and friend.

"How long have they been there?" he asked.

"Three days. They have not attacked, but have laid siege to the castle." The attaché had seen the responsibility that the King bore. Most of the time he stood strong, but tonight the burden of royalty weighed heavy on him and the slight slump of his shoulders revealed the King's fatigue.

"What of our northern troops? Have they broken off their engagement with border skirmishes?" The King took a sip of the wine a servant had placed in front of him.

"A day after the ships set sail they systematically broke their regiment into four battalions of 100. They staggered their retreat as ordered and rendezvoused north of the palace." Word of the Danes' plans had reached Charlemagne early, and as eager as the King was to bring them under his rule, he didn't relish focusing the inevitability of war on Aachen. Yet, allowing the Danes to waste energy and resources on a temporary siege would allow him to surround Sigfred's position from the north and the south, and once and for all break the reluctant king's back.

"When Sigfred's forces arrived at the palace messengers were sent, but none of them made it through." The attaché paused, as the loss of any soldier grieved the King.

"And what of Antwerp?" the King asked.

"It was looted as expected, but the people escaped as ordered. There were a few casualties." The attaché hesitated seeing the King's brow furrow. "Some residents stayed to protect their belongings. Our reports say that all were swiftly killed. That is to our advantage, lord."

The King slammed his fist against the table. "There is no advantage in the death of innocents, even if it seems strategically so. We lay waste to the enemies of the Kingdom for the glory of God and for no other reason." He softened his tone, "But yes, you are the messenger of bad news, not its perpetrator. You have done well, you are dismissed."

Sleep was a luxury, and that evening his haunting dreams held rest at bay. *What is it you want?* the voice spoke from deep within the dark.

Only to serve you, my Lord.

Is this the righteous act of a man of God? the voice whispered.

I do this for you and for your kingdom. Does not your word say that the whole world will bow to your name? Have you not ordained me to be king over all your people and bring the heathen into your fold? There was silence in the dark; the whisper did not answer. The king strained to hear another word, to give him hope and direction.

Yes, the whisper returned. *Yes, bring them in with the sword. I anoint you an instrument of mercy and judgment. Wield your might in the name of your god. Let no one stand who dares resist your will. In this way you will earn salvation for yourself and all who follow you.*

But what of the blood? the King asked, weariness in his voice. *What of all the men who die in your service?*

They will reap what they sow. there was a hint of mirth behind the words. *They will reap what they sow.*

Light escaped through the flap of the king's tent, and his eyes fluttered open to its penetration. He swung his feet over the edge of his bed, and the cool dirt floor reminded him of where he was. Though the morning bid his eyes to rise, exhaustion tugged at his lids to fall. It would take as much effort to battle slumber as it would the enemy. He lay still for what seemed an eternity wondering what the dream meant. He had experienced several such dreams over the years, and he shared them with no one save his personal priest. The message was always the same, delivered in the same hushed tones, and accompanied by victories over his enemies. The priest had said they were visions from God and he should take heed to be obedient. Doubt, however, always lingered in the recesses of his conscience.

All of the blood.

The priest was always quick to remind him that King David had been a man of violence on behalf of God's people, so too was he called to brandish the sword. It was enough to sooth any guilt that might give pause to his destiny.

Standing outside the tent, his valet waited patiently for his master to bid him entrance and assist in the King's dress. The King seldom spoke as the young man attended to his needs, but this morning he needed words to blow the mist of his dream away.

"Have the men of the circle arrived?"

The young man wasn't sure what to do, or how to respond.

The King was patient. "Do not be afraid to speak. Have the Paladin arrived in the camp?"

"I am not sure, my lord. If you like I will fetch the Sergeant of the Guard. He will know if they have arrived."

Realizing that any attempt to converse with his servant would only be awkward, he dismissed him with a wave of his hand and called for his personal guard to enter. "Quickly call the Paladin to my tent, it is time to march." By the time his inner circle arrived, the King had laid some maps on the center table. He wasted no time as they entered. "Are your regiments ready to break camp?"

"My lord," Roland began, "we are fifteen-thousand strong, and it will take time and a little stealth to make our way to Aachen. May I suggest we send Malagigi to the west up along the River Inde? They should be far enough to remain hidden."

"And who is to block their retreat toward Antwerp?" the king asked.

"I will," said Florismart. "My cavalry is the swiftest. We will be able to make Hasselt and march west by the time the King has arrived at Simmerath."

Charlemagne pored over the maps. He was concerned about the guards and staff in Aachen. "We must act quickly once we get there. We have camped long enough in this valley." The small hamlet of Auw bei Prun lay on the river Our between the crest of Schneifel and Rustenschwil and provided ample coverage for his troops. But the King knew that remaining there too long would endanger their secrecy.

A disturbance outside broke their concentration, and Soloman slipped through the tent flap to see to the matter. When he returned, three guards accompanied him along with a man bound at the wrists.

"My Lord, this man was found on the other side of the river. He claims to bring news from Aachen."

Charlemagne motioned him closer. "Tell me your name."

The captive's wild eyes belied the clothes that he wore, and his stare did not exhibit the fear a poor farmer would have shown. "I am Vidfari."

"From your accent and your name I dare say you are not from this realm. Why have you been found skulking in our midst? Are you a spy?"

Vidfari looked at each of the soldiers and knew that his end was sure. He had nothing to gain now in betraying his people and nothing to lose by telling the King all. "I did not come to spy, I... I came to warn you."

"Ah." The King raised his eyebrows. "And why would you betray your people? Are you a Christian, or did your king do you some ill?"

He had heard the stories and Vidfari didn't relish the choice of converting or dying. He thought a lie would be easily spotted, but the truth was just as dangerous. A diversion would be a better plan. Ignoring the question, he offered information. "King Sigfred has surrounded Aachen and plans to destroy the castle and all who are in it. I came to expose his plans to your majesty."

"I see, and now that you have told me what shall I do with you? A traitor to one king is possibly a traitor to another. If I send you on your way how do I know that you will not betray me? If I imprison you, I use resources. Executing you seems ungracious to one who has risked his life to bring me important news. Do you see my quandary?"

"It is not for me to determine my life or death. The fearsomeness of the king is well known. My death was fated when I decided to leave my people and betray them for revenge. Live or die, it doesn't matter. I am in your hands to do with as you see fit." At this point Vidfari was tired of playing this game and death was welcomed. "If I am to die my only request would be to do so with a sword in my hand."

"That you might be ushered by the Valkyries into Valhalla, I assume?" The King walked around the table and looked deep into Vidfari's eyes. "There is a warrior in you, certainly, but death will only bring you greater suffering. The gates of Hell await all who refuse faith in God's Son. Why not convert and enter into heaven and eternal paradise instead of the perpetual war and death offered by your gods?"

"If death comes whether I stay true to my gods or abandon them, what difference does it make? And if I abandon them just to live, then what honor do I have? Give me a sword and let me die like a Viking."

"Yes, I see that you are a man of honor and would rather die in battle. Then I give you this one option: live out your life in the dungeon of my castle, a prisoner of your own choices, or join me in battle against the king you have betrayed. If you die in the process your soul will find what death truly brings; if you live you have your freedom in hopes that you will see the true Son."

"But sire," Roland interjected. "How can we take into battle someone we cannot trust? He could betray us at any time and it could mean the death of our own men." The other Paladin nodded in agreement.

"Are we so weak as to think the honor of this man is not true, that he would not keep his word in the face of death? I see the struggle in his eyes even now, wishing he had not abandoned his king and yet knowing it was the right thing to do. If I extend him this grace am I less a man—a king—for it, and do we all not wish for mercy in the face of our enemy?" Reaching for his dagger the king slipped the blade between Vidfari's ropes and cut him loose. "Give him some food, fresh clothes, and armor. He will walk with the infantry and when the time comes, he will have an opportunity to prove himself in battle. That is my decision." Dismissing the prisoner and the guards, he returned his attention to the battle plans. "What you have laid out is sound. We march at first light."

Further instructions were unnecessary. They had served the King in battle and their tasks were evident. All but Roland left. "It is not my place to question the King, but…"

"But you do so anyway. Do you feel my compassion is dangerous, misplaced, and even reckless?" Charlemagne sat in his chair holding the chalice of wine.

"My Lord, I fear more what it will do for morale when the troops hear of the traitor's presence. We are about to engage in what is surely the final battle to subdue the Danes. Would it not be more prudent to inflame the hearts of your servants by displaying your power and authority over the enemy?"

"You mean executing a man who has brought us news, though it be old news. He has not betrayed us, but his own people. Our soldiers may despise him for that, but should we as their leaders, or I as their king? He is one among thousands and will be swallowed in war soon enough. Live or die he will have served your King, and is that not worth some compassion? Your concerns are noted and appreciated. Now be off; you have a march to prepare for."

The King closed his eyes and prayed. *May my compassion, Lord, bring blessings tenfold. Scatter my enemies before me, crush them in the press of your righteous wrath, and bring into your kingdom all who bow their knees before you. Amen.*

The evening came and went as quickly as the summer rain and their march toward Aachen began at sun's first light.

Attack
768 AD

The servants scattered as cups, plates, and other objects flew from the tent. "Get me Borgar, and the rest of my incompetent command!"

"What is it my King?" Borgar was the first to enter the tent and when he saw the King's anger he slowed his pace. Everyone knew the King's expectations would be difficult to meet, but they worked night and day and it still wasn't enough time. There were delays due to the lack of materials and skill. Nasi had proven to be an apt engineer, but he couldn't rally the Viking warriors. He was condescending and impatient, and the more the King pressed him, the more he pressed the men. It was spiraling to a standstill.

"Need I explain the obvious dereliction of your duties? Do you not remember my warning of speed? Do you think word will not get to the ears of Charlemagne? We must storm the castle or we will lose the opportunity, and yet there is one delay after another and the soldiers in the palace mock us daily. Is there not one catapult or siege machine ready to deploy that I might silence their insolence?"

Nasi dared not speak without direct address, and he wasn't sure whether this question was rhetorical or not. He decided speaking was better. "My lord, one of the catapults is ready, but the problem is the stones. They are much too large and it has taken a while to cut them to a proper size."

"Are you telling me we don't have the wherewithal to use something other than a single stone? Can we not fill it with smaller stones? Get out there and make it happen. If they are not ready by tomorrow I will launch *you* at the wall!" King Sigfred kicked Nasi out the door, and the old engineer scurried away, less determined than ever. The King looked at his captains. "And what have you to tell me that I don't already know?"

"Charlemagne's army marches from the south. They have broken into three battalions and have cut off our escape to Antwerp. Our only recourse is to head north." Borgar was hoping the King would abandon his attack and head back toward the safety of their own borders. He wasn't one to run from a fight but he would rather not be the victim of a massacre.

"Do you see this in my hand? I received it just moments before you dragged your worthless self in here. There is no northern escape. We have been outwitted and Charlemagne's northern forces have been waiting for as long as we have been here. We are surrounded. We either surrender or fight. I for one will not give up without taking that pagan king for all he is worth. Attack the castle, destroy what we can, and punch a hole in the smaller army to the north, but we have to start tomorrow or it will all have been for nothing."

"It would be more prudent to march at daylight. The castle holds nothing of value. If we stay any longer we will be consumed." Borgar knew the King and treaded lightly, but it had to be said.

Sigfred's ire was waning, but his lust for victory still simmered in his heart. "Who is greater, our father Odin or Charlemagne's dead Jesus? Who offers glory for fallen warriors? Whose son wields the hammer of the gods? There is more at stake than the loss of mortal life. In life we fight for honor and in death honor becomes our own.

No, Borgar we will not run like children afraid of a bully. We will stand and fight, live or die, but we will be victorious!"

Even Borgar's heart was stirred, and with obedient assent all the commanders left to rally their troops.

This would be the battle to end all battles. Sigfred divided his army evenly around the castle. He would defend his position long enough to ravage the palace. If he were to die he would do so as Charlemagne's prized city lay in rubble. As the second day loomed and the dust of an approaching army could be seen, King Sigfred donned his armor and prepared for battle. His cavalry was small, some of their horses brought by ship and other equines confiscated on their march through Antwerp. The King mounted his steed and rallied his men.

"Know nothing else but this: to live is victory, to die is to enter the halls of Valhalla!" A great cheer rose in the air and its sound shook the hearts of the soldiers in the castle.

By the time the two armies faced one another, the sound of missiles flying through the air could be heard for miles. Rock against stone and the final screams of the dying, yet King Charlemagne held his forces firm. They neither rushed nor stood still, but silently marched forward. King Sigfred would not be baited. He stood his ground and waited. His smaller cavalry would have to quickly punch a hole in the front line and swing around before the superior army enclosed him.

"Steady!" he yelled to his commanders. "Don't rush ahead and exhaust your horses or yourself. Let them come to us." It was difficult to restrain the beast within, the fury that lusts for battle and blood. The horses could feel the electricity and they stomped and snorted with great anticipation. When the energy could be contained no longer he gave the command: "ATTACK!"

With great force the armies slammed into one another, swords clanging on shields and helmets clashing with metal. Bodies fell and blood soaked the ground, and as all good kings do, Charlemagne and Sigfred stood at a distance, shouting commands and watching men die. In the end the army of the Danes was no match for King Charlemagne, and when the superior force could be held no longer, a cessation of hostilities was proclaimed; King Sigfred was vanquished.

Charlemagne sent word to the King of the Danes that he had two days to gather the bodies of his dead. A mass funeral pyre was built and its flames could be seen for miles. The stench was a reminder to the defeated of their humiliating loss and an aroma of triumph to the victors. When the dead were sent to their respective rewards, the two kings gathered for the final word in the matter.

King Sigfred stood before Charlemagne, who was seated in the great hall of his castle. All around his throne were strewn fragments of stone, pummeled by the catapults' barrage. To Sigfred it was a reminder of his failed attempt, to Charlemagne, a picture of victory rising out of the ashes. "It is with glory to my God that this day brings victory for my army. What was meant to be has now come to pass. The land of the Danes falls under the jurisdiction of my realm. It is for peace that I allow you to stand before me today. The custom of our fathers is to cut off the head of the serpent so that it will not rise again, but that is not the Law of my Heavenly Father. His desire is to see all come into his kingdom, of which I have been anointed steward in this life. Therefore I chose another tack, one that expresses mercy and allegiance." Sigfred's confused look pleased the King, but what was given him swept the Dane's heart with dread.

"In this sack was the hope of the King of the Danes, but he too fell victim to our sword." The King motioned to the guard who reached in and pulled out a head. "This, I believe is the head of

Gowon, body guard of the King's son. I am told he fought bravely in your service but in the end it was fruitless." He waved to another guard and, to Sigfred's relief, Ogier was brought before both vanquished and victor. "Today marks a new era in our relationship. In order to assure your compliance to this hard earned peace, your son, Ogier, will become my guest for the rest of his life, a down payment to assure your obedience. In the event that you transgress our armistice, your son will forgo his life." Signatures were applied to paper and oaths given and received in the name of their respective gods, and peace reigned between the two nations.

All this was chronicled in the books of the King where the son of Sigfred became the son of Charlemagne. Ogier lived as such with the honors bestowed upon him by the King when he became a member of the Paladin. To this day he serves with distinction as both soldier and confidant.

Sole King
771 AD

Men who lust for power or men who live to serve by duty, Charlemagne thought, *desire crowns.* His crown sat on a pedestal in his bedchamber while he slept. It was the last thing he saw when he went to sleep and the first when he woke. Whether made of iron or gold, a crown was the heaviest ornament known to man, and the responsibilities it engendered were not for mere mortals to contend with. For that reason alone Charlemagne believed that God had given it to him as his destiny. He sighed as his attendant entered with bowed head and offered to help the king dress.

Rudolf had been at his side for five years, always ready to serve. He was tall and slender. His light brown hair was cut short and made his already thin face look gaunt. *He needs to eat more,* the King thought. "Rudolf," the King began, "do you find your work satisfying?"

His valet didn't know how to respond. He never thought about whether he was satisfied or not. He served out of obligation. He wasn't of noble birth and if not for the kindness of the King would have lived in poverty. His parents were swineherds, and pigs were all he knew. It was an honor to serve in the court of his Majesty, though it was dangerous, too. Kings had the habit of acting on whim and a servant's misstep could bring a king's wrath upon his head. As the King's valet, Rudolf was privy to many secrets, as he was often unnoticed. He had seen the King angry, which always kept him alert, but the King's ill temper had never been directed toward him. No, it was a better lot than he could have ever imagined.

"Serving my lord is my life," he said cautiously. "It is my breath; how could I not be satisfied with the air I breathe?"

The King stood and thought about the reply as Rudolf helped him with his blouse. The answer was astute, and rather political. If his captains were as savvy, bringing the Saxons under the kingdom would not be too difficult.

"You are a loyal servant and your service has not gone unnoticed." The King was careful, too much familiarity would breed contempt, which could lead to conspiracy and rebellion. On the contrary, with the loyalty of subjects like Rudolf a kingdom could stand forever. The King, however, was well aware that kingdoms rise and fall by the grace of God—no less true for his own.

"Thank you, Rudolf," said the King, and dismissed him. When he left the door open, the king could see the guards outside. The bedchamber was large with a canopy bed that stood at its center. Around it were various couches and cushions that were more decorative than practical. A dark wood paneling covered the walls, carved and lush in their extravagance. The door was the only way in or out that most knew about. A secret passage through one of the panels led to the lower levels, through a series of tunnels, and out to the rear of the estate and several other passages that intertwined and converged. Few knew of them and even fewer knew them well. Even the king wasn't sure whether he could navigate them without getting lost.

The guard was there for his protection. One didn't conquer a continent without making a few enemies. He trusted the guards with his life, and for that they were well paid. The King was never really alone; there were always the servants and guards, and then the official court of dukes and duchesses that formed his council. But his was not a civilian rule, and so he depended more on his military aides and the Paladin for advice and counsel.

As religious as he was, the king relied little on the priests for guidance. Their spiritual input was appreciated, but the politics of the church were more tiresome than in the arena of civil government. At the same time he was indebted to the church for his salvation and, when necessary, threw his weight behind the pope. The insurgence of the Saxons and the fighting over the control of Rome made it necessary to keep an army in both regions. This required him to travel back and forth depending on the nature of the political environment. Travel was exhausting, but the thrill of battle extinguished his fatigue and he could stand as strong as a lion in the face of the enemy.

"My lord." The soldier entered the room. "The council has gathered and awaits your presence."

"Tell them I will be there momentarily." Walking to the corner of his room, he picked up his sword. It was a gift from his father, crafted out of the finest steel, forged by the best craftsmen of the kingdom. The hilt was interlaced with ivory and jewels. The carvings were delicate with the dual heads of lion and wolf. The lion was that of Judah, the King of Kings, and the wolf the image of Holy Roman power. He wore it with pride and brandished it with the skill of ten men. As a military tactician none was his equal. As driven as he was to ride into battle his commanders restrained him to the rear so that he might direct his troops. He strapped his sword around his waist, adjusted his crown, and walked regally through the door.

The guards fell in line, two at the front and two in the rear. Even in his own palace the guard was necessary. Treachery hid behind the walls and ears of betrayal would steal any gossip to use as weapon for his downfall. As they proceeded down the corridor the walls widened and the ceiling began to extend upward in majestic ambiance that rivaled the palaces of Rome. Its height drew his gaze until it was lost in its quest for heaven. For the priests it spoke of God as lofty sovereign; to the masses and vanquished, it represented the power of the King. For Charlemagne the two were inseparable.

When they entered the grand room a circular table stood at its center, around which sat sixteen men with two empty chairs for the King and his brother, Carloman. Since his father's death, the King had ruled alongside his brother. Theirs was a volatile relationship, conversations often ending with shouts and oaths. Though they ruled together, it was obvious to all that the King held the final word, which infuriated his brother. Carloman sat among the peers as a matter of necessity, but he was often ignored. The Paladin were the peers of the King, and he gave deference to their advice over his brother's.

As was his custom, the King greeted each by name and accorded him a word of thanks for his service and fidelity. There was Roland, his favorite nephew; Salomon the king of Brittany; Turpin the Archbishop of England; Ogier, the Dane; Malagigi the old enchanter; Rinaldo, the cousin of Roland; and Florismart, the good friend of Roland. Others had come and gone, but these were the staunch of heart, the fearless warriors and brothers at arms.

After greeting the Paladin, he moved to sit down, but the doors flung open announcing his brother's arrival. "Glad that you could join us," the King said glibly.

"It is my brother's pleasure that I seek, and with gratitude that you have waited." Neither spoke sincerely; the rest of the Paladin held their sneers for another time.

After taking their seats, the court pounded their fists against the table in unison to signify the meeting coming to order. Each of the peers gave account of his respective land, and with each report the Saxons' undertones belied the irritation that had remained even after his father's death. Out of the corner of his eye he could see Carloman and his impish grin. He took pleasure at the King's expense. With each word of difficulty he looked for a foothold to dislodge the King's esteem among the peers.

Admiration was not too strong of a word for how Ogier felt toward the King. It was an odd relationship; one born of the necessity of kings and peace, but through it all Charlemagne held the young knight in high esteem. Even when the tensions between his father and the king were at their highest, and Ogier their pawn, he could not help but hold the king with the warmest of affections. And now sitting at the table he was counted as one of the Paladin. There were times, however, that he wished his relationship with his father was as congenial. Since the battle at Aachen peace with the Danes had been strained, and if not for Ogier's presence war would have been constant. Yet, King Sigfred could see his son growing closer to Charlemagne, becoming more Frank than Dane; it infuriated him.

"Brother," Carloman began, "the Saxon army is a gnat in the face of your strength. How is it that they still persist in their rebellion?"

Charlemagne couldn't prove it, but he knew his brother colluded with their enemy. "You are responsible for the third cavalry; why have you not followed through with patrolling the northern border of Frisia? When we make inroads our foes seem to escape in your direction each time."

"It is true that they slither back behind their rocks, but it isn't my responsibility to advance into their lands." He gave a quick glance at Ogier. "You, with the help of these fine nobles…"

Charlemagne slammed his fist on the table. "Enough of this, Carloman! How are we to rule our father's lands if we are at odds?"

Meeting gaze for gaze Carloman shot back, "Because it isn't for our father that you rule; it is for yourself! You would divest me of my kingdom if you could. Let me take what is mine and rule it myself."

"Are you suggesting that we divide the kingdom? That would be ruinous. There is power in unity. We cannot fend off the Moors to the south and the Saxons to the north if we are not united!" Charlemagne's exclamation was met with agreeable oaths from the council.

Carloman knew there was no love for him in the room. They would gladly see his head on a spike if not for his brother, but their rivalry had peaked—one or the other must be sole king. He knew he could not face his brother outright; the key to his fall was hidden in the shadows. "This is not the first time I have expressed my desire, but it will be the last time in this court."

Charlemagne eyed him with cautious curiosity. *What is my brother up to?*

"I will take my army to the borders of my lands and fulfill my obligation to the kingdom. Unless you have some specific need for my presence there is little call for me to attend." Seeing that there was no one to restrain his departure, he stood up and left.

Intrigue
771 AD

The room was still for what seemed an eternity; all were astonished by the meeting's events. Roland finally broke the silence. "My lord, if I could be so bold? It is for the best. You are now rid of that constant irritant and can pursue your good course without interruption."

"Hear, hear," the others responded, but the King stood silent.

For a split second he wasn't sure how he felt: he was racked with disappointment at not being able to hold his brother's confidence and his father's last wish, but he also felt betrayed that his brother would throw away their family ties for a broken kingdom. He even felt pity; he knew that his brother was devious, and the kingdom could fall if not united. But it was only a split second.

"The union of the kingdom must stand, but how that will be accomplished is unclear. I do not want a war with my brother." He pondered a while as all sat waiting. "Tonight neither revel with your friends nor make love to your wives. Spend the time of forgone pleasures seeking God that he would bring about his will and the advance of his kingdom." He dismissed the Paladin and when the last man had departed, he felt the weight of the crown.

Roland loved the King more than life itself, and knew that Charlemagne loved his brother the same way. The lure of power could overcome any man, and Carloman was as weak as they came. If something was not done immediately the King could lose everything. When he returned to his room he set himself to writing a letter, to be delivered in secret and handed from person to person in the darkness. When he was finished he had his page bring to his room a man cloaked in an old ragged robe.

"Take this to our mutual friend. Has everything been set in place?" Though Roland had just decided to take action, the plans for such an event had been in the works for months. He believed, along with the others, that only a kingdom under the helm of the Charlemagne could stand. Not all were willing to lift a hand against Carloman, so this valiant man of war would act alone. It would be best this way. Too many conspirators and the king would find out— they would all be undone.

The robed agent acknowledged that all was ready, took his leave, and disappeared into the shadows. The lone rider was faster than Carloman and his entourage, and arrived at his castle two days ahead of the group. Three others would assist the agent in this intrigue. Amaury, Christophe, and Denis were all willing to die for their cause.

The cloaked figure handed the letter to a man twice his size who sported a beard that had grown long and unkempt. To his side was a man as tall but not as broad, less stout but not skinny. The smaller man was the more interesting. His hair hung about his shoulders and he wore light armor like the King's royal guard. The note was finally passed to him and he read it with great earnest:

My dear friend,
The time is at hand. The royal house is on the verge of disarray
and the princes are on the brink of war. As we have discussed, we

are in need to act. You are free to engage at your discretion, but sooner, I fear, is better than later.

Those details not immediately apparent soon came to light as Amaury laid out his plan. It wasn't an exceptional plot, but its simplicity increased its odds of success. Amaury was in Carloman's employ, and over the past year had increasingly offered himself for various ingratiating opportunities; as a result he was now the sergeant of the night bodyguard. Though not the most prestigious appointment, it did give him access without too much notice.

The larger men were brothers, Christophe and Denis. Their father was a spice trader who had traveled as far east as Constantinople. There he had dabbled in lethal concoctions similar to what they were ready to deploy. Their father had met his fateful death at the hands of Carloman, so their recruitment into this intrigue had been easy.

"What do we have?" Amaury asked.

"You must be careful with this." His accomplice held a small vial of a milky substance. "It is called pong-pong by the natives and suicide tree by others."

"Will it kill him?"

"Most definitely," said Denis, "but he must eat it all. The taste isn't too strong, but if it's noticeable he might not finish whatever you put it in. Make sure it's covered with lots of spices."

"How will he die?" Amaury inquired. "We don't want anyone realizing that he was poisoned."

"His heart just stops. There is no vomiting or thrashing around. He will just fall over and die."

"Good," Amaury said. Looking at the cloaked figure he asked, "Are you staying to help?" Without answering the man turned on his heels and left. "That's our answer. Christophe, do you know what you have to do?"

They ran through the plan again.

Betrayal
771 AD

His objective hadn't been to rile his brother, but Carloman had a knack for stirring the tension between them. Their father, Pippin the Short, had favored Charlemagne and Carloman's jealously festered beneath the surface and broke through at times, as had just happened in the council chamber. Carloman was determined to be his own man and not be ruled under his brother's shadow, but he lacked Charlemagne's charisma to garner the favor of his subjects. Carloman was a man of cruelty and fear. Men had worked for him, but loyalty to him was bought rather than inspired.

His closest friend and confidant was Munderic. They had known each other since childhood and were cut from the same cloth. Both had older brothers, both had been overlooked by fathers, and both had ambition that God seemed to withhold, but which they were determined to claim. Munderic, however, was not of royal blood. His father was neither knight nor noble, but had worked as a servant of King Pippin. The difference in rank had never been an issue between the two, for the young didn't care for such matters. It was only when adults reprimanded them for things they didn't understand that the ideas of upper and lower classes were formed.

"You spend too much time with the servants," Pippin had said to Carloman. "You are of an age where you need to distance yourself from the commoners."

Munderic's father wasn't any different. "You can't speak to the prince that way. You need to address him as *Your Highness*, bow, and show respect. Too much familiarity could cost us our place, even our lives."

In public they performed as expected but in private they were as equals. Even today Carloman and Munderic were closer than Carloman and Charlemagne would ever be. In public Munderic was his chief of staff, the head of the military, and his closest advisor. In private they spoke as brothers and often disagreed, but in the end Carloman was of the royal house and his word was law.

"He is so infuriating!" Carloman pushed the words between clenched teeth. "He has the world by its tail and treats me just as he would the Paladin." He took his horse's reins, looking sternly at the servant who had offered them. The message was clear: any reiteration of Carloman's outburst would be met with death. He mounted the horse, jerked its head, and drove it through the castle gate.

After a mile the Prince slowed. Munderic was close behind and was able to lend an ear to his friend. "My brother," he began. They used the familial term for one another in private. "What dishonor has Charlemagne bestowed on you this evening?"

Carloman shook his head. "He stopped just short of accusing me of treason toward the crown, of colluding with the Danes in their continual rebellion toward the realm." He stopped his horse and turned toward Munderic. A smile crept across his face. "I believe that we will need to step up our timetable. Charlemagne's suspicions will soon be verified."

"What do you think he will do when he finds out?" Munderic asked.

"Hard to say, but my brother"—he used the word more from spite than love—"has a soft spot in his heart for family. He doesn't want to go to war with me. He has too many distractions on every front to be concerned about what we are doing in the north. He is more concerned about how our actions affect his relationship with King Sigfred."

Their camp lay two miles from the castle. Carloman didn't like being a guest to his brother and preferred the security of being surrounded by his own men. As they approached two sentries asked their identity and when told submissively allowed them to pass. The Prince was naturally paranoid, a trait instilled in all successful dynasties. Royalty had its privileges but it also had its dangers. Someone was always trying to usurp the throne.

Dismounting, they stood by the fire as a servant brought them plates of food. It wasn't good, but it was filling. "My lord," Munderic began, "even though your brother doesn't want war with you, we must be vigilant. He will stop at nothing to preserve the integrity of the realm."

"My thoughts exactly." He took a long swallow of ale. "I am less concerned about my brother than about the Paladin. They are intensely loyal. They may influence him beyond his own conscience and force him to send troops into Frisia as a reminder of who he believes is the true king."

"Do you think he would attack right out?" Munderic asked.

"No, he knows we are no match. He may station them in close proximity to hinder our collaboration with the Danes. They are the key to overthrowing the yoke of my brother's royal oppression." Carloman's mind was racing. He was not as good a tactician as his brother, but he knew his way around strategy. For him to be successful he would have to be one or two steps ahead of his brother. "Charlemagne is too sentimental when it comes to family. Tomorrow

I want you to head for King Sigfred's court with this message." He called for his servant to come and write a dispatch.

To the honorable King of the Danes:
Charlemagne is becoming suspicious of our activities and it is of necessity that we meet. If we are to join in any fashion to overthrow the shackles of the tyrant we must do so with haste. The man who delivers this message is my heart and ears; whatever you say to him you say to me. Make arrangements with him and we will meet on the first full moon.

Carloman affixed his signet ring to the correspondence and placed it in a courier's pouch. "At first light make haste to the Danes' castle. When you have made the appropriate arrangements, come and fetch me; we must not waste any more time."

Assassin
771 AD

When Amaury reached his post Carloman had finally arrived and called all his sergeants of arms to his meeting room. Explaining some of what had happened with his brother, he colored the responses of the Paladin to shed a good light on himself, and proceeded to double the guard in the event that his brother would be foolish enough to attack. But it wasn't Charlemagne's army he should have feared. When evening came and the changing of the guard was completed, Amaury was where he belonged. It was mealtime and Carloman was having his supper prepared and brought to his room.

If Christophe and Denis acted too quickly, Carloman would be alerted or not ready to eat, too late and Amaury would be caught in the room at the time of death. The other tricky part was getting the suicide milk in the food. Amaury made his way to the kitchen.

"What is on the menu tonight?" he asked the cook.

"For you, the same slop as the night before. For the Prince, quail with a honey glaze. He requested it specifically."

"Lucky for me I don't like honey." He laughed trying to put the cook at ease. "I am heading back to the Prince's chamber. Shall I take his food?"

"That would be appreciated…but wait, the Prince has asked that nothing be changed. He insisted that I bring his food personally. I think he is afraid of being poisoned."

"Careful, my friend. Those are treasonous words." Amaury's words had their desired effect. The look on the cook's face made a ghost look black. "But if you don't want my help I will take my leave." He turned and started to walk out.

The cook was confused and worried. On the one hand he had been instructed to bring the food himself. On the other, the sergeant was part of the guard. Still, if he didn't bring the food himself he could be in trouble. Then again if he did bring the meal and something happened, he would be accused. "Wait, it is almost ready. Maybe you could take it, but make sure you explain to the Prince that you insisted on taking him his food." Amaury agreed and waited for the tray.

An assassin using poison might think it an easy task to mix the concoction and wait for the results. When dealing with a paranoid Prince, however, getting him to trust something out of the ordinary could prove difficult. The greater temptation was the smell of the food he carried down the corridor. The lustful eyes of men could themselves cause rebellion, but at least their eyes focused on the food and not the face of its courier.

Amaury knocked on the door and entered when invited in. "My lord, I have brought you your meal."

Carloman looked at him suspiciously. "Where is the cook? I instructed him to bring my food."

"I was passing by and insisted he let me bring you your meal," Amaury said. He was placing the tray on a nearby table.

"That would seem very kind…or not." Carloman followed the guard with distrust and suspicion. "These are days in which trust and loyalty can't always be taken for granted. Filial devotion is best demonstrated. For who are you willing to give your life?"

"My lord, I am your guard. I am willing to give my life to protect you."

"You would throw yourself on this blade if it meant saving my life?" he questioned.

"Surely I have demonstrated that before in battle," Amaury answered.

"Yes, battle, but what about treachery? What about the assassin in the night? How would you give your life for me then?"

"What do you mean?"

"Take this food. It seems delicious, but there are poisons that can't be seen, that act quickly and painfully. Did you know that the cook tastes all my meals in front of me? He offers his delicacies and his life each time. Now you are here in his place. Are you offering the same?" Carloman was watching Amaury's face for any sign of mistrust—he saw surprise in his eyes.

"My lord, I was not aware. Could he have done something to the food all the while using me as his unwitting accomplice?"

"Or," said the Prince, "maybe you have done so, and find yourself in an untenable predicament. If you refuse to eat it you are either a coward or an accomplice. If you eat it you display your courage but could die." They stood face to face. "There is only one way to prove your devotion." The Prince held the dish of quail out for the knight to taste.

Without hesitation the knight took hold of a piece of the quail and chewed it vigorously. Moments after he ingested the meat Carloman gave him a quizzical look and laughed. "You are still alive, retaining both your courage and my admiration." He took the food, waved a dismissive hand, and ate his dinner in private.

A small window was cut into the wall off the hallway just outside the Prince's chamber. After twenty minutes Amaury waved a white piece of cloth out the window. Within seconds shouting and fighting broke out in front of the castle gates.

"Stay here and protect the Prince!" he shouted to the nearest two men. He took the others and they rushed to find the source of the commotion. As was planned Christophe and Denis had enlisted ten other men to stage a brawl that spilled into the court of the castle. It was so raucous that it drew everyone's attention, waking up all the guards, both junior and senior. When the dust had settled and the last thug was under lock and key, the captain of the guard went to check on his master, only to find him hanging off the side of his bed. He had obviously tried to lie down after his meal.

"Guards, come in here quickly!" Sigibert called for his men. "You, go get the court physician, on the double." Looking at the other two he asked, "Who was stationed at his door?"

Amaury looked at his companion who was first to speak. "I was at the door sir, along with Willichar who went for the physician."

"Was anyone in here before or after the commotion?" It was unnerving talking with the prince lying indignantly on the bed.

"I was sir." Amaury thought it best to depict the details of the evening so they cast suspicion away from himself. "I brought the prince's dinner and served as his taster. When the commotion started, the Prince directed me to find out what was happening. I did as instructed, leaving Willichar and Agiulf to guard the door." He paused to look at the Prince's body. "He was alive when I left." Which was true, and a half-truth would be more convincing than a full lie.

Sigibert eyed them both with misgivings; that was his job. He had recruited both of these men and they had served with distinction, Amaury especially. As he was trying to figure out a motive, he was interrupted by Willichar.

"The physician, sir."

Pulling back the cover Sigibert had laid over the prince, the physician carefully and respectfully examined the body. Opening the eyelids, he found the pupils were contracted, which meant his face had not been covered. Usually if someone was smothered, the skin around the mouth and nose would be pale. The physician was quite certain his death was from another means. After thirty minutes of looking over the corpse, the doctor finally spoke.

"He wasn't suffocated, there is no evidence of struggle, and he wasn't poisoned. Poison would be accompanied by foaming around the mouth, yellow discharge from the nose, and bleeding out of the nose, eyes, or ears. It looks as if his heart just gave out. My conclusion is that he died of natural causes."

"Are you certain?" Sigibert questioned.

"As certain as I can be. It is possible that the Prince died in some mysterious or magical way, but from what I can determine his heart just stopped." The physician pulled the cover back over the Prince's body, bowed, and gave himself leave.

Sigibert looked at Amaury. "You were responsible for the Prince's safety; it just seems odd that his heart gave out right when there was a commotion in the courtyard."

"If I might ask, sir,"—Amaury ventured to interject an alternative—"did the Prince have anything on his mind that could have caused so much stress his heart could not bear it? I know it isn't my place, but under the circumstances I ask to speak freely."

"Say what is on your mind."

"The cook said the Prince was a bit more agitated and suspicious of late, and when I was with him, just before the commotion, he seemed more distressed, confirming the cook's concerns." Amaury left it at that, hoping the sergeant would let the matter drop.

Sigibert wouldn't let it go, and an investigation ensued, but no guilty party could be determined; the cause of death was decided to be mysterious but natural. The cook remained silent for fear that his intimation of poison would point fingers at him. The guards posted outside the bedchambers confessed that nothing had been out of the ordinary save the brawl, but no one could figure out who started it and for what reason. The greater challenge was reporting the incident back to the King.

Oaths
771 AD

The King of the Danes disliked all the Franks, even those with whom he conspired. He wasn't oblivious to their ambitions and felt insulted that they believed him to be their pawn. Yet, they were useful, and he would use the rift between the sons of Pippin to his own advantage.

Munderic had been waiting two days for an audience with King Sigfred. It was typical to keep people waiting as a show of preeminence, and Carloman had done the same. Nonetheless time was of the essence and Munderic grew impatient. Midmorning of the third day he was again waiting in the outer court for the King to give him admittance, and to his relief the courtier approached him.

"Sir Munderic, the King is available to see you now." The courtier's air of superiority still irritated the knight, but he was glad to finally have an audience. The castle was not as opulent as Charlemagne's but formidable. Its walls were thick and its defenses strong. These observations would come in handy if the need ever arose to turn the tide in their relationship.

Royalty was the same no matter where in the world one traveled. The majesty of the ruler had to be acknowledged and obeisance offered before the audience could begin. Munderic bowed to the King's authority and handed Carloman's message to a courtier who in turn gave it to the Danish sovereign.

A small man stood to the right of King Sigfred and was handed the note. He then whispered its contents into His Majesty's ear. The message wasn't long, but its content caused the King to furrow his brow and nod his head.

"Why do you Franks need my help to ferret out your differences? Cannot your master wield enough power against his brother to liberate both kingdoms to his cause? What assurances do I have that after I have given you my help that you will not turn your armies toward my lands?"

"It is with great admiration of the King's resolve that my master, Prince Carloman, seeks to enter into a treaty, by which each kingdom would find benefit. Neither would be subject to the other, but both would stand as equals and find mutual commerce and respect. All Prince Carloman wishes is to possess what is his by birth. His brother is ambitious and desires to rule the whole world. There is no room for other kings in Charlemagne's mind. Prince Carloman has tried to reason with his brother, but to no avail. He was shunted to the north and fears Charlemagne will remove him from his rightful throne."

"I have no love for the tyrant Charlemagne," King Sigfred hissed, "but his strength is beyond yours or mine."

"Yes, but together we can stay his aspirations and hold at bay the old wolf. My lord, Prince Carloman only asks that you would meet with him before the new moon. It will soon be upon us and he feels that Charlemagne will not sit still much longer."

"Your words are as sweet as honey, and as tempting as a young maid. However, you have over looked one obstacle. Charlemagne holds my son captive, and any aggression against his kingdom will bring death to my heir." A hint of grief caught in the old father's throat, but something lay hidden that Munderic couldn't quite discern.

"It is not my place to inform Your Majesty of what I have seen and know about the prince, Ogier. I can only speak on behalf of my master."

"But I bid you to speak of my son, if you know something that would soothe my heart."

"Your heart is my concern, for what I know will only cause it pain." Munderic was crafty and he knew that if he could speak the right words into Sigfred's ear he might turn the King's heart from grief to war.

"Do not hesitate to speak the truth, whether it brings joy or sorrow. Your life is safe in this hall," the King said.

"Then I will tell you what I know. Ogier has been turned from the house of Sigfred to the house of Charlemagne. No longer does he call you father, but addresses the tyrant so. He has been brought into the confidence of your enemy and sits at Charlemagne's coveted table as a Paladin." A commotion burst out in the court as Sigfred was noticeably shaken. He knew that Charlemagne was a crafty tyrant, but to stoop so low as to turn his own son against him.

"It grieves my heart and that of my master to see the King so afflicted. It is for this reason and more that we extend our hand of friendship to you." Munderic could see the wheels of Sigfred's mind turning, the cloud of grief turning to anger, but then that flicker came again, something that the King was not telling, something he was holding back. "My Lord," Munderic continued, "if I might intrude on your moment of grief. There seems to be something that Your Majesty wishes to say, which has been set aside because of this terrible news. Would you grant me the grace to inquire about the message?"

Sigfred was lost in his own emotion and almost forgot the revelation that had been handed him last night. It was nothing to him, but he knew it would change the course of his plans. "Yes, yes, there is something that you must know. I have withheld the information for after our discussion, but I see it is time that you knew that your master is dead."

Munderic stood in stunned disbelief. "Surely Your Majesty is mistaken. I left him but days ago. He was in good health and spirits. He looked forward to your meeting. Your information must be faulty."

"I assure you it isn't. How it happened is unclear. All I have been told is that he is dead." Munderic's obvious grief didn't faze the King whatsoever. His own sorrow lay at the surface of his heart as he spoke. "There will be no alliance between your people and mine. Charlemagne will take possession of all your master's lands and will have his eye toward mine. If what you say about my son is true, then I have no reason to fear his death—he is dead to me already." Sigfred stood, waved his hand in dismissal, and turned to leave.

"My lord!" Munderic looked up and exclaimed emphatically, "I am dead to Charlemagne as well and wish to submit my sword to your majesty's sovereignty!"

Turning toward the knight, Sigfred looked intently into his face. It held no guile, no sense of betrayal, but the pain of a lost soul. Stepping down, he approached Munderic and directed him to kneel. Unsheathing his sword he tapped him on the head three times. Then he commanded him to stand, and, taking an ax hanging on the wall, he moved it from head to chest and from right to left saying, "In the name of the great god Odin, his son Thor, and all that is holy I welcome you as a soldier of my kingdom. Take your place among my ranks for the protection of the Danes and the life of your sovereign. This do you declare?"

"With my dying breath," Munderic swore.

"Then live or die, your life is now mine." He instructed his guards to take the new recruit and enlist him in their ranks; then he called his war council to convene.

Paladin
771 AD

The Paladin were called for an emergency meeting. The death of Carloman could destabilize the kingdom and leave it open to invading armies. Though the Prince's activities were limited to the north, the distraction provided a temptation to all who would see Charlemagne fall.

The King was standing at the window when the sixteen entered. They silently took their places and laid their swords on the table. All knew their master's heart was grieved, and they dared not intrude on his silence. Waiting, they prayed for his comfort as their lord taught them. When their liege turned, they could see that his anguish had become resolute.

"What my enemies would use for evil my God will turn for good. Carloman was a scoundrel, but he was of royal blood and my brother. Though his death has been declared natural, I am not so sure. The details surrounding his demise are suspect, and if I knew that the culprit was connected to any person or kingdom, I would bring it down with the wrath of God." He knew these men to be loyal and wouldn't rule out their inclination to orchestrate such folly on his behalf, but he could not bring himself to accuse them outright. He needed them united now more than ever before.

"My lord, we see the pain that you bear and wish it were us instead of you." Turpin was a mighty warrior as well as the

Archbishop of England; when he spoke of God all listened. "Allow us the honor of hearing the King's grief, that you might not bear it alone." His words were accepted by all present.

"My grief runs deep for the loss of my brother, but would run as deep for you. I am honored to call you brothers, both in arms and in spirit. How can I lay before you what only I can endure?" The King sat in his seat at the table, feeling the weight of the throne.

"I am the least of my brothers at this table, but have the distinction to be called your son." Ogier walked around the table and sat next to Charlemagne, in Carloman's usual seat. There were mixed looks at this presumption, but all relaxed when the King didn't react. "We all know that the Prince conspired against my lord, and with none other than my fleshly father. It is with this that I speak my mind, because I understand the pain of loss, if not in death, at least in substance."

"In all the years you have served in my court I have known you only as my son. It is your heart and mind that I cherish; speak freely." The King sat back and Ogier continued.

"As I am sure you have heard, Munderic has sworn his allegiance to the King of the Danes. This speaks of the treasonous actions of both him and his master. Now the world knows, and looks to you for guidance. If you falter in taking action against those who oppose you, it will only invite others to test your resolve." He turned to his fellow knights. "We have a bond that only battle can forge. We have found a home when the world would have us orphans. We have pledged our lives so that the oppressed can find freedom and the lost can find salvation. This, my lord, we have learned from you, and for you we live and die."

"Hear, hear!" The Paladin pounded their fists and stood in unison, honoring the King.

"I must echo my brother's sentiments," said Roland. "We must in a show of force send troops to Frisia and bring the house of Carloman under your realm. I volunteer to lead my knights on such a noble quest."

"And if it pleases the King I will give assistance as well," said Florismart.

Charlemagne raised his hand and bade his fellow knights to sit. For a moment there was silence and he fought back a tear as pride welled up in his heart. He stood up and said, "My grief is comforted in knowing you are by my side. I pledge to you both life and death in order to serve our great God and King. We will resolve to claim what was given to me by right of birth and bought with the blood of soldiers and countrymen. Yet, there is time to mourn the loss of Carloman. His army is in disarray and many have made their way to our castle looking to join our forces. When the time is right I will hold you to your word and send you to hold the northern lands." He paused and took a deep breath. "For now I have instructed Carloman's body to be interred in the hall of kings. A state of mourning will be called, after which Roland will march." He asked his brothers to stand and led them in a prayer, then dismissed them to prepare for the days ahead.

Mystery and intrigue abounded in the rise and fall of kings throughout history, and often coups would result from squabbles between families competing for the throne. As antagonistic as their relationship was, Charlemagne would never have killed his brother to solidify the kingdom. But his death was a relief. The country prepared to mourn the royal son of Pippin, and no expense would be spared to honor him. Though Charlemagne mourned his brother, he did not grieve.

When the days of mourning were over the King stood before his throne surrounded by his court and priests. The pomp and circumstance of this moment far exceeded that of his brother's funeral, for the king was being crowned sole ruler of the Franks, sovereign of his lands. The pageantry exceeded any of that from the ancient world, and the oaths he was about to proclaim would secure for him the crown of his father and the devotion of his people.

The Archbishop of Rome had come for this important event, sent by the Pope as the official representative of the Church. "Your Majesty," he began, "are you willing to take the oath of this high office?"

Falsely or with deep sincerity—none but God truly knew—and with the deepest look of humility, the King said, "I am willing."

The Archbishop had a large Bible brought forth on which the king laid his hand. "Will you solemnly swear to govern the peoples of the Franks, of Brittany to Bavaria, of the Spanish March to the Saxons, and of all territories our sovereign God delivers into your hand, according to the laws of this kingdom?"

"I solemnly promise so to do," he stated.

"Will you in mercy dispense law and justice to be executed in all your judgments?"

"I will," the King answered.

The Archbishop straightened a little taller as he proceeded to the next part. "Will you, to the utmost of your power, maintain the Laws of God and the true profession of the Gospel? Will you to the utmost of your power maintain the teachings of the Holy Church? Will you maintain and preserve for every living person in your realm the supremacy of Christ and the Holy Catholic Church, the presence of Christ on earth? Will you support and promote the furthering of the gospel among the pagans, for the glory of God and the saving of their souls?"

With a resounding voice the King declared, "I will." The page standing at the Archbishop's side offered a decorative pillow on which lay the signet ring of his father, Pippin. He had worn it before, but for the ceremony had given it in trust to the Archbishop. Once again, before his court, his people, and the throne of God, he took the ring and slipped it on his finger. In this act he was finally, once and for all, declared sole king.

A cheer could be heard throughout the great hall, as royalty from all over the kingdom filed out and into the banquet chamber for a great feast. The King, however, was not in the mood to eat. His eyes fell on the Danish representative and the treachery that lay just beneath the surface. When the celebration was over, when the music ceased its jubilation, the king sought a word with Munderic.

Final Respects
771 AD

On this night, this very night,
   Every night and all,
Fire and fleet and candlelight
   And Christ receive your soul.
When you from here away are passed
To Thorny Moore you come at last
If ever you gave stockings and shoes
Sit you down and put them on;
If stockings and shoes you ever gave none
The thorns will prick you to the bare bone.
From Thorny Moore when you will pass,
To Bridge the Dread you come at last;
From Bridge the Dread when you come to pass,
To Purgatory fire you come at last;
If ever you gave meat or drink,
The fire shall never make you shrink;
If meat or drink you ever gave none,
The fire will burn you to the bare bone;
This all night, this all night,
Every night and all,
Fire and fleet and candlelight,
And Christ receive your soul.

Sigfred refused to attend Carloman's funeral. As a sovereign king he had no obligation to be there, but it would show disrespect to Charlemagne if no one from his country came. Being a thorn in the side the King of the Franks brought Sigfred pleasure, and after much thought on the matter he summoned Munderic.

"My loyal soldier, it is good that you have come so quickly."

"It is but my pleasure to serve Your Majesty. I hope that you have heard of my dedication and loyalty," Munderic said.

"Yes, you are well spoken of. I am sure it has been difficult to serve in a less prestigious position than when you were advisor to Prince Carloman."

"My high estate was an honor, just as my low estate before you is an honor. At least here I am accepted. The alternative would not have been so gracious." Munderic had an adjustment period where he learned the ways of the Danes. But his acceptance by Sigfred's soldiers was a different matter. He was seen as a renegade and held aloof. With time, hard work, and skill, he had demonstrated that he was worthy of their trust. Yet, it wouldn't be until they fought together in battle that he would be accepted as a brother.

"Your service as a soldier is appreciated, but I have another duty for you to perform. It will be dangerous and your life could be forfeited."

"Your Majesty, my life is yours. I have pledged it and it is so." Munderic snapped to attention.

"I knew I could count on you. Diplomacy is as much a skill as wielding a sword. I have documents in this pouch that will guarantee your safe passage. I am sending you to the court of Charlemagne in my stead." There was a notable reflex in Munderic's expression. "I see that this bothers you."

"No, my lord," he responded.

"Now, now, let's have honesty between us," the King urged.

"It's just that I am not sure what diplomatic advantage I could bring my King." Munderic would rather give his life in battle than face the disdain that would greet him at Charlemagne's court.

"It is not an advantage I seek, but a thorn in the king's flesh. You will be a reminder of all he has lost, and the perpetual antagonism of our kingdoms. Will this be a problem for you? Is your fear too great to keep you from your king's request?" It wasn't a request. King Sigfred wasn't a man to be trifled with, and if Munderic showed any further hesitation it would mean his life. The most he would have to endure at Charlemagne's court would be embarrassment and humiliation.

"My word is my honor, and I have pledged both to you. I will ride to Carloman's funeral at first light." After being dismissed, Munderic came to terms with his assignment and rather relished the opportunity to mourn the loss of his brother. It was surely the most difficult task he had been called upon to complete, but he would do it with the strength and courage of a true knight.

The town swarmed with people as visitors from all over the realm came to pay their final respects to Prince Carloman. There were no parties or celebrations, but hushed words and long faces of mourning. It was easy for Munderic to slip in unnoticed, which he hoped would be the mark of his visit, but to his surprise the two soldiers that had been sent with him by King Sigfred announced their presence to the guard of the gate. It didn't take long for word of his arrival to fill the streets.

As the grand advisor to the Prince he was well known, and his cruelty was as renowned as that of the dead ruler. Add to that his allegiance to Sigfred and his fate was sealed. So, the humiliation began, but at least he was spared the indignity of vocal recompense in light of the time of mourning. In the crowded street sojourners gave him a wide berth and allowed him to pass by un-jostled.

He would have rather stayed at a tavern on the outskirts of town, but all dignitaries had accommodations within the castle proper. He was vigilant; he knew the death of the Prince had come from within these walls and he feared they would attempt to kill him, too. His companions didn't have the luxury of being guests of the King, so they gave Munderic their leave and settled into the stable area with other men of their station.

When Munderic arrived at his room a young man stood at his door. He would be Munderic's servant for the duration of his stay. The boy opened the door and poured water into a washbasin. "If, my lord, you need any assistance there is a bell on the table next to your bed. I will be outside at all times during your stay. Is there anything else you require?"

"Not at the moment; you may leave." Munderic threw the bags he had brought into the corner and fell back onto the bed, hoping to get some rest before the evening meal. The King had prepared a feast of mourning for his guests and all were required to attend.

He closed his eyes, but sleep was elusive. All he could see was his friend and brother Carloman. He cared little for the trappings of royalty. He yearned for the warmth of their friendship, their bantering companionship, and the ambition that drove them both. He was alone in the Danish court and he was alone in the court of Charlemagne. If not for his dread of hell he would have killed himself and joined his master and brother in the afterlife.

Shiny Ornament
771 AD

The roosters' crow woke Munderic with a start. Disoriented, he sat straight up in bed. For a moment he couldn't figure out where he was. The room looked familiar but the day and time puzzled him. *Where is Carloman?* he thought. Fearful anticipation that his dream was reality crept over him, but as his head cleared the sadness of his friend's death returned.

He had missed the feast of mourners and knew his absence would infuriate the King. Fresh water had been left in the basin, and after washing he hastily clothed himself, leaving his servant undisturbed. "I am sorry, my lord, I didn't know you were awake or I would have come in to assist in your dress," the servant said apologetically.

"You should have roused me last night in time for the King's feast," he said angrily. Munderic pushed the boy, dismissing him, and continued toward the chapel.

People rushed around in the never-ending activity of the royal court, but the mood was subdued as they displayed their respect for the King. Carloman's passing would not have garnered such an air of grief if not for Charlemagne. It was the King's mood that concerned the masses, for they loved their sovereign.

Munderic had turned left at the end of the hall, hoping to take a longer route to the chapel, avoiding as many people as possible. His steps, however, were watched continually upon his arrival, and when he reached the rear courtyard he was met by three imposing figures.

"Are you my escorts to his majesty's court and my master's funeral?" Munderic asked sarcastically.

"If it were my will we would be your escort to hell. It seems you have dishonored the king by your absence last night. Do you have regard for neither Charlemagne nor your master Sigfred?" Ogier spit on the ground.

"Why do you, the grandson of Sigfred and the son of Gudfred, hold me in such contempt? Are you not their servant, and the slave of Charlemagne?" Munderic knew full well the position Ogier had attained in Charlemagne's court.

"You know nothing of me and my family. You are both a traitor to the King, Charlemagne, and a pawn of my grandfather. Do you think he cares for you past the irritation you bring to this court? If you were to die he would not even remember your name."

"As he has forgotten yours," Munderic spat.

Ogier drew his sword and stepped toward the traitor, while the guards put their hands on their hilts, cautioning Munderic from any action.

Munderic stepped around Ogier and continued. "You know, Ogier, we are much more alike than you think. We live in the halls of kings that are neither kin nor clan. We hope for scraps of kindness from their tables, and long for a home that is no longer attainable." He turned to face his opponent. "Don't tell me you haven't missed your grandfather and father."

"We may be the same, but the masters we serve are far different. His Majesty King of the Franks is a compassionate sovereign. He seeks nothing but the welfare of his subjects. Contrast that with my grandfather, who used me as a bargaining chip for peace. If not for the gracious kindness of King Charlemagne I would be nothing but a servant. Instead I am a trusted advisor and son. Can you say the same?"

"You are naïve. It was your King who set the terms of peace. You are but a shiny trophy on the wall of Charlemagne's ego. He can point to you and tell his kin how wonderful and gracious he is for lavishing the kindness of God on his enemies, all the while he slaughters them and burns their homes."

Ogier's anger got the best of him and he pushed Munderic to the wall. Pressing the hilt of his sword against his adversary's throat he said, "You dare blaspheme against your God and His appointed servant? I should slay you here and now, and no one would shed a tear. These men would testify to your insolence and I would be rewarded for ending the treachery of your line."

Munderic showed no fear and knew better then to draw a sword against these men. He might have been able to win in combat, but he would never make it past the walls. "Let's be done with the charade. If you are finished displaying your bravado, either kill me or let me pass. I assume you do not want to start an incident on the day of your King's sorrow?" Munderic tilted his head and smiled. He knew full well that Ogier wouldn't harm him. After a moment of hesitation Munderic continued, "Just as I thought. I will take my leave and join the mourners of the King's brother." He grabbed Ogier's hands and gently pushed them away; as he expected there was no resistance.

"You have not heard the last from me!" Ogier shouted at him. "You think you are safe, but neither Frank nor Dane who hears your name but laughs at the joke you have become."

Holding his head high, Munderic would not allow this whelp any satisfaction. He may be the laughing stock of two realms, but he was a knight and would live and die with some shred of honor. He could feel Ogier and his guards behind him as he wound his way through the castle to the large chapel were his brother and friend lay.

Taking his seat at the far back of the room he avoided further interaction. The room was filled with people who came to pay homage to Charlemagne. The corpse that lay in state was merely a prop to show the King's sorrow. No one cared that Carloman was dead save two people: the King and Munderic. He felt alone.

Compassion
771 AD

After the funeral was finished and the coronation of Charlemagne as sole king of the Franks was complete came a moment so awkward the collective gasp could have emptied the room of its air. Charlemagne stopped while exiting and requested Munderic's presence.

The procession, after the momentary engagement, was more uncomfortable than Munderic had anticipated. The women looked away and the men glared with contempt and hatred. If not for the occasion, he would have been dragged through the streets, placed in stocks, and then drawn and quartered. Even his encounter with Ogier had been less threatening.

When he returned to his room the thought of packing up and riding back to Sigfred's protection was tempting, but he knew from the guards who followed him that any such action would be met with immediate death. He would trust that Charlemagne's famed 'kindness' would be extended to him as well. Yet, the King was an enigma. He was cruel in battle yet kind to his servants. He would offer life to those who converted, but certain death to the unrepentant. If any glory to his God could be gained in Munderic's death, it would be certain, but if mercy did the same then maybe there was hope.

The afternoon did not fly by quickly. There was too much time for reflection and anxiety, and Munderic's nerves were relieved when a knock on the door finally came. He and the guard needn't trade words; they both knew what was expected. The silence was haunting as they marched toward the King's chamber, and the fondly remembered halls of his youth now rang with dread.

To Munderic's surprise, he was not taken to the hall of kings, the chamber where Charlemagne entertained dignitaries of other countries. Instead he was led to the room of the Paladin. There in the center was the round table where Carloman had sat among his peers. Munderic was familiar with it, as he had stood with his master on many occasions.

His surprise, however, turned to trepidation at the sight of the table filled with those ready to cut his throat. All the chairs were occupied save two: Carloman's and Charlemagne's. The King sat instead on an elevated throne, signifying his supremacy in all matters. Munderic was led to face Charlemagne and kneel in obeisance before the throne.

Charlemagne had Munderic remain on his knees for a moment to humiliate him, but soon told him to rise. "I was surprised to see you here, Munderic. Was this your own suggestion or Sigfred's?"

"It was King Sigfred's idea that I come, but it was my honor to be present at the burial of the Prince."

"It has been a while since you played in these halls. Your friendship with my brother was always a sore spot for our father. He would have rather him play with no one than play with a servant. But he couldn't see the danger."

"And what danger would that be, my lord?"

"Contamination. Instead of learning humility and service, he was contaminated by the world and grandiose ambition. Where else could that have sprung from but the roots of the common?" Charlemagne asked.

"Seeing that my death may be imminent, may I speak freely before the King?" The Monarch nodded his assent. "I have spent my life around the King's house and it seems to me that grandiose ambition is but part of all who seek to rule others."

"Watch your tongue!" Roland stood and yelled, but the King held up his hand and the knight fumed silently.

"Yet, there is a difference in serving God by bringing light to a dark world and gathering lands and wealth for personal pleasure and gain, is there not?" the King asked.

"Not from where I sit. The opulence of a 'righteous' king is no less than that of a tyrant."

Charlemagne smiled. "Yes, but the means by which it is extracted is different. I work to serve the needs of my people, and they prosper when I prosper."

"I am not sure the Danes would agree, my lord."

"You have learned a lot from my brother; I know that you loved him dearly." Charlemagne ignored his jab and continued down another line of questioning. "But I must ask you, why would you abandon all that is of this realm and pledge your allegiance to an enemy?"

Feeling the steely eyes of the knights behind him, Munderic dared say, "The Prince's sudden death is suspicious and since, as the King knows, the Prince was in deliberations with King Sigfred, the possibility of the assassin coming after me was certain."

"You dare say that one of my knights was complicit in this matter? There is no evidence of this and you risk your life by saying so."

"My life is in your hands, but as for your knights, their love for you outweighs all other concerns. If my or the Prince's death is to the benefit of the King, would they not act on your behalf?" Munderic spoke what the King expected but would not articulate. Charlemagne believed in the sovereignty of God—this outcome would only serve to strengthen the kingdom and bring glory to the King of Kings. To accuse one or more of his knights of collusion would not serve the kingdom or the church.

"Yes, it is the way of kings to conspire and kill one another for the sake of their own ambition, but I would never give consent nor act to kill my own flesh, no matter what the cost. My Paladin are of the same mind, and would not have lifted a hand against the realm without my permission." The King could see the skepticism clearly on Munderic's face. "If I ever found that this were so, the perpetrator's life, wealth, and family would be forfeit. To act against the King's wishes is to act against the King." He emphasized this so that any who might have conspired in the matter should know better than to bring it to light.

"This is all well and good, my Lord, but what do you want from me? I am at your mercy," Munderic said.

"I have watched you all my life and I know beyond a shadow of doubt that you loved Carloman, and that any action you have taken is from that heart. Your mistake was not to have come to me in the first place. I want to give you an opportunity to come home." The table of knights erupted in opposition. "You see that my Paladin opposes my suggestion, and in this room all matters are open for discussion."

Ogier was the first to speak. "Then I offer my objections. He has served the house of my grandfather with total disregard to the welfare of my King. To allow him safe return would be dishonorable to your name."

"I agree, my lord." Roland had much influence on the council. "Your brother fought you at every turn; why would his servant do less? I say we give him a traitor's due."

All but Florismart cheered. The King saw this and asked if he had a contrary thought.

"I am but a simple man, my lord," he spoke softly. "And if not for friends like Roland, and the grace of the King, I would be a lost soul. Love is a strong bond, and to condemn a man because he loved much is to cast aspersion on what I have here. Munderic obeyed his master until his death and served an enemy in fear. From what I know he has not lifted a hand against the King and, as far as his involvement in conspiracy with King Sigfred—that has always been speculation. If he wishes to come home I would be in favor."

"How can you speak such nonsense?" Malagigi asked. Though less outspoken, he could hold a crowd with his oratory, and when he did speak, which wasn't often, people listened.

The King finally stood, and all fell silent. "I have never been one to conform to popular opinion or tradition. I have sought God in this matter and my decision is final. My Paladins have spoken their minds, which makes my decision more difficult, and their—and your—task that much more challenging." He went to sit at his place at the round table, all eyes following him. "I have decided to give you the benefit of the doubt and offer you my brother's place at the table." Every Paladin stood; from the evident confusion the outside world would think a war was at hand.

The King allowed the men freedom to express themselves and then he held up his hand and continued. "Munderic had much love for my brother and if he is willing to pledge that love to me and this table, I believe it will strengthen our cause and reveal to all the mercy of God."

Munderic stammered, "I am not sure what to say, my lord. Why would you offer me such grace when I willingly pledged my allegiance to your enemy?

"I am not asking for your allegiance," the King said. "I am asking for your love. Allegiances can come and go, but love forges a bond stronger and longer lasting than anything else. Do you pledge me your love?"

Munderic could see the astonishment in the Paladins' eyes. If he agreed to this they would never fully trust him, and he would have to continually prove his worth. The alternative was banishment, a life no better than a slave to a manipulative king. Every knight's hand went to the hilt of his sword as Munderic drew his from its sheath.

"With my sword I pledge this day my love and life for the king. If the first ever falters, may these men make the second true." Munderic laid his sword in the place of his old master Carloman.

"Well said." Charlemagne looked at the rest of the knights at the table. "I can see your emotions run high and that there is much to talk about in the coming days. This act of mercy and compassion is not without design. It signals not only our ability to show forgiveness, but that the schemes of others cannot stand against the bond we have in the love of Christ." He looked each knight in the face. "In time I hope that you will come to embrace the newest member of our council." Charlemagne stood and embraced the new Paladin, Munderic.

Beware the Wolf
771 AD

The two guards that had accompanied Munderic were not enthusiastic about returning to King Sigfred. They had been sent to help in the event that the Franks accosted Munderic. This turn of events would not bode well for them as the bearers of bad news.

"My King, we could do nothing to prevent this from happening. We were held in the livery and permitted out only occasionally." They hoped the King would not take his anger out on them.

"This was not how it was supposed to happen! I don't care about the worthless traitor; he was only a means to an end." Sigfred wanted only to irritate Charlemagne, but the wily wolf had turned the tables and brought embarrassment to the Danes. "Out of here, all of you! And tell my Volur that her presence is required."

When the doors of the throne room opened, a cool breeze blew in and sent a shiver through Sigfred. He didn't like this woman, but she had proven herself useful over the years. Her long, grey gown flowed as she walked, rustling where no wind blew.

"How can your humble servant be of service to the King?" Her voice was low and the whisper wafted across the room.

"I fear my enemy Charlemagne may have once again robbed me of my dignity. I have no recourse but to abide by my treaty for fear of my grandson's life. What do the gods say?" he asked.

"Your fate is in your faith in the gods. Do you believe that Odin can deliver you or do you fear the raised fist of Charlemagne's god?"

"Ah, the praise with which he extols his god is but the parroted words of their church. He says them like an incantation to justify the slaughter of our people," Sigfred said.

"Then gather your people together and face them like men." She offered advice, but was it the words of Odin or her own folly? Nonetheless, of all his advisors she alone dared speak truth to him.

"What do you know of war? Do you steer down a course that will bring only blood and the fall of my kingdom? Charlemagne is shrewd and has paid the people of the north to keep their distance from me. The Norsemen pick at my shores, unwittingly doing Charlemagne's bidding. If they knew what ruin it brings they would rise up against him."

The old lady wore her shroud low and only her hair could be seen falling across her breasts. Her seclusion added to her mystique, and as she began to sway back and forth, the mystery that enshrouded her intensified. She groaned, then began to speak, not in the usual whisper but in a deeper, manlier voice.

"Am I not your Father Odin, creator of the world and protector of man?"

Sigfred stepped back as the ominous voice continued.

"You have allowed the charlatan of the Franks to send his emissaries into your land. They have built their altars and swayed your people into abandoning the gods of their fathers. Am I to reward you in this? Am I to give you victory when you allow such sacrilege to stand?" The Volur was holding something Sigfred could not see, and when it dropped from her hand smoke began to swirl around her. "Rid your kingdom of this pestilence and see the mighty hammer of Thor rescue you. Send your warriors against their cities, against their houses of worship, and you will see the might of Valhalla descend!" With each sentence the Volur's swaying increased; her fevered pitch inspired fear and trepidation. With the last word she fell to the ground and her robe enshrouded her as if she had disappeared.

The King stood like stone, awed by the experience, but fearful of its meaning. Odin had spoken to him; how could he not be successful if he rode in his name? He stepped down and cautiously approached the Volur. Her breathing was heavy, and the garments rose and fell to its rhythm. He touched her arm and when she did not resist he took hold and helped her stand. She kept her gaze down and he was unable to see her face, a practice she had observed in all her years in his service. He had never seen her face.

After she stood, the Volur took a deep breath, and in her quiet whisper said, "Beware of the wolf. He is crafty."

"Yes, you have said that before," he responded.

"Beware of the wolf and his pup. Find the hunter who is destined to face them both. Do not let your pride stand in the way."

"Who is the hunter?" the King asked.

"He is the man of sorrow." The Volur stood straight, pulled away from the King, and strode out the doors, her robe sweeping behind her.

The man of sorrow. She could only mean one person: his son, Gudfred. Since the loss of his wife he had done nothing but brood. His sorrow had brought calamity on their house. This must be the recompense that would restore its glory. He sent for his son.

When Gudfred appeared before his father he had neither bathed nor taken care of his appearance. His wits were barely about himself when he addressed the King. "Why have you bothered me? Can you not see that my soul is vexed?"

Sigfred had given up on his son years ago. Even when the exchange of Ogier took place Gudfred had hardly noticed. He could no longer let him wallow in his misery. It was time he took his place as prince of the realm to lead his people against the wolf.

There was never much hope that Gudfred would amount to much. He was a tender boy, youngest among his siblings, and spent more time with his mother than with the King. She had named him Gudfred in hope that he would bear the *peace of the gods* in their midst, but his emotional instability had taken root and the death of his wife spiraled him into uselessness. This was an opportunity for him to redeem himself.

"Stand straight boy, have you no pride? It is time for you to serve your people or die in the attempt." Sigfred explained what the Volur had said—in the loss of both wife and son, Gudfred's sorrow was greater than any in the realm. Surely he was the wolf hunter that would bring down King Charlemagne and whatever pup he had sired.

When all was told he sobered his son and called his war council to arms. It was time to rid their country of the pagans who had infected their people. Gudfred would take up arms and lead his men to bring judgment against the blasphemers. He was careful to instruct his son not to cross the border into Charlemagne's land. They would first test the King's resolve when he saw the might of Odin against the might of their crucified god.

The countryside was filled with the smoke of burning churches. Priests were put to the sword and newly converted Christians were given the choice offered by Charlemagne. They could convert back to the old ways or suffer the same fate as their priests. All the people wanted to do was live in peace but the battle of the heavens waged and they were the victims of the gods' culling.

Deventer was the final stop on Gudfred's march. In this busy trade town that had been built by Lebuinus, an English priest, morning mass had just completed when shouting broke out in the streets. The priest instructed his worshippers to wait while he went to see what had stirred the excitement. When he walked out the door he was met by the dreadful presence of Gudfred, Prince of the Danes.

Bowing slightly, the priest asked, "What brings you and your troops to our small town?"

"Don't be coy, priest. I know word has reached the town of the King's judgment. Where are your fellow clergy?"

"You have no authority here. Deventer is a possession of King Charlemagne. Unless you wish war with the King, I would encourage you to leave straight way."

"No river can separate what Odin offers as our prize. Your priests in every village and town have died for the cause of a dead man. Submit to my authority and I will make your death quick, refuse and I will burn you in your own church." As they spoke, men and women from within the church tried to scoot their way past, but the soldiers corralled them into the street.

"There is no need to harm these people. They have done you no ill," the priest begged.

"They have turned from the old ways and displeased the gods. Their fate is within their hands. They can return or suffer the fate of their god." He turned to the twenty-three people who were gathered and offered them this choice. Their eyes pleaded with both the Prince and the priest. How could they make such a decision? Surely God would understand? Were they to die for a simple confession? Of the group only two stood with the priest.

"So be it." Soldiers dismounted and dragged them into the church, closed the door, and hammered it shut. Taking pitch and fire they set the building to flame, and the last sound that came from within was the singing of the condemned.

The Prince gathered the people to the center of the town where stood a large *Irminsul*. It was the symbol of their ancient religion, a sacred tree that bound the children of Odin together. The Prince dismounted and bowed before the tree, and the priest who had tended it all these years began to sing.

Out of the shadows and into the light
Odin created Midgard.
Out of the shadows and into the light
Odin fashioned a man.
Out of the shadows and into the light
Odin protects our lands.
Out of the shadows and into the light
Odin upholds our clans.
Out of the shadows and into the light
Odin lays out our plans.
Out of the shadows and into the light.
Odin calls us to take our stand.

When the song was sung and the Prince had stood, a rousing cheer filled the air. It bolstered his confidence and fed his fervor to redeem himself before his father and his people, to wreak havoc on the man who had stolen his son.

Insulae
773 A.D.

"Who ought to be the king of France, the person who has the title or the man who has the power?" —Pippin the Short

Beams of light burst through as the large double doors swung open into the hall. Rays streamed through the four stained glass windows casting a heavenly hue across the stone interior. The King, surrounded by his generals and bodyguard, reverently entered the Holy Church. Five priors stood at the front waiting to bless him and his army. King Charlemagne and his generals knelt before the elegantly clad priest, who laid on each tongue the body of Jesus and said,

"Blessed are you, Lord, God of all creation. Through your goodness we have this bread to offer, which earth has given and human hands have made. It will become for us the bread of life."

Lifting the chalice of wine he continued,

"By the mystery of this water and wine may we come to share in the divinity of Christ, who humbled himself to share in our humanity. Blessed are you, Lord, God of all creation. Through your goodness

we have this wine to offer, fruit of the vine and work of human hands. It will become our spiritual drink."

He handed the chalice to the soldiers, who each took a sip and gently returned it. When the last soldier had finished, the priest turned to face the large crucifix that hung on the back wall, and making the sign of the cross against his chest, he prayed for the Holy Spirit to grant them unity "through him, with him, in him," to the glory of the Father. He then removed the thurible—the container of incense—from its stand and proceeded toward the back of the church. Each of the priors fell in line behind the priest, and the King and his men followed silently.

Guards held open the large doors until the final solider walked across its threshold and into full view of the waiting army. Cavalrymen, 3,000 strong, dismounted from their horses, and along with 7,000 infantry, kneeled before God in an attitude of prayer. When the King turned and knelt, the priest stood on a raised platform and swung the incense from side to side. Lifting his voice as loudly as he could he prayed,

> *"Through Michael the Archangel, oh Lord, defend us in battle. Be our protection against the wickedness and snares of the devil. May God rebuke him, we humbly pray; and do Thou, O Prince of the Heavenly Host, by the Divine Power of God, cast into hell Satan and all the evil spirits who roam throughout the world seeking the ruin of our souls."*

King Charlemagne rose to his feet and mounted his horse, and like a mighty wave on the ocean the army stood and marched toward Saxony.

Pippin the Short had left a legacy of power and domination to his ambitious son. Pippin hadn't been satisfied co-ruling with his own brother, and in 751, with support of Pope Zachary, had his brother arrested and imprisoned. Pippin began to consolidate and expand his kingdom from as far south as the Umayyad Caliphate, to the north toward the shores of Denmark. Throughout his life Pippin could not totally subdue the Saxon people, and after he died Charlemagne continued his father's vision to expand his rule. Like his father Charlemagne had to deal with the treachery of sibling rivalry.

King Charlemagne was shrewd and knew that the conquest north was heavily resisted. He took advantage of tribal divisions among the people of the north, and sent emissaries to forge alliances with the kings of the Swedes. He felt that by cutting off any help from the fierce Norsemen he would have an easier time bringing the Saxon people into submission. However, Charlemagne had not intended to march north. He was engaged in a conflict in Italy when he received the message that the Saxons had attacked and burned churches in Deventer. Immediately he had sent word for his armies to gather for war.

Now, mounted on his horse, he turned to those closest to him, and in kingly fashion raised his voice and said, "God has ordained the kingdom of the Franks, guardians of all that is holy, to bring the gospel of the Christ to the pagan nations of the world. We are engaged in a battle that is far more dangerous than the wars of men; we are engaged in a conflict for men's souls. Word has reached my ears that our churches in Deventer have been burned, that our priests have been killed, and our treasures have been looted. To stand by and let heathens ransack God's house is to participate in that most unholy act. Today we ride, to bring the battle to the enemy, not just to restore God's possessions, but for the salvation of their souls and ours." Lifting his sword in his hand he ran through the ranks as they parted. Banging their shields, the soldiers yelled, raising a cacophony that would awaken the dead.

One week later found Charlemagne's army not at Deventer's gates, but southeast of the city, on the outskirts of Paderborn, at Eresbury. The King had the bishop brought to his tent. "Tell me," the King began. "What is happening in this region? I hear reports that the people are reverting back to their pagan ways?"

"It is true, my lord. My priests and I barricaded ourselves in the Abbey for fear of our lives. What began in the north has spread south, and I fear a revolt is imminent." He was visibly relieved to be in the presence of the king. Charlemagne had founded Paderborn and the priest knew he would not allow it to fall into pagan hands.

"My lieutenant says that the pagans in Deventer have erected a symbol to their false god, Odin." He looked at one of his men. "What is it called, an *Irminsul*?" Charlemagne had pronounced the word fairly well. Over the years he had made it his habit to learn the languages of his subjects. He was often heard to say, "To have another language is to possess a second soul." Though he had never learned to read or write, his ear for languages was unique.

He stood and walked out of his tent. Motioning to one of the men he said, "Lieutenant, gather an ensign and four knights. We will ride into Deventer and have a look at the situation."

Charlemagne and his squad approached the city from the west where a bridge crossed the River Pader. They slowed their pace as they crossed, keeping a close eye on the horizon, not wanting to get caught off guard. But they didn't meet any resistance. Seeing their approach, the residents hid themselves to avoid a conflict, but what they left standing in the city center was enough to set the King's blood to boil. He dismounted and walked around the structure, his breathing becoming labored with anger. The monument wasn't beautiful—it was artless, straight, but with a simple strength and power. He nodded to the sergeant. "Go round up the pagan priest who commissioned this atrocity." The sergeant and one of the knights rode off to find the town's mayor; he could tell them what they wanted to know. Looking at the ensign, he said, "What do you think they do with this thing?" He didn't expect an answer.

It took an hour before the sergeant returned with the priest. He was clearly frightened from the stories he had heard about King Charlemagne's cruelty. He fell to his knees. "My lord, please, how can I help you? I am a simple merchant."

The King walked around him evaluating the man's stature. "A simple merchant who has built quite a monument. Who is it to?"

"It doesn't mean anything; it is just a pole."

"Yes, a pole, but a pole for whom?" The King was tiring of this game. "Tell me what I want to know or I will burn this city to the ground, starting with your home."

"Please, my lord, it is just a pole like those our forefathers erected to the god Odin, nothing more." He kept his head bowed, hoping for leniency.

"Isn't Odin your god of war? If you have a pole dedicated to him, maybe you hope that he will deliver you from my hand." He waved his sergeant to find the pagan believers. "As we speak your followers are being summoned." By the time the King finished speaking his soldiers had gathered twenty men and woman who were identified as pagans. They were made to sit in a circle around the pole. "Your brothers have desecrated the churches of God, they have sacked and mutilated God's anointed priests, and now you have chosen to turn from the path of truth and follow the lies of Satan. I want to give you a chance to turn from your wickedness. Come and

kiss the cross in my hand and you will live, refuse and you will die."
As a couple of women began to cry he added, "Look, do you want
your children to go motherless or fatherless? I don't do this to cause
you harm but to save your souls. Come kiss the cross."

Slowly four women and two men came and kissed the cross.
They were escorted away from the city center so they did not have to
watch what came next. Two knights took axes and chopped the
Irminsul to the ground as the fourteen remaining unrepentant
heathens watched in horror. They thought that surely Odin would
throw thunderbolts down and destroy the city, but when that didn't
happen all they could do was weep. After the pagan monument fell to
the ground, the recalcitrant men were beheaded and their lifeless
corpses staked outside the city for all to see.

As with any forced conversion, not all the former pagans were
sincere. Before Charlemagne had time to muster his troops, two men
left the city heading north to warn their brothers. They were able to
move more quickly than the large company of soldiers, who wouldn't
break camp until the next day. They arrived ahead of the army by
three days, hoping it would be enough.

The people heard of Charlemagne's march and abandoned their
towns for the nearby hills. Only Bjorn, the city's chieftain, and his
most loyal warriors stayed. He was a competent leader; his name
meant bear, and he fought with the same ferocious nature as his
namesake. When he heard that the King of the Franks had desecrated
the *Irminsul* he was angered and dispatched a rider to inform Sigfred,
King of Denmark. Sigfred saw this as an opportunity from the gods.
He sent messengers to the far north, calling the kings to abandon
their differences and fight as one against the incursion of the Franks.
Bjorn knew the King's call to arms couldn't come soon enough, so
after gathering his warriors, he set out to face his enemy.

Charlemagne wasn't a fool and decided not to attack Bjorn's forces head to head. Instead he divided his army into five divisions. Each division was assigned a specific region and instructed to ambush the enemy and take as many noblemen as they could prisoner. As they maneuvered north they would converge again at Deventer in triumph.

Bjorn and his men were competent adversaries. They swung sword and ax with skill and cunning, but they were no match for the well-trained and experienced soldiers under Charlemagne's command. When the King's forces broke through the tree line, the quick onslaught of cavalry scattered Bjorn's men. In the panic they were easily defeated, their metal blades falling silent with each last breath. When the final pagan was released from his life a victory clamor rose that was heard for miles and set any remaining warrior to flight.

After a month of fighting Charlemagne's army assembled again at the town of Deventer. Charlemagne called his soldiers together and brought his horse to a stop at the front of a burned out church. He stood in his saddle and lifted his sword in triumph; the cheers of 10,000 men filled the air. "It is the grace of our God in Christ that has saved us from our enemy. They dared to mock God and the Church by setting this place of worship to flames. Yet, today we stand victorious because God has gone before us. We will bring his glory to the pagans of the north, and the gates of hell will not prevail." As Charlemagne rode among his men, each soldier beat his sword against his shield until the noise was so loud no one could even hear his own voice.

Outside the town, Charlemagne had the noble prisoners gathered near the river. They were divided into groups of fifty, and a lieutenant and a priest were assigned to each group. They were offered the opportunity to repent, believe in the gospel, and be baptized, or they would be freed from this life to face their fate in the next. That day 5,000 noble pagans died.

Two weeks later a horn blew in Birka calling all capable men to war. Magnus kissed his wife and hugged his son goodbye; he turned to join the gathering storm.

Coming Storm
774 AD

Charlemagne had forged a truce with the kingdoms of the north; they promised not to interfere with his campaigns against the Danes. This was helpful to the northern kingdoms, which often fought the Danes and each other, moving borderlines back and forth during the summer months of war. They knew the Frankish king's intent to expand his borders and march against the Danish king, but as long as the fighting stayed along the southern shores they were satisfied to leave well enough alone.

"My lord," the commander began, bowing before Charlemagne. He handed the King a message from the Pope, Leo III. The Dukes of Fiuli and Spoleto were rising up against the king and threatening the church's authority. Charlemagne's assistance was requested immediately.

"Assemble my bodyguard and the first battalion. Have them ready to march by morning. We head for Italy." He called an attaché to his side and dictated this letter,

> *To the most Holy Father in Rome,*
> *Peace and grace be with you. I have received your request and want*
> *you to know that I make haste to come to your assistance. I have*
> *sent word for my southern forces to march toward the north of*
> *Italy. They are to hold the border until I arrive. Do not fear, Your*

277

Eminence: we will deal harshly with the treachery of Hrodgaud and Hildebrand.

After dictating a second letter to his commanders to the south and affixing the royal seal, he dispatched them right away. The rest of the evening was spent with the leaders of his northern army, instructing them on how they were to maintain order with the capture of the Danish lands. His sleep that evening was restless, his dreams filled with war and conquest.

Charlemagne's soldiers were ready to ride by first light. He ordered the rest of his army to maintain their position and reinforce their fortress. He didn't want to lose ground after fighting so hard to subdue the Saxons. But he was not aware of the effect of cutting down the *Irminsul* pillar. The structure played a central role in Saxon paganism and the beliefs of the people of the north, and though many in Sweden and Norway knew little of its practices, it became the rallying cry of the Danes. Within two weeks word had spread throughout the region of the Christian King's disdain for the gods of the north. It was a humiliation that needed to be rectified. Without a central king, and the constant fighting among themselves, the Scandinavian people were reluctant to join together against Charlemagne. They may have been ready to fight, but assent and organization came from the local Thing outward.

Sigurd stood silent as the men of Birka entered the hall. When the last man stepped over the threshold and the door closed, he pounded his staff on the raised wooden platform. "Men of Birka, you have been summoned for an important matter, one that affects us all. Give attention to the Earl as he explains the outrage." *Outrage? What outrage?* His words caught everyone's attention.

"Yesterday evening this man entered my home with an important message." All eyes turned to a tall, thin Saxon. "He has brought news from his home country and their war with the Franks." Those present stirred and murmured. They knew of the war, but paid it no mind. What was it to them that Saxons could not hold off an invading army? The *lovsigemann* stamped his staff. "They have come asking the assistance of the people of the north in their struggle."

"Why would we spill our blood for theirs?" a man in the back yelled out.

"Have they not tried to subjugate us as well?" another asked.

"I, too, was skeptical when he came," the Earl continued. "The messenger explained that King Charlemagne cut down the *Irminsul* tree in Deventer, and that he mocked our god Odin as inferior to his own." Again the men spoke among themselves. Some were angry at the atrocity, but others saw it as inconsequential.

Magnus stood up to speak. He was respected among his peers and held in high regard by the Earl. His words carried a lot of weight. "Do you not have any pride? Should we stand by while our sacred places are desecrated? If this king believes that he is greater than our father Odin, will he not cross the waters and attack the homes of the Swedes as well? Do we fear the sword of the Christian army, or are we confident that our battle-spilt blood ushers us into the halls of Valhalla?" With every question the crowd's response grew in its affirmation. "Then let us put our honor to the test, as well as our lives. Let us join our brothers in battle and bring glory to our houses!" It took Sigurd five minutes to quiet everyone.

"Order, order. Listen to your Earl," he finally said.

Torstein stood and stepped off the raised platform. He put his hand on Magnus' shoulder and addressed the crowd. "Magnus, you have spoken well. Our hearts are one; our anger is one; our swords are one; and our might is one." He drew his sword, lifting it toward the sky, and said,

> *Lo, there do I see my Father, and*
> *Lo, there do I see my Mother, and*
> *Lo, there do I see my Brothers and my Sisters and*
> *Lo, there do I see my people back to the beginning, and*
> *Lo they do call to me, and bid me take my place*
> *Among them in the halls of Valhalla,*
> *Where the brave will live forever.*

As he chanted the words each warrior mirrored them with his own lips until the whole assembly was of one voice. They were ready to set sail at that very moment, but their enthusiasm was tempered when they were told that their fight would have to wait. "I am to bring representatives from our clan to the Uppsala Thing. We will be meeting in a fortnight at the Temple in Uppsala, where clans from all over will give assent to the gathering. Along with Sigurd and myself I would like to take Magnus and Trygve. What say you?" Everyone vigorously agreed.

As an adult in the community, Arne was in attendance; standing close to his father he beamed with pride. He hoped that he would get to accompany him to the Thing of all Swedes in Gama Uppsala. He decided he would ask his father on the way home. Going home, however, wasn't on anyone's mind. Ale was brought and the company of warriors spent the evening drinking, singing, and retelling the heroic deeds of their respective families. It was late when Magnus stumbled out of the hall. Arne, who didn't enjoy ale, helped him make his way down the path toward their farm.

"Father?" Unsure if now, while his father was drunk, would be a good time to ask; Arne didn't know how to proceed. He decided the situation might prompt a more positive response. "Can I go with you to the Uppsala Thing?" Magnus didn't respond. "Father, can I attend the Uppsala Thing with you?"

Standing straight and looking into his son's eyes, Magnus slurred, "I would love for you to come with me." He tripped and almost fell to the ground. That was the answer he wanted, but Arne wasn't sure his father would remember in the morning. However, he had said yes—Arne might be able to leverage his words as if they were a definite promise. He would see.

All Sigrunn could do was shake her head and put her husband to bed, but she and Arne stayed up talking. "So they have decided to go to war?" she asked.

"Yes, mother. Father gave a great speech and everyone voted unanimously to go and fight."

"Death in battle is a glorious thing, my son, but don't be too quick to seek it." She sat quiet, lost in her thoughts, and Arne put his hand on hers.

"It will be alright mother. With Odin's lightning and Thor's hammer we will prevail."

They sat in silence for a moment. "I don't doubt you will prevail." She looked tenderly into his eyes. "But death comes in every battle, and I am steeling my heart to the loss of either one of you."

Arne had not considered his own death and he shuddered. Sigrunn gave her son a kiss and sent him off to bed, where his dreams turned to nightmares and the smoke of Valhalla filled the skies as the Valkyries carried off the glorious dead.

Two days later as morning broke, Arne followed his father out the door. "Don't you have chores to do?" Magnus asked.

"Mother is taking care of them so I can come with you." Magnus stopped and looked at his son; his puzzled look questioning the statement. "The other night at the Thing you said I could go with you to Uppsala. You gave me your word."

"My word, did I?" Magnus squinted his eyes. Arne was not given to lying, so he must have sworn his word while drunk. "Well, boy, my word is my word." He ruffled Arne's hair and they picked up their pace toward town. By the time they reached the dock the boat was ready to set sail. Gamla Uppsala was the religious center of the Swedes, and it wouldn't take them too long to travel the hundred or so miles through the sounds and rivers. It was there that the clans of the Vikings would gather to declare their intentions toward King Charlemagne.

"I thought we would have to leave without you," Torstein chided.

"Typical," Trygve muttered.

"What was that, my friend?" Magnus stood in front of him.

Torstein stepped between them to get on the boat. "Leave your animosity in Birka. We have more important matters ahead of us." Arne grabbed his father's arm, pulling him in the direction of the boat and away from Trygve. He didn't like Eirik anymore than his father liked Trygve, but Arne was caught up in the excitement of going to Gama Uppsala. He had never left Birka before, and traveling beyond the horizon was the longing of most Vikings.

Trygve chafed at Magnus bringing his son. Bitterness and resentment colored his heart toward the Earl's favorite citizen, and though he obediently hid his feelings, they were still there, seething until the moment he would exact revenge for his humiliation. For now he would be the stalwart warrior, representing his city and clan in what was to be an honorable battle.

Arne settled in as the oarsmen set their hands to their task. Through most of the sounds, and especially up all the rivers, the sails would be tied and the strength of men would carry the ship over the waters. Magnus sat next to his son, and amid the cadence of the oars slapping against the water he spoke to him. "Son, the Thing of all Swedes is no ordinary Thing. It is usually held only once a year, and all freemen come and participate. It is here that our vow of allegiance to the King is renewed."

"I thought we had no king. Are we not free men?" Arne asked.

"That we are, and we are not ruled like the Franks. Our king has power only by our word. We give him authority to make laws and fight wars. If he is not honorable and just, we can depose him."

"What is the purpose of a king if he only does what the people say?" Arne asked.

"Men need leaders, free or not. They judge between matters just like the Earl. He is not a king, but he leads our people and establishes order in Birka. The King does the same thing, but for all in his realm."

Arne thought for a moment and then asked, "If the Thing of the Swedes is for all men, then why aren't all the freemen joining us?"

"You have a keen mind, my son. Four days after we arrive in Gama Uppsala, men from every corner of our country will arrive. They will participate in the discussions the King lays out before us."

"Then why do we go before them?" Arne asked.

"There are too many warriors for all to stand before the King. We go as representatives. We will hear what the King has to say, and then present it to our clan when they come for the great assembly. They will give a yea or nay to the declaration of war and we will bring it back to the King. If the majority is in favor the King will give us further direction."

The rest of the trip was uneventful; the weather was clear and cold, but the warm early March sun took the nip out of the air.

When they finally reached the end of the waterway, they disembarked next to other ships from all over the country. Arne's eyes were wide trying to take in the differences in ship design, shield colors, and the array of dress. These were the ferocious Vikings who were known as the scourge of the earth.

The city of Gama was not next to the sea. It lay a few miles inland, so the men had to carry their tents and provisions on their backs. Arne couldn't have imagined anything like this great city. As they entered from the south, they saw a hill on which stood the great Temple of Uppsala. It was adorned with gold and behind it rose three mounds.

"Father, are those burial mounds?"

"Thor, Odin, and Freyr lie in the *Kungshogama*. They protect the city and the Kings. When a great king dies in battle his remains are placed in one of the mounds, a tribute to his just and honorable rule." He pointed to the Temple. "In the Temple stand statues of the three gods. Thor stands in the center of the chamber because he governs the thunder and lightning, the winds and rains, and the fair weather and crops. Odin and Freyr stand on either side. "

"Will we go into the temple?" Arne was hopeful.

"It will depend on the Thing and the festivities. If we have time we will go in and make an offering." Stopping and looking down at his son, he continued, "It is for Odin that we are here. He is our champion in war and we will want his good pleasure above all." Magnus shuddered as he remembered the Wild Hunt and the terrifying presence of Odin and his hounds. His fate was not his own, and he hoped that whatever came his death would be with honor.

While most of the city was preparing for the upcoming festivities, the representatives gathered at the central Hall. It was a large and spacious building. The double doors leading into it were huge, and opened to reveal a raised platform at the end of its length, where the King would sit to preside over the assembly. The hall in Birka seemed minuscule in comparison. As Magnus and Arne walked in, they were absorbed into the collective of Viking Norsemen vying for a spot close to the front. No one noticed the *Lovsigemann* of Gama rise, standing quiet before the assembly. He stomped his staff on the floor until all present fell silent.

"Give your attention to King Olaf, Ruler of Sweden, Lord of the Vikings, dispenser of justice, feared by his enemies." The *Lovsigemann* nodded toward the King and stepped back.

Rising to his feet, Olaf stood high above the men of the north and addressed them. "This is the feast *Disting*, the Thing of the Swedes. It is a time of rejoicing for the blessing the gods have bestowed upon us. Yet, this year, it is a time of great grief. We as a people are faced with a decision. The King of the Franks, Charlemagne, has desecrated our sacred shrine in Deventer. He has cut down the *Irminsul* pillar and killed 5,000 of our kinsmen. By the hammer of Thor we will not let this go unavenged! What say you?"

To a man they raised their swords, axes, and voices to the call of the King. Olaf stepped down from the platform and mingled with his brothers, encouraging them in their quest and solidifying their fealty. Their campaign would not be a direct assault, but ships would sail along the enemy's coasts pillaging Charlemagne's lands of their wealth, cutting off his peoples' desire of conquest, restoring the heritage of their people, and reclaiming the honor of the gods.

Olaf had come up behind the Earl and greeted him. "Torstein, who are these two stalwart warriors with you?"

"This is Magnus and his son Arne."

"Glad to meet you, and I look forward to going into battle with you." He lifted his cup of ale and walked off. It was his custom to meet the representatives personally—the force of his personality was what drew men to his side. He was a distinguished warrior and cunning statesmen. Magnus felt proud to be associated with him, and Arne just stood there, eyes wide and mouth gaping.

After he left Arne exclaimed, "That was the King!"

Magnus smacked him playfully on the back of the head and they spent the rest of the evening feasting and drinking with their brothers, looking forward to the coming months.

Gamla Uppsala
774 AD

Sigrunn decided not to make the trip to Uppsala. The baby was due soon and she didn't want to risk delivering so far from home. She disliked being by herself, so her sister stopped by on occasion to see if she needed any help. She was glad of the company. Freydis had been a topic of conversation for some time after her husband, Olaf, had made known his baptism as a Christian. He was an able-bodied man and a good provider, but his new faith conflicted with the beliefs of their people and was a cause of frustration and arguments.

"Freydis," Sigrunn began to ask, "How are you and Olaf getting along? Is he still trying to convince you to be baptized Christian?"

"We don't talk about it much, because I don't want to hear about it and he gets upset." She was kneading dough to make some bread. "He wouldn't let me go to the Thing of the Swedes. I had looked forward to going and petitioning the gods for a son, but he didn't want any of that. He said if his God wanted us to have sons then he would grant them to us."

Sigrunn put her arms around Freydis and encouraged her. "I am sure he will abandon this new way. Loki must be playing mischief with his heart. Olaf is with Magnus and the others; during this time he will feel the presence of the gods and come to his senses." It wasn't that the Vikings were intolerant of this new faith, but they couldn't abide abandoning the gods of their fathers. They believed only a corrupt heart turned from Odin, who had provided for and protected them all these years. It would be difficult for Freydis if Olaf were too outspoken. "Do you love him?"

"You are thinking I should leave him. He has been good to me, and"—she paused as a tear rolled down her cheek—"I do love him. Olaf has never raised a hand to me, nor caused our children any harm. If it were not for this Jesus I would stand proudly next to him in the assembly. Instead I carry his shame, but no, I won't leave him."

"You are my sister and all I want for you is happiness." Sigrunn put her hand on her abdomen. "The baby just kicked."

Freydis smiled as she felt the baby's movement.

"I think he will be coming soon."

"Are you sure it's a boy? Maybe Freya will give you a girl."

"A girl would be nice, but I know Magnus would like a boy. He has already picked a name, but don't ask; it would be bad luck. I just hope he makes it back before the birth." The rest of the day the women baked, slopped hogs, fed chickens, and chopped wood. By the time her sister left Sigrunn was exhausted and ready to lie down for a good night's sleep.

Christians had made their way to the north and established churches in a number of towns. Their missionary activity had been slow, but its fruit became apparent as small numbers of Vikings and their families were baptized into the Christian faith. But all that was going to change; this wave of hostility focused on anything associated with the King of the Franks.

The festive nature of the Thing was curtailed because of the topic of war. Though revelry was second nature to Vikings, they were an introspective people and made their way to the temple. Magnus was ready to go home, but he would not leave without seeking guidance and hope in his offering to Odin. The wild hunt had left a displeasing taste in his mouth, and the fear that this battle would be his last loomed over him.

"Father," Arne said as they stood in front of the three statues, "have you ever seen the gods?"

"Few have ever seen them, and those who have speak little of it. They come in storms and dreams, and they speak in riddles. We offer them tokens in hope that they will honor and protect our life and death."

"I hope to see them one day." Arne stood mesmerized as his father set his offering before his god. On the way they dropped some coins into the priest's basin, a gesture to remind him of an offered prayer.

"You may someday, but tomorrow we head back home. We have little time left to prepare for war, and I don't want to leave you, your mother, and the baby without provisions."

The enthusiasm for battle was intoxicating, and the wave of animosity toward Charlemagne and the Christian religion was having repercussions across all of Scandinavia. After the Thing of the Swedes warriors went home and burnt churches and threatened death to those who did not recant their faith in the god, Jesus. Those who would not were either killed or chased from their homes. It was a difficult time as families were cut off from their communities and forced to leave in humiliation.

News of the cleansing spread quickly and Magnus feared for his brother-in-law. Olaf had been baptized on a trading mission to the south. Impressed with the cathedrals that expressed the majesty of the Christian god, plus the wealth and power that the church displayed, he had come to believe that Jesus was greater than Odin. Olaf accepted the power of a god who could rescue people from their own sin, but he had been isolated from other Christians, and what he understood about his faith was rudimentary. All he knew was that he was different.

Magnus approached Olaf's home and called out to the family. No one answered. Olaf must be out in his field, but where were his children and his wife? Magnus feared that he was too late, and others in the village had already come and done their mischief. He was startled when Freydis opened the barn door, hitting him in the back.

"I'm sorry," she said, "I didn't see you there. Are you looking for Olaf?"

"Yes, when will he be back?" Magnus was looking around.

"Soon. It is about time for the noon meal. If you want to wait under the shade tree, I will get you something to drink." Freydis was always polite and hospitable to Magnus. The couple had three boys, all of age to work with their father as men. They were probably helping him plow.

"Magnus." Olaf's voice was deep and booming. "What brings you here in the middle of the day?" The boys were with him, but they were more interested in food and drink than their uncle.

"I just thought I would stop by and see how my old friend is doing." He wasn't sure how to broach the subject. He never understood why Olaf was so adamant about renouncing the gods and being Christian, but he was his friend as well as his brother-in-law. He took another sip from the mug Freydis had brought him. "What do you think of the pronouncement at the Thing?"

He had lived with the tension for a long time, and felt that his family and friends in Birka would accept him and forgo any conflict. "I am not worried. What happened in Deventer is unfortunate, but that has nothing to do with me."

"Don't be a fool, Olaf. The battle lust blinds people. Reason and tolerance blow away in the wind. If you are not careful it will come to Birka, and you are the sole Christian. Your family could become the target of the blood lust."

"What am I to do, leave? This is my home; my family and friends live here. I have known these people all my life; why would they turn on me?

"Because they believe you have turned on them by denouncing the gods."

"And what of you, Magnus, do you think I am a traitor?"

Magnus was hesitant to say, but he couldn't avoid it any longer. "I think you are foolish to tempt the gods' favor by rejecting them. You have avoided mischief because you are well respected and your family has a long tradition of loyalty to the Earl, but times have changed. What happened in Deventer was an affront to the gods and the tides are rising toward war. You and all who claim to be Christians will be washed away in its current." He stood and set his cup down on a stump next to them. "I am here to warn you that you are no longer safe. If you do not renounce your beliefs or leave, I cannot protect you."

Olaf stood and replied, "I appreciate your candor, my friend. I will not leave my land; it is my home. I was born here and here I will die." Magnus understood. A Viking didn't shrink from battle, and didn't run from his enemies, let alone his friends. Magnus would not participate in what was sure to come. He would spend the next week preparing his family for his departure, making sure they had enough while he was away. Much still needed to be done, so he excused himself and left.

Friend's Death
774 AD

"No!" Magnus was adamant.

"Why not? I am a man, and I have a right to defend my country." Arne was ready to pick up an ax and follow his father into battle.

"There will be time enough to test your courage in battle. But I need you here to tend the farm. With the baby coming your mother will need someone to be in charge and provide for the family." Magnus was trying to sharpen his sword and ax.

"Her sister can help her—" Arne was cut off with a stern glance.

"It is settled. Any more talk and I will treat you like the man you want to be and knock you on your butt, and you will see how ready for battle you are." He abruptly stopped speaking. Above the trees over Arne's shoulder smoke rose in the air. It was coming from Olaf's farm, and Magnus knew the deed was done; his friend was lost. "Arne," Magnus spoke more gently, "go get your mother." Arne saw the smoke as well and quickly did as he was told.

When they broke through the tree line nothing was left but a pile of ash. "I don't see any bodies," Sigrunn hoped. "Surely they would have escaped."

Arne went to where the barn had stood and kicked through the ash and wood. He could see under the debris the lifeless bodies of his kin. When Sigrunn stepped to his side she buried her face into his shoulder and wept. They had known this could happen, and no amount of protest to the Earl would have stopped the carnage.

"What are you doing?" Arne asked. His father had found a shovel under some of the rubble.

"I am going to bury them like Olaf would have wanted. However false his beliefs they were his, and we will honor them one last time." In silence Arne began digging the hole as Magnus and Sigrunn carefully gathered the remains. It took most of the afternoon and dusk was settling in as they finished. Standing back, tired and dirty, Magnus put his arm around his son and said, "I don't know what is to come; our fates lay in the fickle nature of the gods. I need you to stay here for my sake." No other words were needed between father and son.

The whole town of Birka came to see their warriors load and board the ships. These four ships were to meet up with five others sailing south. The decision had been made not to confront Charlemagne's forces head on, but to strike at his smaller forces along the coast, pillaging what they could and demoralizing the peoples' resolve. Nothing was more ferocious than a Viking raiding party and nothing more terrifying than a warrior bent on entering Valhalla. Once the oarsmen were set, they began the monotonous rhythm that would carry them to the winds that would blow them to the distant shore, and war.

By the seventh day the crews were eager to set aground at the mouth of the bay that led to Lubeck. A tiny fishing village lay at its entrance and the small fleet weighed anchor and went ashore to gather information about Frankish troops in the area. The villagers were used to seeing ships enter the bay and head up river, but seldom did they come to port. Cautiously they watched five shiploads of

Viking warriors disembark. The chieftain stood on the beach with three large men at his side.

"Welcome to our village. How can we serve you today?"

Rolf was King Olaf's representative to this fleet of ships. "We are answering the call of our brothers from Deventer who have been subjugated by the King of the Franks. We know that there is a camp in Lubeck; we were hoping that you might tell us how many soldiers are there."

"We don't venture that far south, but we've had word that only a few men are hiding in a small fortress. Their central camp is in Hamburg. But you can reach it only by sea, unless you want to walk through the forest."

"We will go where necessary," Rolf growled. "As for now, my men need a place to eat and sleep. We will require provisions." The chieftain understood perfectly that it wasn't a request, and faced with an armed armada he had best comply. Rolf instructed the captain of each vessel to maintain order among his men. They were to treat the villagers as brothers and only take what they needed to consume. Magnus was placed in charge of setting up sentries even though their presence was unlikely to be noticed by the Franks. He couldn't be too careful.

You Worry Too Much
774 AD

The evening was uneventful and they set sail by morning light. The trip upriver took only a few hours and by the time the noon meal arrived they were unloading their weapons and preparing for an assault. Nine men were sent ahead to scout the fort's defenses, and when they returned an obvious confidence colored their tone.

"It is a small fort, and the wall can't be more than ten feet high. I am sure we can lure them out easily."

"Were you able to see how many men were on the wall?" Rolf wanted a full report.

"No more than three patrolled each side. They were scrawny and we could dispatch them each with an easy blow." Rolf ignored their bravado. It was good for bolstering confidence, but it was useless when preparing a strategy. He would lean on his experienced warriors for a better solution.

Magnus stood ready to fight, but he had been a trader most of his life, and though there were times that his sword was needed he was better at negotiations. He would leave the strategy to others.

The decision was made to send fifteen men to stand outside the gate to test the fort's strength.

"We wish to speak to your leader," Rolf called out.

"Who should I say requests an audience?" was the reply.

"I am Rolf, representative of the King of the Swedes. I wish to establish trade with this region." The Frankish commander wasn't a fool. The gate opened just enough to allow four men to step through. They were dressed in the metal armor of the Frankish army, and as they strode out archers on the wall held their bows at the ready.

"My name is Benoit. I am the second in command of this regiment. My commander has sent me to greet you and invite you to be our guests. However, you will need to leave your weapons outside the camp."

Rolf just smiled. What he had hoped for was about to come true. Every eye on the wall was watching him. As soon as he raised his sword a group of his men attacked the fort from the opposite side, which drew the archers' attention just enough for the Vikings to rush the gate. As they did more warriors broke from the tree line and engaged the Frankish soldiers, pushing them back into the fort and slaughtering everyone in sight. The battle took less than thirty minutes, and it was brutal. In the end fifty-five Franks lay dead. Three of Rolf's men had been struck down, but only one fatally. When the last Frank dropped to the ground a roaring cheer rang throughout the fort.

"Today we have won a great victory for Odin, and the power of Thor's hammer has struck a mighty blow against our enemies." Again cheers rang out. "But our quest is not over. We will send the plunder back with ten men, and the rest will push toward Hamburg and strike at the heart of the beast." Blinded by blood lust every man held his weapon high and cheered to the glory of Odin and the King. "Hang the bodies from the walls of their fort, and tonight we will feast and rest. Tomorrow we will march on!"

That evening, after most of the men were sleeping, Magnus approached Rolf. "I do not want to overstep my boundaries, but may I have a word with you?"

"Come, sit with me. We are brothers and there is no need for formalities. What is on your mind?"

"We have won a great victory, but I am concerned about trudging through the forest to Hamburg. We are supposed to stay on the coastline. Wouldn't it be more prudent to sail around and approach the Franks from the water?"

"You worry too much Magnus." Rolf offered him a cup of ale. "Drink with me. The journey can't be more than a couple of days. We will have the element of surprise. Besides, our brothers have sailed around the land of the Danes. By the time we get there we will be able to offer an attack from the opposite side. We have proved today that Odin has granted us favor. He will not withdraw now that we have obtained a glorious victory."

Hamburg
774 AD

Sleep escaped Magnus. He did not like leaving the ships and trudging across land, and when the next day came and the hung over warriors loaded up their provisions he hoped that they would return to this place, as Rolf believed. The road between Liubice and Hamburg was little more than an oxcart path. Their forces walked single file most of the day, which meant that they were open to attack and could easily be picked off by archers in the forest. These men were not just seafarers, however, they were hunters, and they were just as much at home in the dark forest as on the sea. Yet, Rolf had misjudged the distance and by the second day his forces were beginning to grumble. On the third a few of them became sick.

This is not good, Magnus thought. He turned to Hakon, one of Rolf's closest friends. "This sickness is going to run through the ranks if we don't find fresh water soon." Hakon was not one to complain, but he too was becoming disillusioned with this trip, and on the fifth day, after burying one of their men, he spoke to Rolf.

"You said two or three days, and now it has been five. Maybe we should turn back."

"I know it looks bleak, but we have fewer days ahead than behind. If we turn back now it will have been for nothing. No, we will be there soon." His own doubts were crowding out reason. "You are not afraid of death, are you Hakon?"

298

"No glory lies in dying of sickness. I would rather enter Valhalla as a warrior than as a decaying corpse." They were interrupted by one of their advance scouts. He had ridden ahead on one of the captured horses to see how much further they had to march, and the news was good.

Gathering his warriors together, Rolf said, "I have just received news that we are a day and a half from Hamburg, and that our brothers who parted with us at Liubice have arrived. Word was sent to them of our trek across land. They are encouraged to have our support and will await our arrival. I know the journey has been difficult and longer than expected, but the prize is just ahead." The news came at the right time and even Magnus' spirits were lifted. Maybe the omen of the Wild Hunt had passed.

There was no revelry that night. Men sat around low-burning fires, warding off the night's chill, and remembering their dead friends, both present and past. They knew that the next battle would be more difficult than the last, and they steadied their hearts with a song of long-passed heroes.

Fire shall devour and wan flames feed on the fearless warrior
Who oft stood stout in the iron-shower,
When, sped from the string, a storm of arrows
Shot o'er the shield-wall: the shaft held firm,
Featly feathered, followed the barb.
Then about that barrow the battle-keen rode,
Atheling-born, a band of twelve,
Lament to make, to mourn their king,
Chant their dirge, and their chieftain honor.
They praised his earlship, his acts of prowess
Worthily witnessed: and well it is
That men their master-friend mightily laud,

Heartily love, when hence he goes
From life in the body forlorn away.

The Franks' fort at Hamburg was larger than that at Liubice, but its basic construction was the same. When Rolf's forces came through the forest at the north end of the city, they were surprised that little notice was given to their approach. Charlemagne's forces, under the command of Ogier the Dane, seemed overconfident in their fortress. Rolf ordered his men to make camp and keep a low profile, and then Hakon, Magnus, and he traveled the road along the river to where their brothers had been waiting.

The King, Olaf, came out of his tent as they rode up, "I am glad to see you Rolf, though I must say it is unexpected. You were to stay in the area of Liubice, but I see you had other plans."

Rolf nodded his head in deference to Olaf and replied, "I hope my lord is more pleased than surprised. Looking at the Franks' position I believe it is most useful that we are here."

"So it is. Come, we are making plans for our assault." Magnus and Hakon remained outside until Rolf was finished. When he came out of the tent he simply motioned for the two to mount, and they quickly returned to their camp.

Once there, Rolf assembled the leaders and explained King Olaf's plan. It wasn't much different than the one they had used in Liubice, just on a larger scale. They would be the ones to attack from behind when everyone's attention was focused on the larger forces to the west.

That evening each warrior prepared his weapons and his soul for the upcoming battle. Magnus wanted to make sure that he had everything in order. He prayed for protection, but mostly for honor and that if he were to die his soul would be taken to Valhalla.

When morning broke so did the camp. The warriors positioned themselves behind the fort, barely within the tree line, and waited for the battle to begin. King Olaf led his forces to the front of the fort just out of the archers' range. When he had established his position, the gates of the fort opened and the Frank cavalry galloped out, lining up their impressive force before the oncoming Vikings. After much yelling and shield slapping, Olaf advanced his men, forming a shield wall that would protect them against the archers. When they were sufficiently close, the Frank cavalry charged.

Hearing the noise, Rolf and his men broke the tree line and advanced on the wall. They were surprised when archers appeared and rained arrows down on them. Several men fell before Rolf shouted for them to form the shield wall. They quickly came into formation with the shields over their heads and shot arrows that hit their intended targets. Slowly they moved forward until they were fifteen feet from the wall, when a gate to the rear opened and soldiers filed out of the fort like ants. The shield wall formation held as the approaching soldiers wielded their swords. Magnus was positioned at the point of the wall and was the first to take a blow. He pushed out and opened the shield wall to pull through a Frank soldier, who was quickly killed. Magnus pushed out again but stumbled, and found himself standing outside the wall, face to face with a soldier. He managed to raise his sword just as the enemy struck.

First Command
774 AD

The Paladin council stood around the table waiting for word of the King. Charlemagne had been south for a long time and they wished he were present. Roland had been left in charge and the council's confidence in him was unshaken, but the Viking infestation was causing alarm and they needed to make a decisive move.

Munderic spoke first. "It is my hope that I have won favor in the eyes of my brothers and that you will listen to what I have to say."

"The table yields to my brother," Roland said, voicing what they had all come to believe. Charlemagne had been right to forgive and trust Munderic, and his addition to the Paladin was indispensable.

"I have lived among the Danes long enough to know that they will utilize the strength of the Norsemen against our most vulnerable cities. But don't be mistaken; while we are off chasing them through the hills they will mount an attack on the closest city that will cause us the greatest defeat. I believe that they will strike hardest at Hamburg."

"But that isn't anywhere near the sea. The Norsemen have kept to the shores and ventured only a few miles inland." Rinaldo had seen firsthand the Vikings' skill in combat.

"Yes, but when they have felt the lust of blood and its taste of victory will embolden them to march inland. Prince Gudfred will encourage them with Valhalla and they will die in a vicious onslaught.

"The citadel at Hamburg is well fortified and its well-trained, armed battalion can defeat any attempt to take it. What we need is someone with a keen mind for strategy." All eyes fell to Ogier.

"My brothers honor me, but I am the least at the table," he said.

"Least only in age. You have fought well and learned with earnest from our King. He is proud of you and you would do him honor to take up this charge." Approval resounded around the table and the council was dismissed.

Ogier was nervous about this assignment. He knew how to lead men into battle, but the council's confidence in him was daunting. He hoped to prove his father's pride was not misplaced. Charlemagne had brought him in as a means to peace, and that peace was ever elusive. But Ogier had always felt like a son. The memory of the King's last words to him would forever reinforce his place in the King's family.

Charlemagne had taken his son aside. "Ogier, I am proud to call you son and glad that God has brought you into my life. You represent what our heavenly Father has done for all who believe. As we are adopted enemies into his family, so are you in mine. Of all my children, none save you exhibit the character that can sustain the kingdom." He took from his tunic a pin in the form of a wolf. "This has always reminded me of my destiny and God's call to continue the dynasty of order begun in the Roman Empire. The wolf is the symbol of her power and might. As I have been called the wolf king, so now you will bear the mantle." Ogier had tried to protest. He could never be king. "Others may wear the crown, but you will carry the burden."

Since that moment the wolf pin had not left his person. He would wear it in peace and war. When morning came Ogier was already astride his horse, and his contingent of men started for Hamburg.

Days later at the Hamburg fortress, Ogier called out, "Open the gate, it is the flag of Ogier, the Dane." The title the Dane was given him initially with derision, but he bore it as a badge of honor. He was proud of his heritage and hoped one day that his people would come to understand the glory of God and the majesty of His king. Until that time he would fight with the grace of his master.

"Where are your commanders?" he shouted to the guard.

"They are in the main hall," came the reply.

Ogier dismounted straight away and left his horse in the hands of a stable boy. When he walked into the hall the tables were filled with food and the commanders were lounging as if no war was upon the horizon. At the sight of Ogier they stood, brushing off stray morsels of food.

Afton stood at the head and approached and greeted the Paladin. "My lord, we were not expecting you so soon."

"That is obvious. Do you not realize that there is a horde of Vikings heading your way?" Ogier looked around the room sizing up his commanders.

"We have scouts in all directions. We will know within two days of their approach. We will be ready for them." Afton was a little nervous. He was a competent soldier and would die in the service of the king; his momentary lapse of discipline was embarrassing.

Ignoring the commander, Ogier walked up to a man at the end of the table. "You, what is your name?"

"Kenton, lord, son of Kingsley."

"Well Kenton, son of Kingsley, tell me the state of your troops."

"What do you mean, sir?"

"I mean are they prepared? How many archers, how many cavalry, how many swordsmen are at the ready? Do you have plenty of guards at the towers and what is your plan for a breach?" It was obvious that Kenton didn't know and that disturbed Ogier.

"I...I don't know, lord," he stammered.

After looking at the other commanders, Ogier spoke to Afton. "Whose fault is it that so many are unprepared?"

Afton hesitated and faced Ogier. "It is mine, lord."

Ogier then addressed the leaders. "If the least of your commanders do not understand the condition of your troops then in the heat of battle all will fail. The enemy is at our door and we must be ready for him." He called for the servants and instructed them to remove the food. "Now, Afton, instruct us on the fitness of your army."

For the next two hours the knight went step by step through each of the three battalions, the cavalry, all the way to the squads. He outlined the strategies of the archers, swordsmen, and wall battlements. By the time he was through Ogier was convinced of the man's competence.

Nodding his head affirmatively, Ogier looked again at Kenton. "Do you see the big picture now?"

"Yes, sir," he responded.

"Do you know what your responsibilities are in the event the walls are breached?"

"To fortify the wall battlements and keep the high ground."

"Good. Rehearse this knowledge until you are dreaming about it." Ogier then looked at Afton. "Good job, commander. I think we will be ready." The exercise was as much about establishing himself as their leader as it was about learning what they knew. A well-disciplined force was stationed at the castle of Hamburg, the commanders just needed to know that Ogier was now in charge. When he left that evening, he felt that he had established himself well. A disciplined force and solid chain of command would be necessary in the days to come.

Significant Casualties
774 AD

"Archers, steady your bows! Make every shot count. It is better to take time to aim than fire aimlessly!" Ogier stood tall among his soldiers; he was proud of their skill and confident in their resolve. The Vikings proved to be more devious than he had anticipated. Their cunning approach and attempt to lure rear defenses away from the wall was admirable, but this wasn't his first battle and he would not leave his rear unguarded.

Kenton proved to be an apt solider and Ogier had recruited him to be his personal assistant. There was always a need for someone to rally the troops and convey important information to other commanders. "Kenton, where do you see a weakness in our enemy?"

From on top of the furthest tower Ogier had a vantage point of much of the battlefield.

"They have no offensive machinery to scale the walls. Their attempts to breach the gates have failed."

"How long can we be sieged before we have to advance beyond the walls or wait for help to arrive?" Ogier asked.

"We prepared enough rations for a month, but lord, if we choose to attack, I believe we have sufficient forces to run them back to the sea," Kenton responded.

"Yes, but at what cost?" Ogier was fierce in battle, but like his master he didn't relish the death of his men. Yet, at the end of the day they would be victorious or vanquished. He pointed off to the distance. "What is that?" Out of the trees four large towers were being rolled before the castle.

"Siege towers, sir. They constructed siege towers." Kenton's eyes went wide with this unexpected turn of events. "What is your command sir?"

"Retrieve Afton," he said softly. It didn't take long for Kenton to find his commander; he had already been on his way. He too had seen the machines and knew that they would have to reinforce the walls.

"I have already sent additional units to strengthen the walls to the west and north. They are closest to the woods and the easiest to advance. But it looks like it will be difficult for the archers to penetrate the tower walls."

"True, but the Vikings will still have to come across through a small opening. If we can bottle it up with the bodies of their dead, then it will render the towers useless. Our greatest challenge is the height of the breach machines. The north wall will be slightly lower and their archers will have direct aim on ours. If they are able to stop our defenses there we will lose the wall." Silence fell as they contemplated this change in affairs.

"Flaming arrows, sir," Kenton offered. "If we light our arrows and pierce the wood it could set the siege works on fire."

"Make it so. Take your best archers to the west and north wall and have them ready." Ogier asked Afton, "How are we doing at the east and south gate?"

"They have attempted to set the gate on fire, to draw us out into the open. It has been unsuccessful and we are able to keep them at bay. At the moment it is a cat and mouse game. Once the siege works are in place I am certain they will mount an attack at all corners."

"Are the reserves in place?" Ogier asked.

"Yes, all we need is to give the signal and they will attack."

A reserve of cavalry had been left a few miles south of the castle. They were well hidden and kept silent for just a time as this. When the Viking army was focused mostly on their siege machines their more exposed forces to the west and south would be vulnerable. Ogier knew that if they could, holding a portion of his cavalry in reserve would be advantageous to squeeze the enemy between the cavalry and the castle.

The towers were almost in place, but one of them was billowing smoke. The archers had placed their arrows perfectly and the flames now enveloped both wood and flesh. The other three towers were a different story. The Vikings had covered their walls with damp skins and the arrows were bouncing off them and burning out on to the ground. Viking archers were able to get an advantage on the northwest corner and Frank soldiers were falling from the walls.

"Afton, go and strengthen the wall." His commander ran from his side. Ogier called for Kenton to go to the southern wall and have

308

an archer send three consecutive arrows into the air. It was the signal that would call for the reserve.

The horses bursting through the tree line surprised the Vikings, and they turned to form a shield wall against the advancing cavalry. But in doing so they exposed their rear and archers on the wall were able to hit their targets.

"Shield circle!" Magnus called, and the Vikings in the different groups spun around to protect both sides. "Protect your back by the wall and dismount the horsemen!" he yelled to his men. The large horses smashed into the Vikings sending them sprawling in all directions. Magnus knew his men would all die if they stayed in the open. "Retreat to the trees! Retreat to the trees!" Without hesitation they obeyed.

On the tallest tower stood Ogier, observing the reserve cavalry and its success. The horsemen did not follow the Vikings into the woods, but took up a defensive position that gave them the most advantage. Ogier was impressed with the strength and resolve of his enemy. Even with death at hand, the Vikings had stood their ground until given the order to retreat, and he knew that retreat was only temporary. The large Viking who gave the orders would not settle for licking his wounds. He would regroup and figure out a different tactic.

The south gate opened and the commander of the cavalry gained entrance. He quickly made his way to Ogier for further instructions. "Sir, we have secured the southern wall for the moment, but we are left exposed if their archers decide to attack."

"Yes, I think what we need is to move your men to the west wall and chase the enemy away from there as well, keep moving around until we thin out their ranks. Then we will open our forces' flood gates and eliminate them once and for all."

The commander relayed the mission to his troops, but they found the task easier said than done. As they swung around they discovered the dislodged Vikings had joined their brothers on the subsequent field of battle. The larger horde made securing the area more arduous. They were killing the Vikings, but they were also sustaining significant casualties. Yet, the cavalry kept advancing until it seemed they had corralled the whole Viking force in the front of the castle. The siege machines were ineffective, and their occupants either fled or died while the machines burned. It was time for Ogier to unleash the wrath of his master.

Young Wolf
774 AD

When the gates opened, the field in front of the castle was littered with the corpses of hundreds of Vikings. The steady cadence of hooves and marching feet reverberated from the ground and the sight and sound alone should have driven their enemy back to their homes. Despite admonitions from his commanders, Ogier chose to ride in the front and lead his men into victory. He was Paladin, a mighty warrior of King Charlemagne, entrusted with the kingdom, and bearer of the sword of retribution. He had faced a hundred men and would face a hundred more.

When the full force of his cavalry and foot soldiers flooded through the gate and filled the field of battle, all the was left to of his enemy was a scant handful approaching through the tree line. A single warrior walked forward carrying a flag of truce, and with Afton and Kenton at his side Ogier approached with caution.

Ogier was an imposing figure sitting tall on his horse. The Viking stood but 5'8" and the battle-weary guards with him were not much bigger. Yet, they were not dispirited and their presence even now was defiant. The two men glared and neither dared to give way.

Ogier chose to speak first. "You have fought well, but are no match for the might of Charlemagne and the glory of my King. If you are ready to negotiate peace, bring to me the commander of your army and we will accept your surrender."

"I am Magnus, son of Vargr, the hunter of wolves." Instinctively Ogier touched the wolf amulet on his cape. "I am the spokesman for our commander, and he has but one answer for you." Magnus never would have expected to be in this position. He was the least of his brothers, but acknowledged to be among the bravest of men. He stood here because many of the other leaders had fallen, and the lot fell to him to stand before Ogier, the Paladin.

"You have desecrated our sacred tree and blasphemed the gods of our people. You have waged war against our brothers for the last time, for today we will rain down the thunder of Odin or enter into the gates of Valhalla!" He raised the flag in the air and threw it to the ground. The response of the Vikings shook the leaves of the trees. With a show of force all who were left stepped from beneath their branches. The army of the Vikings had been drastically depleted but they had managed to encircle the field while Ogier was making his grand procession. The army of Charlemagne was surrounded on three sides.

Ogier did not let the Viking see his concern, but ordered his cavalry to a defensive position. He knew that as soon as they tried to race back to the castle the Vikings would be on them. Better to face them head on than to run. Brandishing his sword he ordered his commanders to stand fast and hold shields high. They would not yield, but they would not be the first to fire. Ogier wanted his enemy to exhaust their store of arrows first, and the air was thick with anticipation. When the first volley was let loose, the skies darkened with their approach, but the Franks did not move. Protected behind their shields few fell.

"Hold. Don't let them bait you to run," Ogier commanded.

The sound of their cheers and taunts rang from the trees. They cursed the Franks' mothers, and drew down oaths from the gods.

They called them cowards and castrates unworthy of honor. Yet, the Franks did not move. Finally, a horn sounded and the rush of Vikings began.

Ogier was surrounded by his guards who took the brunt of the attack. The soldiers on horseback used the size and weight of their mounts to push through while hacking at the advancing Vikings. The surge, however, was proving too much for the cavalry, and they were being forced to the ground.

Ogier's troops still had outnumbered their foe, but the surprise of the rush was a momentary drawback. Once they had regained their wits they stood toe to toe with their adversaries. Eventually Ogier dropped to the ground, his horse no longer an advantage.

"Kenton!" Ogier shouted.

"I am here." Before he could respond, the servant swung his sword at Ogier's head. For an instant Ogier thought he had been betrayed, but as the blade slipped past it fell hard on a Viking skull, and blood spurted onto a grateful Paladin. At this point there was no strategy—it was all about survival, each man pitted against two. The fortunes of the battle seemed to turn against the forces of the Franks.

Magnus pressed hard as his men followed his lead. He gave no thought to life or death, only the victory in either. Adrenaline pumped through his body, driving fatigue away, and the skills he had honed over a lifetime raged without thought or mercy. Sweat and blood stung his eyes and threatened to blind him to his enemy's sword. His arm throbbed with pain, blood soaking his outer garment. Breathing heavily, he looked up and saw the young wolf.

Battle Between Worlds
774 AD

Sigrunn walked over to a stool next to the house and sat down. Her back had been hurting all morning, and at that moment her water broke. She called for Arne who came running to her side. "Arne! I need you to go get your aunt. The baby is coming."

"I don't think I should leave you," Arne responded.

"Go now or you will be delivering the baby." She was panting but talking steadily. Arne looked at her and then turned and ran toward town. When Sigrid arrived Sigrunn had made it inside and laid down in her bed.

"How fast are your pains?" Sigrid asked.

"They are coming faster." She winced as another set in.

"Arne, go get me some water, and some rags." He went right away.

"Take some deep breaths. When the next one comes you need to push." Sigrid had done this four times and was good at helping women with their births. Arne put the water next to her. "Go get Torhild and Hilde. Tell them your mother is having her baby."

The battle wasn't going the way they had planned. The Frank army wasn't as gullible as the outpost. Their numbers were overwhelming and it was all that Magnus could do to keep them at bay. Ten of his men had already fallen, but he was not going to Valhalla willingly. He was holding his ax in one hand and his sword in another. The shield he was using had splintered after a Frank pummeled it with his sword.

"Behind you!" Geir yelled.

Magnus swung around, blocking the oncoming sword with his and swinging his ax through the soldier's torso. Blood spurted everywhere, covering his already drenched body.

Their formation had collapsed, and if there was any hope of victory they needed to regroup. Picking up a dead man's shield, he yelled, "Shield wall! Shield wall!" Others came around him and they formed the wall. It gave them a defense and a reprieve from single combat. They were exhausted, and those who stood behind the wall slashed through the openings, killing whatever Franks they could reach.

"Archer!" Magnus moved out of the way as an arrow flew by his head into the neck of a soldier. "Replacement!" he yelled again, and a warrior stepped in front of him and allowed him to take a breath.

"Hilde, good, you are here." For a moment the pains had stopped and Sigrunn was resting. "Step outside with me."

"How is she doing?"

"I don't know. The baby hasn't turned and I don't feel any movement." She looked around to make sure Arne couldn't hear. "I am not sure that the baby is alive."

"Has she been bleeding? I didn't notice any."

"Just a little. What do you think we should do?" Sigrid was very concerned.

"There is nothing we can do but continue with the birth. Maybe Freyr will be merciful." Sigrunn was cringing when they came back in; she was ready to push again.

"It hurts so much!" Sigrunn cried. "I don't think I can do this. Something is wrong. What is wrong?" Fear shone in her eyes.

"The baby isn't moving. But that could mean anything. I need you to push your stomach to help the baby's head to move." Sigrid and Hilde worked together to move the baby into a position that would make it easier for it to come out. "The next time you feel pain, push."

"Ahhh! I think the baby is going to come this time!" Sigrunn screamed.

Magnus was in front again trying to push the wall forward, but the Franks were too strong, and he felt them losing ground. He knew there would be no victory today, but he would not call retreat. He called for a replacement again, and made his way around to another shield wall where Rolf was fighting.

"We are not going to win today Rolf. We need to retreat and regroup." He knew his words sounded cowardly, but he believed it would be the best strategy.

Rolf said, "We will win or go to Valhalla victoriously. Run if you want."

"I will not run, but all will be lost if we die here today." A large Frank soldier broke through the line and brought his sword down,

316

slicing into Magnus' left arm. He spun around and deflected a second thrust just in time. His arm was bleeding badly but he couldn't feel it. Adrenaline pumped through his veins and he swung his sword wildly; in front of him stood Ogier.

No words were necessary, no pleas or reprieve, only the steely eyes of combatants. Ogier swung first bringing the full weight of his sword against Magnus' shield. It was deflected but the force caused him to stumble. Catching his balance, Magnus spun around, trying to wield his ax and sword low against his opponent's legs, but Ogier stepped over with little difficulty, kicking Magnus' sword away. Trying to regain his balance before Ogier could advance was fruitless, and a crashing blow made Magnus' head spin. All he could hear was the ringing that filled his ears.

Magnus fell to his knees breathing heavily; he could no longer raise his weapon. Blood streamed down his arm and face and when he looked up he thought he could see winged Valkyries swooping from the sky. "Odin, the Wild Hunter, I have failed to kill the wolf. Are you calling me to your glorious hall? Are you carrying out the curse for seeing your hounds of hell? Take me if you must to Valhalla!" A pain shot through his back as Ogier plunged his sword deep, and with one last gasp Magnus fell face first into the dirt.

"The baby's coming, push!" Hilde cried.

"I can't, I am too tired."

"Don't give up now!" Hilde watched the baby's head come through. It was blue and the cord was wrapped around his neck. Torhild had arrived an hour earlier and was now holding Sigrunn's hand. When the baby came out Hilde was shaking her head and Torhild knew the news was not good.

"Is it a boy?" Sigrunn asked.

Quietly she replied, "It's a boy."

"Magnus will be glad. Let me hold him."

Sigrid handed her sister the baby.

"He is cold… he is blue." The reality of the baby's stillbirth sank in and Sigrunn began to cry.

"What's that—no! More blood." Torhild had noticed the dark liquid flowing from Sigrunn. Something had happened when the cord came out; the flow was too much. They looked at Sigrunn's face and it had gone ashen; before they could say a word her eyes had closed and her breathing stopped. Sigrunn lay still with the baby in her arms when Arne came into the house.

"Has the baby been born—?" His question hung in the air as he stared at his mother. He just stood there, and no one said a word.

Epilogue

The air was filled with the groans of men whose thoughts were not of war but of home. In the final moment no one cared if lands and kings were victorious. The glimmer of a smiling child, the soft touch of a wife, the laughter heard around the hearth, and sounds of love were all that mattered. Steadily the light dimmed and the crushing sounds of war disappeared, until only darkness and silence remained.

Ogier stood alone, Magnus at his feet, his army routing the rest of the enemy. A thrill coursed through his body at the victory just won. Yet, his heart was heavy for the souls that were lost, both his kin and his foes. There was no joy in the loss of life, only the hope that this battle could secure a lasting peace.

King Sigfred and Gudfred would now realize that their attempt had failed and only submission to the will of Charlemagne could mean peace for both lands. But the heart of man was defiant toward God, and only the future could know how the Norsemen would respond. Until then the carnage was over and the blood would stand as a reminder of the rebellious heart.

Slowly Ogier made his way to his horse and led him the length of the field, careful not to step on the fallen. There were no wisps of spirit, no wings of angel or Valkyrie, only the silence of the dead. His heart was heavy as he realized that this battle was not won by the strength of man. He knelt and prayed,

The King is not saved by his great army;
A warrior is not delivered by His great strength.
The warhorse is a false hope for salvation,
And by its great might it cannot rescue.

Behold, the eye of the LORD is on those who fear Him.
On those who hope in His steadfast love,
That he may deliver their souls from death,
And keep them alive in famine.

Our souls wait for the LORD;
He is our help and our shield.
For our hearts are glad in Him,
 Because we trust in his holy name.
Let your steadfast love, O LORD, be upon us.
Even as we hope in You.

Yet, on another shore the moon hung low, its crescent silhouette vainly trying to light the sky. Out on the rocks the wolves stood watch to see if Fenrir would consume the orb, but the cries of men, in the terror of night, wailed in hope that it would not be extinguished. For no man desired to die in the gloom of night where he might not find his way to Valhalla. With one voice they broke the silence, their howls chilling the soul, rumbling through valleys and canyons until they reached a lone soul standing on a pier.

A shiver ran through Arne's body, the chilling of lost souls. He turned and looked to the hills and the mourning cry of the wolves announced Magnus' death. He knew his father would not return. The loss of his family weakened his legs and the gentle swaying of the pier forced him to sit. He felt betrayed by his father for not taking him, betrayed by his mother for leaving him, betrayed by Odin for forsaking him, and his sorrow was turning to anger.

Out of the darkness stepped the Earl and those who followed. They were bearing torches to light the way of the fallen. Word had come that the war did not go well and the community came to stand watch for the dead. Specks of light and wisps of smoke lit the ways for the fallen to follow to the ship of the dead, and a quiet chant filled the air.

For you who died the sun has set,
Midgard has lost her allure;
The halls of Odin open the door,
And usher in the fallen.
Let not our heart of sorrow cease,
Unending joy and feasting,
May we take comfort in your stead,
One day we will be joining.
One day we will be joining.

It was for another shore, not Valhalla, that Arne would set his heart. Anger had pushed aside sorrow where even love could not penetrate. He would avenge his father's death. He would cross the shores and make them pay. There was nothing to hold him down and nothing to hold him back. He would shake off the curse of Odin and embrace The Wild Hunt.

Other Novels by the Author

Centurion: From Glory To Glory

Viking Chronicles Book 1: Call of the Wolf
Viking Chronicles Book 2: The Wild Hunt
Viking Chronicles Book 3: The Priest's Son

For other books go to:

Amazon.com

www.cravingsomethingmore.com

Printed in France by Amazon
Brétigny-sur-Orge, FR

11032549R00185